When the Stars Collide

When the Stars Collide

Alexis Harris

RESOURCE *Publications* · Eugene, Oregon

WHEN THE STARS COLLIDE

Resource Publications
An Imprint of Wipf and Stock Publishers
199 W. 8th Ave., Suite 3
Eugene, OR 97401

www.wipfandstock.com

PAPERBACK ISBN: 978-1-6667-3497-3
HARDCOVER ISBN: 978-1-6667-9152-5
EBOOK ISBN: 978-1-6667-9153-2

JANUARY 3, 2022 11:11 AM

Dedicated to the first people to buy my book when it came out. Thank you for your support! Christina Haldeman, Sarah Carter, Teresa Webb, Lauren Breed, Tabatha Hogueison, and Robbin Harris. Also, a special dedication to Vondre Green (Dredon), the villain of this tale.

Contents

Orion

1

"Orion, come on!" Epsilon shouted. He had black hair, dark skin, and a warrior's build.

"Coming!" Orion replied. He had black hair as well, and his skin was a mixture of light and dark. His mother was from the land of Duwazo, which was a land famous for its light-skinned residents. His father was from the land of Cardeas, which was mostly darkly complected individuals. It wasn't often the two came together, so he was the product of an unusual love affair.

Orion had been best friends with Epsilon since they'd met at the age of eleven, when they'd journeyed from their homelands to the land of Abyumo, and the realm of the dragon riders. He'd grown up in Cardeas, and Epsilon had grown up in the land of Gachichken, just south of Cardeas. Orion's mother had moved to Cardeas to be with his father, giving up a life of wealth and status to be with a poor peasant. In spite of that, the three of them had been happy.

He had grown up on stories of the riders, as had all Cardeans. As soon as he was old enough, he'd begged his parents to let him travel to Abyumo to join the next class of potential riders. It was there he'd met Epsilon, and they'd gone through the process of being selected to go before the eggs together.

When he'd been allowed inside the room where the eggs were kept, his heart had been pounding in his chest so hard, he thought he might faint. All his hopes and dreams had rested upon that day. Truthfully, he wasn't sure what he would've done if an egg hadn't hatched for him. He would've had to head back home, ashamed and disappointed.

He'd strolled through the rows of colorful, shiny eggs, hoping. A bright, blue egg had caught his eye. When he'd approached it, the smooth, shiny shell developed a small crack. The crack had traveled down the side of the egg, and the shell had exploded away, revealing a tiny, blue dragon. It had looked up at him with its sapphire eyes and squeaked at him.

His brown eyes had turned blue that day—the mark of a rider. His precious little Saphron had fit so perfectly in the cradle of his arms. How quickly that tiny baby dragon had grown! He was now the size of his parents' house! And, he wasn't done growing. That was the most amazing part. Who knows how large he would wind up being in the end.

Epsilon's white dragon, Moonstone, was a little bit larger than Saphron. Even though it was normal for their eyes to change color, it was hard for Orion to adjust to his best friend's white eyes. Still, at the end of the day, there was no one he could relate to more. They'd been training together and hanging out together for the last ten years.

Today was no different, as Orion put on his black bodysuit with blue lines—the uniform of the riders. Epsilon's was the same, but with white lines. The only riders who didn't wear bodysuits were the royals and the dragon rider council. They opted for colored armor instead.

The two of them lived with a group of dragons and riders in a mountain stronghold just outside the city of Cabri, which was ruled by Lorena, the recently crowned queen of the riders, daughter of their previous queen, Kirstiana. She had brown, flowing hair and bronze eyes, like her dragon, Aeramen.

The stronghold was tucked inside a massive cave, and each of the eleven of them who lived there had a bunker they shared with their dragon. Orion and Saphron's bunker was toward the bottom of the stronghold, as they were considered to be lower on the food chain by the others' standards.

It annoyed him, but he thirsted for the opportunity to prove them all wrong. Their nook had a twin bed for him, and a dragon-sized bed for Saphron. They had a nightstand and a wardrobe for Orion's things, and a blue curtain for privacy.

Epsilon and Moonstone's bunker was right above them, so they were able to hang out and chat easily. Their white curtain was already open as Orion peered above him, stretching. Epsilon was an early riser, always ready to train—determined to work his way up through the ranks of the riders. Orion was not a morning person, but he knew he needed to train hard if he wanted to improve. So, he mustered his strength each morning to get out of bed when Epsilon did.

You won't last long against the others if you aren't fully awake, Saphron said.

Due to the strong bond formed when a dragon hatches for its rider, Orion could hear Saphron's thoughts, and he could hear his. It was the way riders were able to communicate with their dragons—something outsiders could never seem to understand.

I know that, he thought, *You know I hate mornings.*

I do, Saphron agreed, *But, you'll have to get over that if we are to gain recognition. No one great wakes up late. Winners start their day early. Wake ahead to get ahead.*

You know I hate when you say that, he thought, rolling his eyes and yawning.

Saphron roared, releasing a great gust of hot air in Orion's face.

Really?

He nestled his massive blue body against the earth in satisfaction and content.

"What's taking so long?" Epsilon asked, swooping down upon Moonstone's back, "Let's go."

Orion nodded sleepily, climbing upon Saphron's back, *Come on, you little hellion. Let's go.*

Saphron snorted, smoke streaming from his nostrils.

With that, Moonstone soared up through the stronghold, and Saphron followed, up and out. No matter how many times they flew, Orion never quite got used to it. It just never ceased to amaze him. The feeling of soaring higher and higher until they reached the clouds couldn't be beat. There was nothing better in the world than the peace and beauty of the world from above. It was so quiet and serene. He always felt completely free, like

. . . nothing could touch him. He couldn't imagine never getting the opportunity to fly. It was all he ever wanted to do.

"Get your head out of the clouds, Orion!" Epsilon shouted, "We're supposed to be training."

Orion shook his head, snapping out of his trance. He drew his jousting stick, beginning a practice fight with Epsilon. Saphron knew what to do already, and didn't need much guidance as far as which way to go, or how to maneuver through the air. Orion couldn't say the same of his own technique, and Saphron had to keep trying to tell him what to do.

Left, right, left, dodge! Saphron thought.

Orion ducked too late, getting whacked in the face by Epsilon's jousting stick.

Come on, Orion, Saphron thought, *Keep up.*

I know, I know, he thought, clearing his head from the blow, *Just fly.*

Don't get snippy with me, he thought, *I'm not the one messing up.*

He ducked and dodged, trying to get a hit in, but it was no use. He'd never been a very good fighter. Eventually, Epsilon knocked him off Saphron's back. His shiny, blue-scaled dragon had to swoop through the air to catch him.

Epsilon sighed, "Come on, Orion. You're never going to get respect if you can't win a single duel. You're my friend, but I need a better practice partner. You're not a challenge for me. I can't improve myself if I don't train with some real opponents."

"What are you saying? You're giving up on me?" he asked in disbelief.

He sighed again, "I'm sorry. You're my best friend. But, I want to be a top rider. It's my life-long dream. And, training with you isn't helping me." He paused, "Just because I don't want to train with you anymore doesn't mean I don't want to be friends."

Orion didn't say anything. He couldn't believe his "friend" would abandon him. They'd been training together every day since they became riders.

"I've held on as long as possible," he continued, "I've been there for you for the last ten years. I didn't want to say anything, because you're my friend, but I feel like you've been holding me back. I could be a much better fighter if I trained with someone who could offer me a challenge."

He remained silent.

Epsilon let out a long breath, "I'm sorry. Truly." When he still didn't respond, he added, "I'd better go. Dredon offered to train with me, and I'm sure that won't last."

"Dredon?" he asked.

"Yeah," he replied, "He's one of the best riders. I can't miss this opportunity to better myself. I'll see you back at the bunker." With that, Epsilon took off, heading to the training mountain. Only the top riders were able to train there. Dredon ruled that mountain. If he was giving Epsilon a chance, it was a huge deal. Dredon was a big, dark-skinned rider with more muscle than Orion could ever hope to have. His dragon was black, and was one of the largest in the mountains. He couldn't even go into the city, because he was too large to land. And, the city was built to be accessible for dragons. He was the mountains' top rider, and in the land's top five.

Orion knew he would never be able to train with someone of Dredon's level. He couldn't even train with Epsilon. He was right to leave. As much as Orion wanted to prove himself, he knew Epsilon was right: he couldn't win a single duel. If he didn't learn to fight properly, he would never amount to anything amongst the riders. He'd wind up like Gregorious—the fat, old rider whose dragon was condemned to light the city's fires, for he wasn't good for anything else.

He screamed internally, frustrated with his situation.

I know how you feel, Saphron thought, *But, feeling sorry for yourself won't help. You need to learn how to fight, properly. I know you have it in you.*

You chose me for a reason, Saphron, he thought, *But, I've never been sure what that reason is.*

Saphron suddenly took off, launching himself higher into the clouds.

Orion had to grab on quick to avoid falling off, *What are you doing?*

Just hang on, he thought, *You shall see.*

They flew up into the clouds until they could see the training mountain ahead. *What are you doing?* Orion thought, *You just wanted to show me how much better they are than me?*

No, dimwit, Saphron said, *I wanted you to see how they train. Copy them. Follow their movements. Think of it as a free lesson.*

Orion sighed. He looked over at the training riders. There were several practice duels going on simultaneously. He caught sight of Epsilon and Moonstone, fighting with Dredon and his dragon, Obsidian. He looked away quickly, *I don't want this free lesson. I wasn't invited to the mountain. I never will be.*

I didn't ask if you wanted it, his sapphire dragon thought, *I said, copy their movements. You're right. You'll never get invited to the training mountain—not unless you can prove yourself worthy.*

He sighed again, *Fine.*

With that, he stood upon Saphron's back, looking through the clouds to the mountain below. He imitated the movements of the other riders; turning, sliding, and swinging his jousting stick, stabbing it through the air. It felt unnatural at first, but he slowly began to get the hang of it.

There you go, Saphron encouraged, *Just like that.*

This is easier than I thought it would be, Orion thought.

I knew you could do it.

Why aren't we all trained this way before we're released?

Because, he thought, *we are expected to learn on our own. We each must embark on our own journey, and earn our success. If we were all taught the same, no one would be exceptional.*

Orion sighed, sliding back down onto the saddle, *When will we be exceptional?*

He watched as the other riders flew off for the day, leaving only a few of the leaders. Dredon gathered in a tight circle with them, talking. As Orion was about to suggest they head back to the bunker, he saw a struggle ensue amongst the remaining riders.

They're not still training, are they? he asked.

That doesn't look like training, Saphron replied.

They watched with horror as Dredon and his followers slit the throats of the other leaders. Their blood dyed the snowy precipice a pure red, as their dragons screeched in agony, circling above. Obsidian led his followers against the remaining dragons, breathing fire across them and ripping into them with their teeth and talons. They tried to flee, but Obsidian's great size overwhelmed them, and they could not outrun him.

No! Orion thought, *What should we do?*

A single dragon escaped, blood streaming down its indigo scales. It dove away from the mountain, gliding between the other mountains in the range while they were focused on the other dragons. He caught sight of Dredon, standing in the reddened snow, laughing, his white teeth bright against his dark skin.

Saphron dove down, back toward the bunker, flying at top speed away from the bloodbath.

What are you doing? Orion thought angrily.

Getting away from here, he replied, *There is nothing we can do against the might of Dredon and Obsidian. If we are to do anything, we must live to tell the tale. Lorena and Aeramen must be informed of this as soon as possible.* He paused, *We should tell Epsilon and Moonstone, too.*

He was silent for a minute, *What for? They abandoned us after ten years of friendship just to get ahead in their training.*

What are you saying, Orion? We shouldn't care about their lives because we were terrible training partners? They could be in danger. We can't let them go back there again.

They spiraled down into the stronghold, and to their bunker.

"How was the training?" Orion asked, glaring up at Epsilon.

Epsilon sighed, looking back at him, "I know you're angry with me. But, I held on as long as I could. I tried to make it work. I really did. Becoming a great rider is the most important thing in the world to me. You know that. I know you want to get ahead, too, but . . . "

"But, I can't even defeat you, so how can I help you learn?"

"Exactly," he said, jumping down to their bunker, "Look, you're a good friend. You always have been. But, this is important to me. The things I can learn on the training mountain are far greater than our little duels."

Orion sighed, "I don't know how to tell you this, but . . . you can't go back there."

"Orion, I know you're mad, but don't make it worse. I can't train with you anymore."

"No, that's not why—"

"You're holding me back. But, I can't let you . . . no matter how good a friend you are," he said.

"But, that's not—"

"Stop, please," he said, "I don't want this to ruin our friendship."

"It's not about our friendship!" he yelled. His voice echoed off the walls of the stronghold, and the other riders and their dragons looked over at them. He paused, waiting for them to go back to their business, and lowered his voice, "It's about Dredon."

Epsilon sighed, "I can learn a lot from him. He's one of the best. I know he intimidates you, and I know you're upset he asked me to the training mountain and not you, but you can't go around slandering his name because you're jealous."

"I'm not jealous," he said.

"Of course you are. You want to be a great rider, same as me, but you're further from that goal than I am, and it drives you crazy. Especially now that we're not training partners anymore, you're realizing just how far you have to go. I'm sorry for you. I am. But I can't let it stop me."

"Would you just listen to me?" Orion cried, "I'm trying to tell you that Dredon and Obsidian slaughtered the other leaders after you left today."

Epsilon paused, looking at him, "Now you've really gone too far, Orion."

"I'm telling the truth."

"Oh, yeah?" he said, "How would you know?"

He sighed, "Saphron took me up today, to watch you guys train from afar, and maybe learn a few useful moves to improve my dueling. I saw you guys training, and, after all the trainees left, the leaders assembled for a meeting. They started fighting, and Dredon and his followers slaughtered them. The mountain runs red with their blood. Only one dragon got away." He looked down, leaning against Saphron.

Epsilon shook his head, letting out a breath of disbelief, "I don't know what's going on with you. I really don't. I didn't know that me moving up in the world without you would make you so crazy, but I guess I should have." He moved closer, "You need to keep your mouth shut, and focus on your own training. I don't know if you really believe that's what you saw, or if you'll say anything to get me to train with you again, but either way, you'd better just go to your bunker, and go to sleep. When you wake up, you'll feel worlds better, I'm sure."

"You don't believe me?" he said, "Why would I make something like this up?"

"I don't know, but it's really sick. I'm going back to my own bunker, and getting some rest. Come tomorrow, I'll be moving up in the training world, and you'll have to accept that you're on your own. Goodnight, Orion."

Why won't he believe me? Orion thought, frustrated.

He thinks we're defacing Dredon's character out of jealousy, Saphron said, *He's not going to listen. All we can do now is tell someone who will.*

And who will listen? he asked.

Lorena, he said, *The queen of the riders.*

Dredon

2

When morning came, and the other riders had left to train, Orion and Saphron set out for Cabri. It was a short flight away from the mountains. They crossed the desert plain quickly, landing beside the glittering gold and emerald palace. Several of the other dragons and riders looked at them with suspicious curiosity, unsure why a mountain rider would be landing in their city.

They walked together into the palace, which was designed large enough for dragons to fit through. They ventured to the throne room, going before Lorena. She was seated upon her golden throne, garbed in bronze armor, brown hair billowing around her. She wore a golden crown, and her bronze eyes matched her sleeping dragon's scales.

Kirstiana stood close by, garbed in golden armor, auburn hair done up with a golden band, amber eyes gleaming. Her amber dragon, Solstra, was asleep beside Aeramen. She nodded to Lorena when they entered, readying herself to help the new queen transition smoothly to the throne.

"Welcome," Lorena said, "What brings a mountain dragon and his rider here?"

"We come bearing news of treachery," Orion replied, "I hate to be the bearer of such tidings, but it is my duty."

Lorena sucked in a breath, looking at her mother.

Kirstiana nodded to her.

Lorena cleared her throat, "What is this treacherous news?"

Orion swallowed, looking at Saphron, and then back to the throne, "A terrible crime has been committed. Dredon and Obsidian—leaders of the mountains—and his followers have murdered the other leaders."

"What?" Lorena gasped.

Kirstiana held up a hand, calming her, "Young man, what proof have you that such an event has taken place?"

"I have no proof," Orion answered, "But please, you must believe us. We were the sole witnesses to the event. Only one dragon got away." He looked down sorrowfully, and Saphron whimpered beside him, nudging him supportively.

"And, where is this dragon now?" she asked.

"I don't know," he said, "He flew off into the mountains. I think he was injured. He had indigo scales."

Kirstiana exchanged looks with her daughter, looking back at them, "You have no proof, and your only alibi fled the scene. How can we trust that what you say is true?"

"Of course he fled the scene!" Orion cried, "They were being slaughtered!"

"How is it you were able to escape?"

"I didn't," he answered, "I was up in the air a short distance away. None of them saw me."

"So, you could see them, but they couldn't see you?" she asked doubtfully.

He sighed, "Yes. I know it sounds hard to believe, but the mountain air is rather cloudy, and I was high enough to see the training mountain, but far enough not to be seen. You have to believe me! Other dragons and riders could be in danger. Who knows who will be next!"

"Mother," Lorena said, "What reason could they have to make something like this up?"

Kirstiana sighed, "One thing you must learn, my daughter, is that reasons aren't always understood upfront. You have to be objective, and not give in to your emotional response. All facts must be considered. Otherwise, you could have the wool pulled over your eyes. They could be telling the truth. But, they could also be sick people, trying to trick us for their own ends."

"We wish only to protect our fellow dragons and riders," Orion said, "Please, you must believe us. We're telling the truth. We have no reason to fly here from our mountain stronghold bearing this news in falsehood."

"Perhaps," Kirstiana said, "What is it you would ask of us, then?"

"Send troops to the mountain. Bring Dredon and Obsidian into custody, along with their followers. The missing leaders, their bodies, and the bloody snow should be evidence enough. Capture him and bring him to justice before anyone else gets hurt."

"Slow down there," she said, "First, we must investigate. If we can, indeed, gather the evidence you suggest, then we will bring him to justice for what he's done. But, the evidence must be collected first. If we have no proof, we have no case against him."

He may have cleaned the scene by now, Saphron thought, *He wouldn't want anyone else to see the blood or the bodies. Whatever he's trying to do surely wouldn't involve getting captured by the troops of Cabri, or even letting the trainees know what he's done.*

You're right, Orion thought. "In case he somehow cleaned the blood and hid the bodies, I would ask that the primary evidence for consideration be the missing leaders," he said quickly.

Kirstiana sighed, "I'm afraid we'd need more than simply for them to be missing. Anything could have happened to them. It wouldn't be enough proof."

"Then, make sure you find the bodies," he replied, "Don't rest until you do. They couldn't be far."

"We'll do what we can," Lorena said.

Orion nodded gratefully to her.

"Ember," Lorena called, summoning one of the servants, "send in Morgalina and Austinian." When Ember had disappeared from the room, she turned back to Orion and Saphron, "They're our best investigative riders. We shall send them and their dragons, Turq and Amaline, to the mountains to look for evidence."

"Only two? But, they'll be in danger!" he cried.

"Only a fool would harm riders from Cabri!" Kirstiana retorted, "If he does seek to keep his treachery a secret, he will not touch them. And, if he's willing to do anything to them, he will immediately be brought to justice. So, either way, you're getting your wish, rider."

He nodded uncertainly, fearful for the lives of the two riders they were sending.

"Now, return to your mountain stronghold and leave the rest to us," she said.

As he and Saphron exited the throne room, they saw the two riders enter. Morgalina had blonde hair and turquoise eyes and armor. Austinian had blonde hair and purple eyes and armor. They appeared to be siblings. They nodded to them as they passed them, wishing them luck in their investigation.

What now? Orion thought.

Now, let us go see the mountain for ourselves, Saphron thought.

When they reached the sky above the snowy peak, it was just as they'd feared. The bodies were gone, and there was no blood. The snow was pure white. Dredon and Obsidian, along with their followers, were training the recruits like normal. The other leaders weren't there, so Orion knew it hadn't been only in his head.

Where could he have stashed so many bodies? Orion thought.

I'm not sure, Saphron said, *It would be difficult to conceal the dragons he killed. Not to mention, cleaning the snow would be a difficult feat in itself. We can only hope that Austinian and Morgalina can find them.*

Something tells me they won't, Orion thought, *What else can we do? He must be brought to justice for what he's done.*

I agree, Saphron thought, *But, I'm not sure what else we can do just yet. I think we should watch over the mountain today, and keep an eye on our investigator friends. If they find evidence and manage to report back to Lorena, or if something happens to them, then we shall know the army of Cabri will descend upon Dredon and Obsidian shortly. If not, we'll know we must think of some other way to bring them to justice.*

Orion sighed, *I suppose you're right. That's all we can do.*

As they watched the dragons and riders training on the mountain, keeping a close eye on Epsilon and Moonstone, they saw Morgalina and Austinian fly in upon their dragons. The great turquoise and purple beasts landed upon the training mountain a little ways past where everyone was training. The two riders dismounted, beginning their search.

They searched the entire mountain, as well as the surrounding mountains, pausing briefly to speak with Dredon and Obsidian directly. With no way to hear what they were saying, they could only hope they weren't giving away too much detail. They could also only hope that they didn't wind up getting killed. Even though it would prove to Kirstiana that they had been telling the truth, they didn't want any more dragons or riders to die.

Austinian and Morgalina completed their search by the time the dragons and riders had finished training for the day. They'd searched the entire mountain range, thoroughly. Not a trace of evidence remained from the previous day. Not one speck of blood or stray tooth was found.

Where did the survivor go? Saphron thought.

He's the only one who could prove what happened, Orion thought, *And, he's long gone.*

He's probably too frightened to return, he thought.

Orion sighed, *You're probably right.*

As the two riders flew off upon their dragons, Orion and Saphron returned to their bunker, defeated.

What now? he thought.

Now, Saphron replied, *We must find the survivor.*

Callisto

3

The next morning, Orion gathered up some supplies for the road, taking all of his money and food, along with some clothes and weapons. He wasn't sure how long their journey would take, but he knew they had to find that dragon.

"Where are you headed off to so early?" Epsilon asked, hovering beside his bunker on Moonstone's back.

"What do you care?" Orion said.

"You're not still mad about the other day, are you?"

Orion was silent.

"Come on; we're still friends, aren't we?" Epsilon asked.

Orion paused to give him a look, going back to loading Saphron's saddlebags.

"Are you leaving?" he asked. He looked concerned and slightly suspicious, watching him load his belongings.

You'd better answer him, Saphron thought, *He might get the wrong idea, and it could put all of us in danger.*

"Yeah," he answered, "I'm leaving. I don't belong here. You said your-self I can't win a duel. I'm never going to be invited to the training moun-tain. This bunker doesn't feel like home anymore. I think it's best if Saphron and I take to the distant mountains, and find a different life."

Epsilon paused, looking down, "Forget what I said. Look, don't leave. I know some riders who could help you train. You'll get to the training mountain, you'll see."

"No," he said, "I have to do this. I need to find my own way to the mountain."

He paused again, unsure, "Will you return?"

Orion looked at him, "I don't know. Maybe, someday."

Epsilon nodded, "Do what you must. I hope to see you again someday."

He nodded back, smiling.

His old friend returned his smile, taking off upon Moonstone's back toward the training mountain.

Let's go, Saphron thought.

Orion leapt upon his back, and they took off out of the mountain stronghold, and off into the mountains. They spent the day searching for the surviving indigo dragon. They flew far and wide, searching the peaks and valleys. By nightfall, they had searched the entire mountain range from east to west, north to south. Still, there was no sign of him. They stopped to make camp on the outskirts of the mountain range.

Where could he have possibly gone? Orion thought.

He could be anywhere by now, Saphron replied, *If he was fleeing for his life, he could have gone anywhere. If he flew out of the mountains, he's at least a day ahead of us. We have no way of knowing which direction he went.*

Maybe we could find where Dredon and Obsidian hid the bodies, he thought, *If we watch them tomorrow after the trainees leave, we might see where their stronghold is, and I'd bet the bodies are there, too.*

No, Saphron thought, *They wouldn't have hidden the bodies in their own stronghold. For one, it's too obvious a place. Morgalina and Austinian would have found them if they did. For another, they wouldn't want to live with a bunch of dead bodies. The stink alone would be unbearable.*

Then, what do we do?

We must go to The Oracle, he thought, *She may be able to tell us where the indigo dragon went. Everyone knows she can see the future. She may even be able to see what Dredon and Obsidian are planning.*

Orion nodded, *Very well. Tomorrow, we go to The Oracle.*

As the sun rose brightly beside the mountains, Orion awoke. He clambered sleepily upon Saphron's back, and the two of them took to the sky, gliding through the crisp, morning air, high above the snowy peaks of the mountain range. The snow glistened in the sunlight, and intensified the light, blinding them at certain points. It took them all day to fly back across the mountain range, past Cabri, and to the realm of the wizards, where The Oracle resided.

From snowy peaks to barren desert to grassy plain, they flew. The border between the realms allowed them to cross, sensing that they meant no harm. When they crossed, they nearly ran into a phoenix, causing Saphron to breathe fire across it in surprise. Luckily, the poor bird's affinity for fire rendered it completely unharmed as it retreated in a panic.

"Quite a way you have with phoenixes," a voice said.

The rider and his dragon looked in the direction of the voice, maintaining their surprise. It was an old witch with gray hair, blue eyes, and pale skin. She wore a blue and silver robe with a rope tied around her waist, and a hood over her head.

Orion cleared his throat, "My apologies. We were startled."

"Yes, I could see that," she said, "What brings you to the wizard realm?"

"We have come to see The Oracle," he replied, "Who are you?"

"I am her keeper," she answered, "My name is Callisto."

"I am Orion, and this is Saphron," he said.

She shifted, looking surprised. After a brief pause, she said, "Right this way."

Callisto leapt upon her white horse, and they followed her steadily, struggling to keep pace with such a slow creature. She led them to an elliptical, ivory structure, which appeared to be glowing from within.

"I'm afraid there's no room for a dragon in the home of The Oracle," Callisto said, "But, you are welcome to enter, rider."

Orion nodded, dismounting from Saphron's back and walking up the steps. The doors blew open, releasing a gust of wind and blinding light. He shielded his eyes, entering. The doors closed behind him. Once he was inside, the wind and light died down, and he was able to see The Oracle. She sat cross-legged in the center of the ivory room. She was glowing, and her hair floated around her, a mixture of gold and amber. Her eyes glowed white, with no pupil or iris. She wore turquoise pants with sheer legs, and a turquoise top with sheer arms that hit above her navel.

"Welcome, Orion," she said in a haunting voice.

He shivered, "H-how do you know my name?"

"I know more than that," she said, "I know everything. I know why you have come, and I know what Obsidian and Dredon have done."

"You do?" he asked in surprise.

She gave him a slight nod, smiling.

"Then, you'll help us?"

"I cannot tell you the whereabouts of the indigo dragon," she said, "I see only bits of the future. Certain fragments come to me, and I cannot control which fragments they are. If he does not wish to be discovered, I cannot discover him. I *can* tell you that you will see him again in the future."

"I will?" he asked eagerly, "When?"

The Oracle sighed, shaking her head, "When the time is right."

Orion looked away, losing hope. After a pause, he asked, "Can you tell me what Dredon and Obsidian are planning?"

"I can," she said, "But, it'd be better if I showed you."

"*Showed* me?" he said in disbelief, "How?"

The Oracle smiled, holding up her glowing hand, "Take my hand."

Orion looked at it uncertainly. After a pause, he inched forward, cautiously sliding his hand into hers. As soon as he had, the room turned white and cloudy, and he could see they were standing atop the training mountain.

"How did you—" he began, but he was cut off by the sight of Dredon, walking toward him. His eyes widened, and he nearly screamed as Dredon walked straight through him as though he were a ghost. He turned to see the massive, dark, Obsidian looming before him, and nearly fainted.

"Dragons! Riders!" Dredon began, turning toward his followers, "Welcome, to the revolution! Today, we fulfill our lifelong dream. Today, the dragon rider realm is ours!"

Obsidian flew higher into the sky, revealing a tied-up Lorena and Kirstiana. Solstra and Aeramen lay dead beside them. Orion watched in horror as Dredon lifted the queen and former queen of the dragon riders up, tossing them into the snow before him.

"The reign of our former queen is at an end!" he continued. "Today, the dragon rider realm is ours," he repeated, "Tomorrow, the world!"

With that, he drew his sword, beheading the former queens.

"No!" Orion yelled, reaching toward them helplessly as the cloudy, white mountaintop faded away, leaving him and The Oracle in the ivory room once more. "Bring them back!" he yelled, "What have you done?"

"Calm yourself, rider," The Oracle said, power radiating from her voice, "I have done nothing. These events have not yet occurred. There is still time to prevent them. I only showed you what will happen if no one stops the black dragon and his rider."

He took a few deep breaths, trying to calm himself, "So, this is his plan? He's going to kill our queen and take over the dragon rider realm?"

"No," she replied, "It's much worse. He's going to slaughter countless dragons and their riders, leaving only his followers. Once he's seized control of the dragon rider realm, he's going to spread his reign of terror across all the lands of this world, following the example of his ancestor: Vidar the Conqueror."

"But, what can we do?" Orion asked, panicked, "Kirstiana won't listen to us. We can't find the indigo dragon to prove what we say is true. If the army of Cabri won't confront him, who will?"

"You will," she said.

"Me?" he asked, letting out a humorless laugh, "You've got to be kidding, right?"

She looked at him with a straight face, meeting his eyes.

"I can't even win a duel against the other riders in my bunker, let alone against someone of Dredon's level. I'll be killed for sure!"

"No," she said, "You won't. It is your destiny, if only you are brave enough to face it."

He paced back and forth quickly, running his hands over the tight coils of his hair.

"You are the only one who can defeat him," she said.

"You've got me confused with someone else," he said, "There's no way I'm destined to defeat Dredon. And, can you imagine Saphron facing off against Obsidian? He'd swallow him in one bite!"

"You need only the right trainer," The Oracle said, "Don't forget that I have foreseen all possible outcomes of this. If you decide to do this, you can win."

Orion paused, meeting her eyes, "Who can train me?"

She smiled, "Callisto."

"Callisto?" he said, "Your keeper? She's not even a rider."

"No," she replied, "But, she has experience in both combat and magic, which is what you need to learn."

He let out a breath, looking around the ivory room, "Where can we train without someone taking notice? And, are you so readily willing to part with your keeper?"

"I have had more than one keeper in my day. And, I've parted with them before when the need has arisen. I shall be fine. To answer your first question, I would recommend the south of Katangalo. It is far enough from here not to draw a wandering eye. And, it is all but abandoned. I can think of no better place." She paused, looking at him, "When you are ready, remember this: Vidar the Conqueror was defeated. Follow the example of Derekkian, and you shall defeat Dredon as well."

"Derekkian?"

"Every hundred years, a row of stars align overhead. When this happens, it usually spells trouble for the world below. But, every millennium, a row of stars collide. When that happens, God rest all our souls," The Oracle continued, "The stars will collide this year. You have until the first pair collides to complete your training, and you have until the last pair collides to return here, ready to face Dredon and Obsidian. Now, go."

"But—" he began.

"I said, go," The Oracle said, "I have already spoken with Callisto, and she will be ready to depart with you at dawn."

He sighed, wanting to ask more, but realizing there was nothing else she would tell him. He exited the doors, and Saphron read his thoughts, learning what had happened in their meeting. For some reason, he hadn't been able to hear him whilst he was inside The Oracle's house.

So, we are to be trained by this witch? Saphron asked.

Apparently so, Orion thought.

"I trust your questions were answered?" Callisto said.

"You should already know," Orion replied.

Callisto nodded deeply, hood falling over her eyes, "You may stay with me tonight. Tomorrow, we shall set out for Katangalo."

Orion climbed upon Saphron's back, and they followed the old witch on her white mare to a nearby hilltop. A little shack sat upon it, and they looked at each other uncertainly. There was a stable built into the side of the hill, and she led them to it first, putting her horse inside.

"Good girl," she said, "Easy, Raynee." She turned to Orion, "Well, are you coming inside, Saphron?"

Saphron looked at him uncertainly. After a brief pause, he squeezed through the doorway, and inside, there was plenty of space for him. The stable was massive, and Saphron had an oversized stall where he could sleep comfortably.

This is impressive, he thought.

Orion gawked in amazement, nodding.

"Don't look so surprised, rider," she said, "You know magic as well as I."

"Magic?" he said, "You used magic to make this place so big?"

"Of course," she replied, "You saw it from the outside. How else would it fit your dragon?"

He shrugged, nodding.

"Come on," she said, "There are a couple of dead pigs in the corner if you get hungry, Saphron, and plenty of water in the trough. It's large enough for your snout."

Saphron snorted his gratitude, curling up in the bed of hay, his warm belly singeing it.

Orion followed Callisto into her house, which was also larger on the inside than out. It was a quaint, rustic cabin, decorated with dark colors. There was a large kitchen and living room, and two hallways with bedrooms and a washroom.

"Make yourself at home," she said, "There's food in the refrigerator, and fresh towels in the washroom. Let me show you to your room."

He followed her down one of the hallways to a guest room. It was spacious, with a large bed, a nightstand, and a wardrobe.

"Thank you," he said, "Your hospitality is most appreciated."

She nodded, heading down the hall, "If you need anything, I'm just down the hall."

He went into the room, sprawling out across the bed. His mind was going a million miles a minute, thinking about everything The Oracle had said. *Am I really someone special?* he thought, *How can she expect me to face Dredon? And who is Derekkian?*

It will do you no good to dwell on these things, Saphron said, as he enjoyed the pigs he'd been provided, *We need to get a good night's sleep if we are to embark on a journey in the morning.*

I know, he thought, *It's just a lot to process.*

Why don't you ask Callisto about it tomorrow? he offered.

Good idea, he thought, *After all, she is supposed to be our trainer.*

When morning came, Orion reluctantly rose, heading out to the barn with Callisto.

We would travel faster without the horse, Saphron thought.

"Do you have anyone who could look after your horse?" Orion asked, "You could ride with me upon Saphron. We'd get there a lot faster."

"I do," Callisto replied, "If that's alright with Saphron, then I shall have my friend watch over Raynee."

"It was his idea," Orion said.

She smiled, "Very well, then. Let's load his saddlebags. I only have to make a call." She pulled out a mirror, going outside to call her friend upon it with magic.

In the meantime, Orion added Callisto's clothes and weapons to the saddlebags, along with the food she'd brought into the barn for them to take. She also had some money to add to the collection. He only hoped his dragon would be able to handle the weight.

Don't worry about me, Saphron thought, *I'll be just fine.*

I'll always worry about you, he thought.

Saphron wiggled with content, smoke streaming from his nostrils.

"He shall be here this evening," Callisto said, re-entering the barn, "So, that's that, and Raynee will be in good hands while I'm gone."

"Excellent," Orion said, "Then let's go."

She nervously shifted closer, and Orion leaped into Saphron's saddle. She eyed the blue dragon cautiously, placing her foot in the stirrup and pulling herself up behind Orion. Saphron walked out of the stable, using his claws to close the doors behind him. Then, he jumped to the bottom of the hill, pushing off the ground and launching them up into the sky. Orion waited for Callisto's scream of fright, but it never came. She squeezed his waist tightly, but she maintained her composure. He had never met a non-rider who wasn't afraid of dragons. They were massive, powerful creatures with huge, sharp teeth and talons. If that wasn't enough, they could breathe fire. But, riders knew they were severely misunderstood. They were wise, kind creatures, with a wide range of emotions, including love. Any creatures capable of love couldn't be bad.

But, as with any other species, there were good dragons and there were evil dragons. Obsidian was the perfect example. He was willing to kill his fellow dragons. He and his rider shared their evil thoughts and schemes, planning to take over the land like Vidar the Conqueror.

The morning sky was beautiful, casting pink and purple hues over the land below. Orion often got lost in his thoughts while flying. The sparkling scales of Saphron's body gleamed in the sunlight, casting shadows over his membranous wings. They could touch the clouds, and he reveled in the peace of the world from above.

They flew all day, making it a third of the way across Gachichken. He knew if they'd brought Raynee, they wouldn't have made it nearly as far. Dragons were much faster than horses. A dragon could traverse in a single day what would take a week for a horse.

Even on their descent into the trees, Callisto didn't scream. When they landed, they set up their campsite, eating a meal of stew. Saphron flew off into the trees to hunt for his meal, as they couldn't very well transport enough food for a dragon.

"How is it you were not afraid today when we flew?" Orion asked as he and Callisto were seated upon a couple of logs, eating.

She smiled, "I have had plenty of experience with dragons in my day. I understand these creatures. Perhaps not as well as a rider, but I like to think I display the proper reverence."

"Indeed you do," he said, "I must say, I'm impressed."

She nodded, "Thank you."

Her blue and silver robes sparkled in the light of the fire, reflecting off her blue eyes. Though she was old—no telling how old—she was beautiful.

"So, how did you become a rider?" she asked.

He looked at her, "Well, I grew up in Cardeas. Half the riders come from my homeland. We all grow up on stories about them, and I was no exception. I journeyed to Abyumo when I was eleven, and joined the recruits. Saphron hatched for me, and the rest is history."

"So, your family is from Cardeas?"

"Well, my father's side," he answered, "My mother's side is from Duwazo."

"Really?" she said, "Who is your mother?"

"Her name is Isadora," he replied, "She was a lady of the court in Chemsson. But, she gave that up to marry my father, Peiter. He's a poor peasant, and they weren't allowed to be together, because of her family. Almost everyone from Cardeas is either a poor peasant or a warrior. Why do you think we all long to be riders?"

"Cardeas does turn out some of the best warriors in the land," she said.

"Yes, they do," he said, "Don't tell me you're from Cardeas."

"No," she replied, "I just know many people from the area. I had several old friends who were Cardeans."

"I see," he said, "Well, I'm sure they were honorable."

"They did their families proud," she agreed.

He paused, "What do you know of Derekkian?"

She smiled, "I was wondering when you would ask. Though, being native to Cardeas, I'm surprised you don't know."

"He was a Cardean?"

"Indeed he was," she replied, "He was the one who organized and led the revolution which ended the reign of Vidar the Conqueror."

"Really?" he asked in wonder.

She looked at him with surprise, "He is hailed highly amongst Cardeans. How is it you do not know the story? His name has even spread to other lands thanks to an outreach program in Duwazo many years ago."

Saphron returned then, satisfied, with a full belly. He nestled into the dirt behind them, ready to get some sleep, *What'd I miss?*

She was just about to tell me about Derekkian, he thought.

Oh, good, he thought, *Then, I haven't missed anything important.*

"I don't know," he said, turning back to his conversation with Callisto, "But, the name was never brought up to me before."

She looked disconcerted, "His strategy was clear: he convinced his friends amongst the other races to join him. Elves, dwarves, and dragon riders came to his aid in Cardeas. From there, it was easy to get the remaining armies of men on his side. Then, he recruited warriors from the lands Vidar had already conquered to join them. Before long, he had a massive army at his disposal, and he led them into battle against Vidar, and won. A poor peasant from Cardeas orchestrated the largest counter-offensive in history, mostly due to his friends from the other races."

"So, that's what I have to do!" he said.

Saphron projected thoughts of agreement as he drifted off to sleep.

Callisto shot him a questioning look.

"The Oracle said to follow the example of Derekkian. I have to get the armies of the elves and the dwarves to join us, and get as many human armies on our side as possible. Dredon is the descendant of Vidar the Conqueror. He plans to do what he couldn't. I'm supposedly the only one who can stop him, by following the example of Derekkian, the one who defeated Vidar!"

She sighed, "I suppose that *is* what The Oracle meant. Very well, I shall help you. I have many friends amongst the elves and the dwarves."

He took a deep breath, "Thank you."

Callisto nodded, "Get some rest. I'll take the first watch."

Saphron

4

The next day, they flew another third of the way through Gachichken. It would take only one more day to make it to the border of Millhaymae, and from there, it would be another couple days to reach the southern territory of Katangalo, where they were to train.

While Saphron was off hunting, Orion sat on a boulder beside Callisto, "So, I told you about how I became a rider last night, and who my parents were. But, I know nothing about you. How did you become The Oracle's keeper?"

"I trained under her last keeper, and when he died, I decided to take over the job," she said.

"I see," he said, "Well, where are you from? Have you always lived in Abyumo?"

"No," she answered, "I'm actually from Duwazo."

"Duwazo? Really?" he said, surprised. After a moment, he said with understanding, "I see. So, that's why you were curious about my mother. You thought you might have known her from Duwazo."

She nodded, "Indeed, I did."

"And, do you? Know her, I mean."

Callisto paused, "No. I don't."

Orion looked away, "If you don't want to talk about yourself, it's alright. I just thought I should get to know the person who's training me a little better."

"I am talking about myself," she said.

When he didn't say anything, she sighed, "It's been a long time since anyone has tried to get to know me. I guess . . . I don't really know who I am anymore."

He looked at her then, "It's okay. I don't really know who I am, either. I'm just a nobody dragon rider with a destiny too great to live up to."

She laughed, "Many people think that."

"Think what?"

"That their destiny is too great for them to live up to," she replied, "But, they are all wrong. The Oracle has never been wrong. If that's what she's foreseen, then it's the truth."

Orion smiled, "I guess we'll see."

As they flew, Orion watched a storm on the horizon. It was always strange, seeing one from afar. It looked like one big cloud, with a waterfall of rain beneath it, while the rest of the landscape remained sunny and dry. Gachichken was a large land, but they were able to traverse it quickly on the back of his sapphire dragon. They reached Millhaymae by the evening, and landed to make camp again.

"Why don't we begin your training now?" Callisto asked as Saphron took off to find his meal.

"Isn't it safer to wait until we reach Katangalo?" he asked.

"We are far enough away from Abyumo," she replied, "Plus, I doubt he has anyone watching you. I'm sure he knows nothing of you, and perhaps thinks nothing of you. He surely doesn't see you as a threat."

Orion looked down.

"We can use that to our advantage. He won't expect us to orchestrate a successful counter-offensive against him. He doesn't even know who we are. Therefore, he's likely not taking any measures to watch us or prevent us from gathering forces."

"I suppose," he replied, feeling the embarrassment of his lack of skill acutely.

"We won't do any magical training, yet, as that would surely attract attention, but I can begin your combat training."

He nodded reluctantly.

"Let's start with archery," she said, "Why don't you show me what you've got."

"Very well," he grumbled, rising and grabbing his crossbow.

"A crossbow," she said, "Very rider-like. I suppose you're not educated with a bow and arrow, then."

"I'm afraid not," he said, "Riders tend to use crossbows more."

"Alright," she said, "I have a basic knowledge of crossbows. I'm far better with a bow and arrow, though. But, let's see what you've got."

Orion shot off arrows at the surrounding trees, hitting each one in the same place. Then, he shot a squirrel that was running through the darkened woods, killing it. "Care for squirrel?" he asked.

Callisto let out a laugh, "Sure. It seems your skill with a crossbow is adequate. We need only to test how well you do upon the back of your dragon."

He looked at her nervously.

She raised an eyebrow, "You'll have to be able to do as well upon his back. Chances are that's where you'll be fighting from. You'll have to be able to perform both feats masterfully if you are to beat him."

He was silent, looking at the ground.

"I see," she said, "So, that's the place that really needs work. Tomorrow night, we shall see how your sword fighting is on the ground. From there, we must work at your combat skills from the back of your dragon. And, of course, we must train in magical combat as well. It's going to take a lot of work."

"Yes," he agreed, "It will."

The two of them flew over Millhaymae, and to the border of Katangalo before they landed to make camp again. It would only take one more day to reach the desolate southern territory where they were to complete his training.

"Let's see how your sword fighting is," Callisto said, tossing him a stick and grabbing one herself.

Orion gripped the stick, nervously taking his stance. Callisto swung, and Orion blocked.

"Good," she said, "Again."

She swung again, and he blocked it. She smiled, and they engaged in a fight, swinging, thrusting, and parrying. Her footwork was impressive, and he found it difficult to keep up. The fight lasted a few minutes, before she finally knocked the stick from his hand.

"Not bad," she said, "Not bad at all. You need only to fine-tune your skills, and you will be a formidable opponent in sword combat. You're not a blank slate, Orion. You have skills from which I can build upon."

He smiled, feeling relieved and proud, and at the same time, surprised and disappointed that he didn't win. But, knowing his teacher believed him able was a good thing. It meant less time spent training, or more time spent on the areas he needed improvement in. He wasn't sure how long they had, and that put enough pressure on him to train quickly.

"Why don't you take the first shift tonight?" Callisto said, "We'll begin your training when we reach the training grounds in Katangalo tomorrow night."

Orion nodded as Saphron returned from his nightly hunt, curling up beside him. Callisto lied down to get comfortable, and Orion leaned against Saphron's side, feeling the warmth that radiated from his fiery belly.

Do you *think we can do this?* Orion thought.

Of course, Saphron said, *I've always believed in you. And I think Callisto will be a good teacher. If The Oracle saw the ways everything could play out, and she saw us succeed, then I'm sure we can. She recommended Callisto to train us, and it seems as though she knows what she's talking about, so I know she'll be the best teacher we could ask for.*

Maybe, he thought, *I suppose it depends upon how much stock you put into the word of an oracle.*

Oracles are famous for their wisdom, knowledge, and understanding of the future, Saphron said, *They're able to see events before they happen. Who could doubt them when they already know what will happen before it does?*

She said she saw all possible outcomes, Orion thought, *So, that means it depends on what we do, and what he does. Basically, either of us can change what will happen. Nothing is set in stone. So, how does her "foresight" actually help us? The only thing she told us that was useful was what Dredon and Obsidian are planning.*

Yes, he agreed, *And, she told us what to do to stop him. She was giving us guidance toward the outcome where we succeed. If we listen and follow her words, we can do this.*

Orion sighed, *I suppose you're right, Saphron.*

The only way to know for sure is to do it, he thought.

The yellows and oranges of the sunrise played over the land below as the three of them made their way across Katangalo. It was windier than normal, and it made Callisto shiver. Orion had his black bodysuit with blue lines, crafted by the dragon riders. It was designed to protect him from the elements, and it kept him warm and cozy. But her hooded cloak didn't offer her as much protection.

He could hear her mutter a spell under her breath, and she stopped shivering. He guessed she knew one which would keep her warm against the cold air. After a while, he could feel the warmth radiating behind him, and he knew it was the spell.

When evening approached, Callisto pointed ahead, "There! We made it. Those are the abandoned training grounds!"

Saphron landed in the center of the barren, dusty plain. It resembled the dragon rider realm; only it was drier, dustier, and devoid of life.

"What is this place?" he asked.

"Well, it was once a thriving city of the human realm," Callisto said, "But, drought struck, and never really went away. The people were forced to leave for their own survival. It hasn't rained here in . . . two hundred years."

"You've been around that long?" Orion asked.

"No," she replied, "I'm one hundred and thirty-one."

"Wow," he said, "Even though I'm a rider, it always sounds like such a long time."

"Yes, well, human mentality does that to you," she said, "You'll get used to it as you get older yourself."

Orion nodded, thinking about the long lives of dragon riders, and what it would be like to be that old. *If I even live through this,* he thought.

"I think tonight we'll work on your sword fighting. We must improve that first," she said, "Then, we can focus our full attention on the other aspects of your training."

A marvelous plan, Saphron thought, *I'm going to go get something to eat.*

Orion chuckled, *Very well, old friend. I hope my sword training doesn't take too long.*

Callisto tossed him a stick, taking her stance. They engaged again, fighting back and forth. She was very fast and graceful, and he had a tough time keeping up. But, he knew the only way to beat her was to learn to read her and be prepared to counter her moves. She shouted out critiques as they twirled around, kicking up dust.

She disarmed him several times, offering him advice each time to improve his skill. Finally, six rounds later, he cornered her by a boulder, knocking the stick from her hand, and placing his against her throat.

"Touché," she said, "Well done."

He smiled, lowering his stick, "Thanks."

"It seems you have your sword fighting down. I knew it wouldn't take long, but one night is better than I'd hoped. You're a fast learner. How is it you were never properly trained as a rider?"

"They don't offer us much training," he said, "We get a fortnight's crash course, and from there, we must train on our own. Our friends help us. If we prove ourselves worthy, we get to go to the training mountain, and train with the top riders. But, I never made it there." He looked down, feeling ashamed and dismayed all over again.

"Perhaps that's for the best," she said, "If you had, Dredon would know who you are, wouldn't he?"

He looked up, "Yes. He would. He rules that mountain." He paused, looking out over the dark and desolate plain, "Which is why I'll never be able to beat him."

Callisto looked at him, "Yes, you will. That's why we're here. This . . . " she gestured around them, "This is *our* training mountain."

Indeed it is, Saphron thought, returning from his hunt with a full belly.

Orion nodded, "Alright. Let's get some sleep. We've got a full day of training tomorrow."

Callisto smiled, "Yes, we do."

"Okay, since I can't hear you talk, Saphron," Callisto said, "We need to work out a system of communication. You can nod your head for 'yes' and shake your head for 'no.'"

Saphron nodded, *That one's obvious.*

Hush, Orion thought.

"That one's obvious," Callisto said, "If you need to go into detail on something, I suppose Orion will have to translate. If you need to go hunt or go to the bathroom, draw a single line in the dirt with your talon. If you're tired and need a break, draw two lines. If you need to speak to your rider, slam your tail against the ground. If there's danger, breathe a jet of flame upwards. We'll work on more later. But, for now, I think that should be good, right?"

Saphron nodded.

"Excellent. Now, it's not me who needs to work on my communication with you. It's Orion," she turned to face him, "The two of you have to be perfectly in sync for you to be able to fight upon your dragon's back."

"We are perfectly in sync," he said, "We can hear each other's thoughts."

"Oh, really?" she said, "Well, let's see it then. Shoot your crossbow into the trees on the edge of the clearing, like you did the other night, but from your dragon's back."

"No problem," he said, leaping upon Saphron's back.

"Saphron, don't make it too easy for him. In battle, you'll have to fly evasively, and he'll have to be able to shoot as you do so."

The great dragon nodded, pushing himself into the air. He flew back and forth, darting past the trees and around the clearing. Orion struggled to notch his crossbow and aim it, the momentum pushing his arms around as he tried to shoot. He fired off his arrows at the trees, and they landed in front of Callisto. When he looked over at the trees, he could see that he'd only hit one of them.

"Again," was all she said.

He sighed, and they circled again, firing off more arrows. Again, he missed his marks. Callisto made them do it over and over, and he only hit two trees in all the times he had to repeat it.

"You have to learn how to compensate your aim for the momentum of Saphron's movements. Once you do that, you'll be able to shoot from his back as easily as you can shoot from the ground," she said.

"The momentum pushes my arms, so it's not simply a matter of changing my aim," he retorted.

"You're correct," she replied, "So, you must build your arm strength to counteract the force against your arms. Keep practicing."

"Why would I not work on my arm strength first?" he asked.

"Your arm strength will increase as you continue to practice," she said, "You need to figure out how to get your aim right."

"Easy for you to say," he groaned, frustrated. They'd been at it for hours, and he wasn't making any improvements.

Saphron flew around again, and Orion tried to change his aim to hit the trees. He managed to hit two of them this time, but he still had a long way to go. His arms were tired, and he needed to rest.

"That was better," she said, "See? You're improving. Now, do it again."

"How many times do you expect me to do this today?"

"Until you get it right," she said, "Now, go."

"No," he said, "I'm done. I'm not getting any better, and my arms are sore. If I don't take a break, I'm going to go crazy."

Callisto scoffed, "Don't be such a baby. I thought I was training a dragon rider, not a weakling. Again."

"And just why do you imagine you're capable of training a rider?" he snapped, "You're not one. I'd like to see you do this."

She raised her eyebrow, twisting her lips. Silently, she grabbed her bow and arrow, walking up to Saphron's side, "Move."

"What?" he asked in disbelief.

"Move," she repeated, "You said you'd like to see me do it."

Orion laughed, sliding out of Saphron's saddle, and standing back. "This ought to be good," he muttered under his breath.

"Okay, Saphron," she said, "Do what you did with Orion, and fly past the trees."

Saphron nodded, taking off and darting around the edge of the training space. Callisto shot off her arrows, hitting every single tree dead center. Orion's mouth dropped open as Saphron landed in front of him, and she slid off his back.

"How did you—" he began.

"Again," she said.

He hung his head, sighing. He felt a mixture of emotions all through him. He was embarrassed that she'd shown him up and done what he couldn't. He was impressed by her skill, and surprised by it. He realized she was a better trainer than he had given her credit for. And, he was still tired and frustrated. But, he gritted his teeth and did it again, hitting three of the trees.

"Take a break and eat something," Callisto said when he returned, "After lunch, keep practicing until you get it down. If this is the only thing you do, over and over, then that's what you'll do. I want you to master this. It's a very important skill to have. And, I know you can do it."

Orion sighed, nodding, and headed off to get something to eat.

The next day was spent doing the same thing. His arm muscles were extremely sore from the previous day, and he could barely hold them up to do it again. Callisto stood by on the ground, having them go in circles until lunch, firing arrows at the trees.

When they'd finished eating, she said, "Let's try something. Obviously, you need some guidance if you are to get your aim right, as you haven't managed to hit all the trees yet. I'm going to ride with you, and help you aim."

Orion paused, surprised, and finally nodded. The two of them climbed upon Saphron's back together, readying to take off.

Pay attention, Saphron thought, *She knows what she's doing. I know we are one, as dragon and rider, but she understood my movements, and where to shift her body, better than you ever have. I'm not saying this to make you feel worse. I'm saying it to let you know she's a good teacher, and she can really help you. I have a feeling this experience will be as invaluable as getting invited to the training mountain.*

Orion projected his reluctant agreement, readying himself.

Saphron flew around the clearing, and Callisto guided Orion's arms, helping him steady his crossbow, and showing him when to fire. When they landed, he could see that they had hit all the trees. She climbed down, saying, "Now, do you think you can do that on your own?"

Orion nodded.

"Excellent. Let's see it."

Saphron circled for the millionth time, and Orion shot off his arrows at the trees. This time, he only missed one.

"Great job!" she shouted, "That was excellent. Now, do you feel the difference between what you were doing before and what you did that time?"

He nodded again.

"Okay, so keep practicing that, until you feel comfortable and confident in your ability to do it consistently."

He spent the rest of the day continuing to circle the clearing, firing arrows at the trees. His aim had improved tremendously since she'd helped him learn when to fire, and he was able to hit at least a few trees every time. When he went to sleep that night, he dreamed of circling the clearing and hitting all the trees as professionally as Callisto had. That thought made him wonder, *How is it she can do that so well? Was she a rider who lost her dragon?*

Saphron stirred, perturbed by the thought. *That could very well be,* he thought, *It would explain a lot. But, it's impolite to ask. What a horrible tragedy to endure if it's true.*

Still, Orion thought, *I wonder . . .*

In Sync

5

"Let's do some drills today to work on your synchronization," Callisto said.

Orion and Saphron nodded, readying themselves for her instruction.

"You can share each other's thoughts, but you need to be so in tune with each other that you think the same thing at the same time," she continued, "It allows you to react quicker, which makes you dangerous in battle. Any advantage you can get is going to help you." She looked from him to his dragon, "The time it takes to communicate your thoughts to each other needs to be eliminated. Once you're on the same wavelength, you'll both know what to do without the added time."

She makes a lot of sense, Saphron thought, *When we dueled Moonstone and Epsilon, I had to keep trying to tell you what you should do, and what I was going to do, so you'd be prepared for it. If we both fought the same way, and you knew what to do and what I would do, I could've focused on the fight, and not worried about you.*

So it's my fault? Orion thought angrily.

Well, yes, he thought, *I'm a dragon. My battle instincts are . . . well, instinct.*

Don't blame this all on me, he fired back, *You could've minded your own business and let me figure things out on my own. You fight the other dragon. I fight the other rider.*

Oh, yes, that's synchronized, he sarcastically retorted, *The greatest teams handle their fights individually.*

Listen, you—

His thoughts were interrupted as Callisto cleared her throat, "When you boys are finished bickering, we'll begin."

"H-how'd you know we were arguing?" Orion asked.

She rolled her eyes, "It was pretty obvious, the way you two were facing each other, making angry faces and gestures. Are you done, now?"

"Uh . . . yeah," he said, straightening.

"Great. Let's begin. To start, you need to feel how your dragon moves. You're going to ride without a saddle, and pay close attention to Saphron's movements, and the way he flies."

"Without a saddle?" Orion said, eyes wide.

Callisto nodded, "Yes. That's the easiest way for you to feel his movements. You'll be able to go back to the saddle later, once you have it down, but for now, it's about getting to know your dragon."

"Well, that might be getting to know him a little *too* well," he said, "Do you have any idea how painful and uncomfortable it is to ride a dragon bareback? The scales are hard, with no cushion, and there are spikes along their spine!"

"Well, I suggest you don't sit directly on those, then," she replied, turning to his dragon, "Saphron, your job in this exercise is to fly through the forest on your daily hunt, and return. That should give him a sense of how you might move in combat. When you return, be prepared to practice evasive maneuvers. I mean you no disrespect by what I'll do, but I must leave it a surprise if I am to catch you off guard."

The great sapphire dragon nodded his head.

"Excellent. Get going."

"How am I supposed to ride without sitting on the spikes?" Orion asked, annoyed.

"Figure it out," Callisto said, removing Saphron's saddle, "Now, get going."

Orion reluctantly walked to Saphron's side, feeling his warm scales beneath his hands. He stared for a moment at the sharp spikes along his spine. He cautiously lifted his leg, clambering along his scales to try to situate himself atop his back beside the spikes.

Easy there, geez, Saphron thought, *It's like you've never climbed onto my back before.*

Well, not without a saddle, he snapped back, *How am I supposed to sit up here without stabbing myself in the crotch?*

Saphron laughed, and Callisto smirked as she watched.

Very funny, you great oaf, he thought, *Just shut up and fly.*

Oaf? he thought, *Oh, I'll fly alright.* He paused, tauntingly adding, *Are you sure you're ready? Or are the spikes too much?*

Just fly!

With that, Saphron took to the sky, launching himself high into the clouds.

Orion had to clutch onto the spikes to hold on as his body slid off of his dragon's back, *Whoa! Not so fast, I'm slipping!*

Saphron laughed again, *Oh, is this too much for you? Well, I guess you should've thought of that before you called me an oaf!*

Saphron!

The great blue dragon spiraled through the air, Orion clinging to him for dear life. The edges of his spikes weren't as sharp as the points, but they still cut into his hands a little. The current of air slammed into him, making him squint, and making his body dangle in the wind.

As he dove down, swooping toward his prey, Orion lost his grip, falling toward the earth below. Saphron quickly changed course, moving beneath his rider to catch him. Orion landed on his back, cutting his arms on the spikes. He cried out in pain, struggling to hang on as his arms bled. The sapphire dragon moved quickly, snatching up a deer and eating it as he sped back to the training grounds.

As he approached, Callisto began throwing rocks at him. He had to maneuver quickly to dodge them, swooping side to side. Orion felt his movements distinctly, and, despite his agony, he could tell the difference from a saddle. He was able to make out each muscle's individual movement. He could feel how his wings caught the different air currents to move, and how Saphron's body twisted and turned.

They landed, and Saphron projected his remorse and his worry, letting him down gently.

I'm sorry, he thought, *Are you alright?*

I will be, he thought, *Don't worry.*

"Orion, you're bleeding," Callisto said, running up, "Here. Give me your arms." She took his arms, healing his wounds with magic.

"Thanks," he said.

"Of course. Now, I know lessons are always harder to learn when you get hurt by them, but were you able to feel his movements better?"

Orion nodded, "I did."

"Good," she replied, "Now, let's take a break and try again. This time, try not to hurt yourself. Maybe I can put a temporary spell on his spikes to make them dull, so you don't cut yourself. Pay close attention to the way he moves, and you'll be able to read him better, and know how to move yourself to compensate."

"You want us to do it again?" Orion asked.

Absolutely not, Saphron thought, horrified, *You hurt yourself once already. It's too risky.*

Relax, Orion thought, *She's right. We need to do this.* "Okay," he said, nodding, "Let's do it."

"Good," Callisto said, smiling, "Glad to see your perseverance increasing." She walked to Saphron's side, uttering a spell, and then stepped back, nodding, "That should do it."

He went beside his dragon, clutching his spikes in his sore hands, and feeling that they had dull edges. He took a breath, climbing onto his back. Saphron took to the skies again, spiraling through the air. Orion held on easier this time, even though the dull pain still lingered from his injury, made worse by gripping the dulled spikes.

He honed in on his dragon's movements, feeling each muscle as he flew, shifting and maneuvering through the sky. He dove down, catching himself another deer, and eating it as he flew. When he reached the training grounds and Callisto began throwing rocks, he dodged them perfectly, and Orion learned the ways he moved, and how to move himself to avoid falling off.

"Excellent!" she shouted when they landed.

I'm most impressed, Saphron thought.

Thank you, he thought.

You learned a lot, didn't you?

I surprised myself how much, he replied.

She's a good teacher. I suppose I was quick to judge her when you got hurt, but she really knows what she's doing. We've never been so in sync.

Orion let out a laugh, *Yeah. I think I'll be able to move with you now.*

"You did beautifully," Callisto said, "Both of you."

Saphron beamed proudly.

"Did you learn something?"

Orion nodded.

She smiled, "Well, let's test that theory."

The young rider and his dragon exchanged glances with one another.

She removed the spell from the spikes and put Saphron's saddle back on, "Do it again, but this time, you'll fly normally. You don't have to catch another deer, Saphron, as I'm sure two of them were plenty. But, just practice maneuvering through the air, twisting, turning, diving, and dodging." She turned toward Orion, "Now that you've learned how your dragon moves, you should be able to keep up, and move with him without difficulty."

He cleared this throat nervously, "Right. Of course." He leaped upon the blue dragon's back, taking to the sky. As they flew, he was able to tune into his movements like he never had before. He couldn't believe the difference a couple of bareback flights had made.

When they landed, Callisto shot them a huge smile, "What a difference! I'm proud of the two of you."

"Thank you," Orion said, "I think we got this whole synchronization thing down."

Saphron nodded his agreement.

"Excellent," she said, "Keep practicing today, and tomorrow we shall work on your sword fighting from dragonback."

Orion was impressed by Callisto's skill and agility as she fought him with a stick to improve his sword fighting from Saphron's back. He rode upon his great dragon, swinging the sword with intensity and moving with him. Callisto swung her sword from the ground, leaping upon boulders and climbing trees to make their duel as realistic as possible.

He was still getting used to his dragon's movements, but he was able to keep up as he would on the ground. His balance was off as he swayed side to side, but he maintained a firm grip with his legs, and focused his energy into strong thrusts and parries.

"Excellent," Callisto said as she stepped out onto a tree branch to fight them, "You're doing well. If we keep practicing like this for the next few days, I think you'll get it down."

"I hope so," he said, swinging his stick and forcing her to leap from the tree, "Because if I'm to fight Dredon, I need all the skills I can get."

"You're not as bad as you think with your sword," she said, "I think the main thing you were missing was your synchronization. Now that you're getting that down, you're improving exponentially! Our main area of focus will be magical combat."

That will be the thing to focus on, for sure, Saphron thought.

What do you mean? Orion countered, *We were trained magically.*

Saphron snorted, *Not so well as I would hope. It certainly won't be enough to best Dredon. I, for one, am glad we're being trained by a witch. Her expertise in that area will certainly be useful. And, I must admit, she's a good teacher. Look how far you've come. You could never win a duel before, you were always falling off my back, and I had to focus on you instead of the other dragon. Now, you can feel my movements, I can focus on other things, and you're fighting like a pro. I daresay you could beat Epsilon, now. You might even be skilled enough to receive an invite to the training mountain.*

You really think so?

I do, he replied.

Orion smiled to himself, redoubling his efforts in their duel. If Saphron had faith in him, he might actually have a chance. Though he was a long way from being able to best Dredon, he knew he'd progressed as exponentially as Callisto had said.

Epsilon

6

"How much do you know about magical combat?" Callisto asked, readying her wand, blue eyes shining.

"Well," Orion said confidently, "We riders are trained in magical combat before we're released. So, I have a fair bit of knowledge."

"Oh, good," she replied, "Then, this should be easy for you."

"What should?" he asked uncertainly.

She smiled, waving her wand, "This." She launched a magical attack at him, knocking him backward.

He got up, readying himself, blue power radiating from his hands. She fired at him again, and he jumped out of the way, launching his own attack back at her. She waved her wand nonchalantly, easily blocking it. They fired back and forth a few times before she knocked him down again, causing him to faceplant into the dirt.

"Yes," she said sarcastically, "That training was very useful."

Orion stood, spitting the dirt from his teeth. He felt his anger rise at his humiliation, and he fired a blast at her. She, again, blocked it with ease.

He began a rapid-fire stream of attacks, none of them getting through her barrier.

"Enough!" she shouted, blasting him back again. She stood over him, eyes flaming, "Never attack in anger. You must use your other emotions, like grief, compassion, protectiveness, or rage."

"Rage...is the same thing as anger," he said as he stood, panting, and calming himself.

"No," Callisto replied, "It is not. When you're angry, your actions are rash, impulsive, and stupid. When you're vengeful, your actions are righteous, powerful, and full of intent. When you act out of anger, you're blind. You lash out like a child, with no real goal in mind besides causing your opponent to feel your pain, frustration, and humiliation. When you act out of rage, you're focused. You have a reason for your feelings and a goal in mind. Don't confuse the two. Rage can help you. Anger cannot."

Orion nodded, clearing his head.

"You've learned how to launch magical blasts," she said, "But, you have no knowledge of actual *spells*, or how to counter those blasts when they're launched at *you*."

He hung his head.

She's right, Saphron thought.

I know, Orion replied, *Don't rub it in.*

"Pride will be your downfall," Callisto said, "Answer me this: what do you have to be proud of?"

He looked at her, dumbfounded.

"You're a rider, yes. But, that was nothing you did. You got lucky. You have something inside you that has the potential to be great. Your dragon recognized that. But, it's up to you whether you fan the flame, or let it go out. If you can't swallow your pride and learn what you must, you'll never defeat Dredon."

He sighed, realizing she was right. He had nothing to be proud of. He was a nobody rider who couldn't even get invited to the training mountain. He only just now figured out how to read his dragon's movements, and he was decent at shooting and fighting from his dragon's back, but he still needed to practice. If he couldn't follow her instruction, he *and* Saphron were doomed.

"I'll teach you how to form a protective barrier first. Then, we'll work on offensive spells," Callisto said, "Once you're able to best me in a duel, you'll have only to keep practicing. If only there were someone you could practice against who has a dragon. That would help you more than facing off against me." She looked off into the distance, seeming upset.

"Did you have a dragon? Before?" he asked.

She faced him then, "No. But, I've certainly lost my share of people I cared about. I've had several mentors, and the one thing I know is: once a mentor has taught his or her student all they can, it's up to the student to prepare themselves. And, knowing they face a threat greater than what you can replicate for them makes you feel inadequate as a mentor."

"No," he said, "You're not inadequate. You've already taught me so much in such a short time. I've progressed further than I ever thought I could."

"Still," she said, "Once I've taught you what you need to know, you need a better practice partner than me."

"Perhaps," he sighed, "But, a mentor and a practice partner aren't the same thing. Your job is to teach me. Once I've learned, I must find a way to practice, and that's not your job."

She let out a humorless laugh, "Perhaps you're right. I never thought of it that way."

"Well, it looks like it was my turn to teach *you*," he said, smiling.

"Alright," she said, "Let's teach you how to form a magical barrier of protection."

A few weeks went by as Callisto helped him practice the skills she'd taught him. He and Saphron's synchronization improved to the point of perfection. His shooting and sword fighting skills from dragonback improved as well. He was able to fight Callisto off with ease, and fire arrows off, hitting the center of any target he aimed at. He learned how to form a magical barrier of protection, and actual combat spells. He was able to best his mentor in a duel, and he knew he was as prepared as she could make him.

I really need a practice partner, he thought, *That's the only way I'll improve enough to defeat Dredon. And, that's the only way you'll be trained enough to defeat Obsidian.*

You're right, Saphron agreed, *But, how are we to get a dragon and rider to practice with?*

Orion paused, *We could call Moonstone and Epsilon.*

No, Saphron thought, *It's too risky.*

They're our friends, he thought, *And they miss us. They didn't want us to leave. They only abandoned us as practice partners because we couldn't offer them a challenge. I bet that now they would be willing to fight with us again.*

The blue dragon sighed, *Very well. But, ask Callisto first.*

He nodded, going over to the blue-and-silver-cloaked witch, "I've been thinking about what you said . . . about getting a practice partner. And I think I have someone. If I could just call our old friends, I bet they'd be willing to come here to practice with us."

She nodded reluctantly, "As much as I'd like to avoid the risk of involving anyone else, I'm afraid it might be necessary. Give them a call."

"Thank you," he said, heading to the edge of the clearing and digging a small hole, "*Dwervo.*" The hole filled with water, and once it settled, he waved his hand over its surface, visualizing Epsilon, "*Balgadeer.*"

His old friend's face appeared on the water, "Orion? Is that you?"

"Yes," he replied, "How's it going?"

"You've been away for months, and all you can say is, 'How's it going?'"

Orion shrugged.

"I've been fine," he said, "How've you been? *Where* have you been?"

"That's actually why I'm calling," he said, "I've been training, and I need a training partner. I know we've had our differences as far as training together, but I think I can offer you a challenge now. So, if you're interested, I need you to come here to train with me."

"Where's here?" he asked.

"Does that mean you'll come?"

Epsilon paused, looking at him uncertainly, "Alright. I'll come train with you. But, this had better be worth it. How far away is it, anyway?"

"We're in the south of Katangalo," he replied, "It's pretty barren here, so we'll be easy to find once you get here."

"Very well," he said, "Moonstone and I shall set out at dawn."

"Thanks," Orion replied, "See you soon."

Epsilon nodded as they severed the connection.

The next few days were spent working with Callisto on the things she'd already taught them as they waited for Epsilon and Moonstone to arrive. It was a five-to-six-day journey from the realm of the riders in Abyumo to the southern training grounds of Katangalo. So, it gave them plenty of time to perfect their technique and prepare.

Orion noticed each night as they lied out beneath the stars that several of them were lining up overhead. It wouldn't be long before they reached each other. Callisto seemed to be growing more and more nervous the closer they got. He figured it was due to the likelihood that these were the stars The Oracle had prophesied to collide.

"Do you think those are the stars The Oracle foresaw colliding?" he asked.

Callisto nodded her silver-haired head as she stared up at the heavens, "I've no doubt."

"We don't have much time, then."

"No," she said, "We don't."

"We have only until the first stars collide to complete my training," he said.

"Your training is already complete," Callisto replied, smiling, "Congratulations. I've taught you all I can. The rest is up to you to practice. That's why your practice partner is coming. You only have until the first star collides to get your practice in, and then we must set out."

"Set out where?" he asked.

"The land of the elves," she answered, "Gliken."

"What is our plan exactly?"

Callisto rolled her eyes, letting out a laugh, "You're supposed to be in charge here. The plan should be yours . . . Derekkian. We must gather warriors to face Dredon and Obsidian and their troops."

"So, we're going to Gliken to get the elves on our side," Orion stated.

She nodded, "Now you're getting it."

As Orion opened a sleepy eye, he saw a white blur streak past him. The gust of wind caused him to jump up and arm himself. As he tried to gather his bearings, he saw that it was Moonstone, and he was launching a surprise attack on Saphron, who was angry and disoriented at being so rudely awoken. He scrambled to climb upon his dragon's back, and Saphron took to the sky as Epsilon tossed Orion a jousting stick.

"Good morning," he called, "Shall we begin?"

Let's go, Saphron, he thought.

The sapphire dragon breathed a jet of flame across the white dragon, and used the distraction to attack. The two beasts locked into a fight as their riders began swinging their jousting sticks at each other. Epsilon was quite a skilled opponent, and fighting upon Saphron's back while he was locked into a duel with Moonstone proved more difficult than fighting Callisto while she jumped around in the trees. But, he focused on moving with his dragon, keeping his balance, and fighting Epsilon.

He was finally able to offer his old friend a challenge, as they dueled back and forth across the clearing. Epsilon and Moonstone had learned things on the training mountain, but he and Saphron had learned things from Callisto as well. The two riders swung their jousting sticks, stabbing and blocking as the two dragons grappled. Finally, Orion and Saphron were able to beat them.

"Whoa," Epsilon said as they landed, "It seems you were correct: you *can* offer us a challenge now. Well done."

"Thank you," Orion said, "We've been working really hard."

"I can tell."

"The two of you have improved as well. The training mountain must have done you good," he said.

"Indeed it has," Epsilon replied, beaming.

"So, you haven't noticed anything strange?" he asked.

"Strange like what?"

"Like . . . with Dredon?"

He sighed, "Again with this Dredon thing? When will you let it go, Orion?"

"Have you seen the missing leaders?"

He shook his head, "No."

"Exactly," he replied, "Because he killed them. How can I let that go? He's a murderer. And, he needs to be brought to justice for what he's done."

"You can't prove anything," Epsilon said, "Even Kirstiana doesn't believe you. How could he have possibly hidden that much evidence?"

Orion paused, looking at him suspiciously, "How did you know about Kirstiana and the missing evidence?"

"She sent two investigators to the training mountain to search for evidence," he replied, "I heard everything. They didn't find anything, and they're the best in the business. If he did what you claimed, where could he possibly hide the bodies of so many dragons and riders that even Morgalina and Austinian couldn't find them?"

"I don't know!" he exclaimed, "But, somehow, he did it. I know what I saw. I'm your friend. Why won't you believe me?"

"Because it doesn't make any sense!" he cried. He paused, sighing, "Maybe it was a mistake to come here."

"Maybe it was, then!" Orion shouted, "If you think so, why don't you just go?"

Epsilon looked at him, eyes full of sorrow, "Alright, Orion. Fine. If that's what you want, I'll just go."

As Moonstone started to take flight, Orion sighed, "Epsilon, wait. Don't go."

He paused, hovering, the dark-skinned rider looking back at his friend earnestly, "If I stay, I don't want to hear another word about Dredon and Obsidian."

Orion nodded, "I promise."

"I mean it," he said, "One more word and I'm gone."

"Okay," he said, "Let's just . . . set up camp. Tomorrow, we'll have a rematch."

He nodded, and the white dragon touched back down, his rider sliding off his back.

"Orion, you didn't tell me our guest was here," Callisto said, walking up.

"Who's that?" Epsilon asked, backing toward Moonstone.

"I'm Callisto," she said, moving closer and extending her hand, "Keeper of The Oracle and trainer of Saphron and Orion."

He shook her hand, "I'm Epsilon, and this is Moonstone. We're old friends of Saphron and Orion. We've come to be their practice partners."

"I know," she replied, "Pleasure to meet you both."

Moonstone gave her a nod, nuzzling her with his snout.

"He says it's a pleasure to meet you as well," Epsilon said.

Callisto patted his snout, giggling.

"We were just going to set up camp," Orion said, "and start practicing in the morning."

"It is morning," she replied, looking confused.

"I know," Orion said, "But they've come such a long way. Plus, we've already had a duel. I think we could all use a break today, and we'll start fresh in the morning."

"Very well," Callisto said, still looking confused, "I suppose you *have* earned a break."

"Excellent," he said, "Besides, we have a lot of catching up to do."

"Indeed we do," Epsilon said, putting his arm around Orion's shoulders. The two sat by the extinguished fire as they told each other what had happened in the time they'd been apart. Callisto sat nearby, unable to partake in their conversation. Saphron drew a single line in the dirt, indicating to her that he needed to hunt. She nodded, and he and Moonstone took to the forest to find their prey.

They spent the next few days sparring with Moonstone and Epsilon as Callisto sat back, observing. She'd occasionally pull Orion to the side to give him pointers, but overall, it seemed her training had stuck. He was able to beat his old friend easily, much to Epsilon's frustration.

"I guess this place has done you more good than the training mountain did me," he said, catching his breath.

"Still, thank you for coming all the way here to help me," Orion said.

"Of course," he replied, "That's what friends are for."

"I think I'm done training," he said, "I'm ready to continue on. Perhaps I'll get more time than I thought."

"Continue on with what?" Epsilon asked suspiciously.

"His quest for self-discovery," Callisto interjected as Orion struggled to find words.

"Yes," he agreed, "My quest for self-discovery."

"That's why you left The Oracle?" he asked, eyeing Callisto, "To help train some underdog dragon rider on his 'road to self-discovery?'"

"Yes," she answered quickly, "The Oracle is a big believer in self-discovery. She can see everyone's possible destiny. Everyone has a destiny of greatness, but not everyone achieves it. When someone is willing to work for theirs, we are all too happy to support them."

Epsilon looked from her to Orion, disbelieving.

"Look, I appreciate you training with me," Orion said, "But, this journey is one I must take alone. I've already become greater than I ever thought I could. I've beaten a rider who's been to the training mountain. Now that my training is over, I must pursue other paths to finding myself. Eventually, I shall return home, to Abyumo. I promise you that. But, until then, this is goodbye." He held out his hand for Epsilon to shake.

He stared at it, a strange expression on his face. After a long pause, he said, "I guess this *is* goodbye."

Orion felt his heart sink as he looked at Epsilon's face, which seemed to be twisted with sadness. He lowered his hand, saying, "I don't want to say goodbye this way. But, I have to do this for me. We're still friends, aren't we?"

Epsilon paused again, looking forlorn. Finally, he nodded, softly saying, "Yeah. We're still friends."

Orion smiled, grateful his friendship wasn't ending. As the two riders embraced and their dragons nuzzled each other's snouts in farewell, they suddenly heard a deafening *crash*. They looked up in time to see two stars colliding with each other. They began to fall from the sky together. Streaks of starlight and chunks of debris emanated from the collision. Another *crash* followed as they impacted into the ground a short way away. The shockwave was enough to knock them all down, even the dragons.

"You're right, Orion," Epsilon said, panicked, "It *is* time for me to go home."

Orion nodded.

Epsilon mounted Moonstone's back, and they took to the sky, fleeing back to Abyumo.

An Old Friend

7

"Why didn't we tell Epsilon the truth?" Orion asked as they made their way to Gliken upon Saphron's back.

"Because," Callisto replied from behind him, "It's not his burden to bear. Also, he didn't believe you about Dredon, so he would likely not support our plan, and he may, inadvertently or otherwise, say something to someone he shouldn't. Then, Dredon would know of our plan, and we'd lose the element of surprise. We shouldn't involve anyone from Abyumo until the ending stages of our plan. The fewer people near our enemies who know, the better."

"I suppose you're right," he sighed, "But still, he's been my friend for years. I tell him everything. It feels wrong to hide something from him, particularly something this big."

"He can be the first one you tell when we reach Abyumo," she said, "Until then, it's best he's kept in the dark."

It took them all day to reach the border of Gliken. They stopped to make camp, ready to speak with the elves the following day. They hoped they could get at least a couple of their kingdoms on their side. The more help they could summon, the better.

As Orion took the first watch, Callisto falling asleep beside Saphron, he looked out over the elven forest ahead. It was as beautiful as it was ancient, and the heavy burden of this quest bore down on him as he stared into the mist. He hoped Callisto's friends would be able to help them get the elves on their side. He knew several elves back home who were riders, but he'd never met a non-rider elf before. The customs of the riders were a blend of human and elven customs, so he felt somewhat prepared, but not entirely.

He just kept thinking, *Is this really my destiny? How will I ever live up to it?*

If you don't quit dwelling on what's to come, I'll never get to sleep, Saphron thought.

Sorry, he thought, *It's just a lot to think about.*

I know it is, he replied softly, *But thinking on it too much will only drive you mad. You won't know until it happens. Just let things happen.*

If everyone just went along for the ride, no one would ever do anything great, Orion countered, *You have to actually* do *something.*

The great dragon sighed, *Well if you want to do great things, you need to get some rest. Focus on something pleasant so I can sleep, and then I'll take over, and you can sleep, too.*

I'll try, he thought.

As they ventured into the ancient forest of the elves, several elven warriors greeted them. Half of them had dark skin and ebony hair, and the other half had pale skin and silvery hair. They all had the pointed ears and angled features of the elves, and the misty blue elven robes of their warriors. Their hair was long and silky, and they wore bands made from precious metals around their heads.

"Follow us," their leader said. They showed no fear of Saphron. Even their horses seemed unafraid.

Saphron flew just above the trees, hovering behind the elves upon their horses until they reached a clearing where he could land. The elven citizens were slowly milling about, but they faltered when they caught sight of the massive dragon, several of them fleeing in fear.

Now that's more like it, Saphron thought in satisfaction.

Orion rolled his eyes as he and Callisto dismounted. *Wait here,* he thought.

With pleasure, he replied, settling into the ground contentedly.

Callisto and Orion followed the elven warriors toward the palace. The elven kingdom was far more beautiful than Orion had thought it would be. He'd known several elves who'd described the kingdoms of Gliken, but he'd never yet visited himself. The entire city was built by the elves' magic, each tree's branches formed into buildings and homes by their enchanting spells. It was illuminated by lanterns and pixies, and the thin streams of light that reached them from the forest canopy.

The palace was positioned higher than the rest of the structures, and it spanned several trees, making it the largest structure there. The beautiful, twisting branches formed a magnificent home for the elven royalty. The warriors led them up the drawbridge, down the beautifully crafted corridor, and to the throne room. Orion couldn't help but marvel at the ornate artwork etched directly into the walls. The throne room was of adequate size. Compared to the throne room of Lorena, it was small, but compared to the average human kingdom, it was quite sizable.

Upon the throne sat a beautiful elven woman. She had dark skin and black hair with dark eyes. She wore an iridescent robe that picked up shades of blue, pink, and purple as she moved. Upon her head sat a golden crown.

"Welcome, rider," she said, "I am Queen Gizella of Garellis."

He and Callisto bowed in respect, "I am Orion, and my dragon's name is Saphron."

"Queen Gizella," Callisto said, "A pleasure, as always."

She smirked, nodding. After a pause, she said, "What brings you here?"

"We have come to ask for your help," she said.

Queen Gizella sat back in her throne. She thought a moment, and as she opened her mouth to reply, a tall, dark elven man glided into the room, interrupting, "What is it you would ask of us *this* time?" He eyed Callisto meaningfully.

"Hello, Boreas," she said, "A pleasure seeing you as well."

"Are you alright, daughter?" he asked, placing his hand on Gizella's shoulder.

"I'm fine," she answered, "Thank you, father."

He nodded, turning back to the two of them, "What is your request?"

"The Oracle had prophesied Vidar's descendant's rise to power," Callisto began.

"Yes, what of it?" Boreas asked.

"It's happening," she replied, "Dredon of the riders of Cabri's mountain stronghold is Vidar's heir, and he has taken up his torch. If left unchecked, he will take over all the lands of this world, without mercy. We must prepare an opposing force to stop him, and we need your help."

"I know this is a tremendous request," Orion said, "And, I can certainly understand you being reluctant. It puts elven warriors in danger. I only ask that you think of how many elven lives—warrior and otherwise—will be at risk if he succeeds. Don't do it for us. Do it for your people. Do it for *all* people."

The previous king, Boreas, and his daughter, Queen Gizella, exchanged glances with one another. "This is not something I can immediately answer," she said, "Marcos will show you to your rooms. We will discuss this request at length before making a decision. It may take a day or two to get your answer." With that, she waved over Marcos, a dark-skinned elven servant, to lead them to the guest rooms.

Before they exited the throne room, Callisto said, "Gizella, there's one more thing you should consider as you make your decision."

The elf queen looked up, "What's that?"

"Orion is Derekkian's descendant."

"I'm what?" he demanded, eyes wide with surprise.

She gave a nod to Queen Gizella, whose eyes were just as wide.

"When were you planning on telling me?" he asked.

She turned to face him, "I'm sorry, Orion. I wasn't sure when the right time would be. The Oracle told me I'd know when the moment came. But, in this moment, I had no choice. That piece of information could change their entire decision. I didn't plan for you to find out this way. But now, you know. The reason she told you to employ his strategy, the reason you are the one who can stop Dredon . . . is because you are the descendant of Derekkian. He was an underdog, too. Nobody thought he was anyone special. But, when Vidar took over, he formulated and executed the plan that stopped him. You, too, shall rise to the occasion. It's in your blood."

He stared at her in disbelief.

"Right this way," Marcos said, walking out of the room.

Orion and Callisto followed him down the hall, and to two rooms. The beds were made of moss, ferns, and other plant life, and Orion was skeptical to sleep upon them. But, he nodded in gratitude to Marcos and looked out over the glowing elven kingdom.

Callisto stood in his doorway, and he could feel her presence behind him. "Are you alright?" she asked.

He sighed, "I don't know." After a pause, he said, "This news is huge. How could you not tell me?"

"I wasn't sure how you'd take it," she said.

"What else don't I know?"

"There're a lot of things you don't know," she replied, "I like to think that I'll let you know the things you need to know when you need to know them. In this case, I got it wrong. I just didn't feel you were ready to hear it. I thought it would put even more pressure on you—that maybe you'd feel like you had too big of shoes to try to fill."

Orion was silent.

"You are your own man," she said softly, "Just because you are descended from a great hero doesn't mean you are him. You have to do this *your* way."

He remained silent, contemplating. This was all too much for him to take in.

"Maybe it's a good thing they're going to take their time deciding," she said, "It will give you time to process it as well." With that, she headed across the hall to the room they'd given her.

This isn't bad news, Saphron thought, *This is great news, actually.*

How's that? Orion asked.

Derekkian succeeded against Vidar. If Dredon is Vidar's descendant and you are Derekkian's, then you are truly destined for victory! You can beat him. You can win!

No, he thought, *Just because I'm descended from Derekkian doesn't mean I am Derekkian. And, just because he's descended from Vidar the Conqueror doesn't mean he is Vidar. This war will be our own. This is not the conflict of our ancestors. We cannot tell the outcome based on what they did. The outcome of this will be based on what we do.*

Saphron was silent. After a pause, he thought, *Not a bad speech, Orion. You're right, too. This will be different. But, the result will be the same. We are going to win. Why? Because we have resolve. We won't give up. We care what happens to the world, and everyone in it. Everyone knows love is stronger than hate. We are on the side of love. Therefore, we have the most powerful force in the universe on our side.*

We'll need more than that, Orion thought, *We'll need more than that.*

When Marcos came to get them that evening for a welcome feast the elves were hosting in their honor, they were led to a table full of elven delicacies. Orion recognized some of them from home, but most were foreign to him. Callisto seemed in her element among the elves, as though she had plenty of experience with them. He guessed she'd traveled to many lands in her time as The Oracle's keeper, maintaining friendships among the races. She devoured their food as though she knew exactly what everything was.

Orion felt extremely out of place, attempting to fill his plate with caution, and hoping Saphron was having better luck than him on his hunt. He was too far away to communicate with his mind, which was difficult for him. He felt truly alone.

"Orion, eat up!" Callisto said, "Elven foods are mild and sweet. They don't eat meat, though, so you have to eat quite a bit to fill yourself up. You'll need your strength for the journey ahead."

Mild and sweet, huh? he thought, *That doesn't sound so bad.* He grabbed a few of the strange fruits and vegetables, and made sandwiches out of them with the bread. It did have a unique flavor that he was unable to define. The sweetness was vague, but pleasant. His taste buds kept searching for more.

When the feast was over, everyone began milling about, finding places to relax. Orion was puzzled that they did not sing, dance, or drink. It was unlike any party he'd ever been to.

"Why the puzzled expression?" Callisto asked.

"Why do they not dance? Or drink?"

"Elves rarely drink," she replied, "And if they do, it is rarer still that they would get drunk. They don't believe in clouding their judgment or their senses. As for dancing, they will. They rest after a large meal, and allow themselves leisure time to digest before partaking in rigorous activities."

Orion gave a slight nod, indicating he understood.

"Their culture is very formal by nature. At first, I thought they were difficult to understand. I was afraid of offending their high manner with a false step. But, once you take the time to understand them, the things they do make perfect sense."

"Is that why you seem so at ease here?" he asked.

She nodded, "It certainly is."

"So, you know the queen and her father. Who are your other friends amongst the elves?"

"I know many, many elves," she replied, "Comes with the territory as The Oracle's keeper."

As he felt Saphron's consciousness come into contact with his own, he thought, *Have a good hunting trip?*

Yes, he replied, *I did, indeed.*

He could feel his dragon's satisfaction at a full belly as he settled into the soft patch of grass in the main square that the elves had cleared for him to sleep.

"Come on," Callisto said, "Let's get some sleep. Tomorrow, I shall introduce you to an old friend of mine who will surely help with your training."

"I thought I was done training," he replied.

"I have taught you all I can," she answered, "But, it never hurts to gain skills from more than one mentor. The more things you can learn, the better. Besides, elves have incredible speed and agility. I'm sure they'll be able to provide you a challenge despite your skill."

"Very well," he said, nodding, "Tomorrow, we shall train."

When the morning sun shone through the window, Orion awoke to the smell of flowers, and the feeling of soft plants smushed against his face. He climbed out of the strange bed, preparing himself for his training. Poor Saphron was bored and restless, with nothing to occupy himself in the square. He took to the skies, flying around and scaring the birds.

Hopefully, their decision won't take too long, Orion thought.

Hopefully not, Saphron agreed.

"Ready to go?" Callisto asked, appearing in his doorway.

He nodded, following her through the elven city to the training grounds of the elven warriors. They were spacious, but not quite enough so for Saphron to fit. It was probably the only area in the kingdom not covered with grass and plant life. It was a dirt patch with lines drawn on it, dividing it into sections.

As the two of them stood at the edge of the field, a dark elven beauty approached them. She wore mossy green robes and a gold band around her head. Her intense hazel eyes captivated Orion. He'd never seen anyone like her before. Her eyes locked in on him, picking up shades of brown and green.

Then, Callisto smiled, opening her arms, "Xharia! So good to see you!"

Her beautiful hazel eyes shifted their gaze to her, and she lit up, opening her arms to embrace her, "Celestia! It's been too long!"

"Celestia?" Orion asked, "You must be confused. This is Callisto, keeper of The Oracle."

Callisto smiled, "Yes, my name is Callisto. But, it *was* Celestia. I changed it when I moved to Abyumo." She turned to the elven woman, "Xharia and I have been friends for years—long before I became The Oracle's keeper. She knows me as Celestia."

"She was the princess of The Great Prophecy," Xharia said.

"What?" Orion said in shock, "The princess who saved the world from darkness? Twice?"

"The very same," she replied.

"There's no need for all of that," Callisto said quickly.

"I guess that's why you knew so much about having a destiny too great to achieve," Orion said, "You defeated *two* dark wizards! You can wield raw power! You even rode a dragon! The only non-rider in history to do so! No wonder you didn't fear Saphron, and you were able to shoot from his back . . ."

"Alright, that's enough," she said, "That was my past life. I'm a different person, now."

Orion gave her a look of confusion and disappointment, "But, why?"

"Things happen in life," she said, "Things that change you." She looked off into the distance, seeming pained.

He wasn't sure what to say, but he didn't like seeing her so upset. He turned to Xharia, "So, you're the friend who's supposed to train me?"

Xharia was staring at Celestia with concern, but she shook her head, turning toward Orion, "Yes. That's why she asked me to come."

"Go on," she said, "Get started. I'll just be over here, meditating."

"Very well," Xharia replied, "Come on, Orion."

"You know my name?" he asked.

She laughed, and it was the most beautiful laugh he'd ever heard, "Of course. Celestia already told me all about you." She led him out onto the field, handing him a training sword. She picked up her own, taking her stance, "Are you ready, rider?"

He took his stance as well, nodding.

Xharia smiled, and they engaged, swinging their swords through the air. "Whoa," he yelled, dodging a blow, impressed by her speed. Callisto had been right: elves were faster and more agile. It only took a few swings before she'd swept his feet, knocking him down.

"Is that all you've got?" she asked, "I thought you'd completed your training."

Orion shot her a wry smile, jumping up, "Not even close."

She smiled again, and they started up once more, swinging and twirling. Again, it didn't take long for her to knock him down, "It seems you need to work on your speed . . . and your footwork."

"Oh, yeah?" he said, trying to hit her with a surprise attack.

She saw it coming, and knocked him back down before he could reach his feet, "Yeah."

He looked down, frustrated and embarrassed, but at the same time, amazed by her.

"Here, let me help you up," she said, sensing his embarrassment. She extended her hand, and he took it as she pulled him up. Once he was on his feet, she continued, "We need to make you stronger, faster, and more poised. If you can learn to beat an elf, you can beat a mere human rider."

He nodded, catching his breath.

"Let's run some drills to improve your reflexes and increase your speed," she said.

Orion trained all day with Xharia, focusing on strength, speed, and balance. By the end of it, he felt ready to take on the world. But, he knew it would take a lot more practice to master the skills she'd taught him.

I thought I was ready when I was able to beat Callisto and Epsilon, he thought, *But, I can't even beat an elven warrior. Are you sure we can do this?*

Of course, I'm sure, Saphron thought, *We can do anything, so long as we're together. Just keep working with Xharia until the elves make their decision.*

No problem there, he replied.

Hey, he thought, *Get your head out of the clouds. This is no time to lose focus. She's here to train us. And, as you said, you need the training.*

Orion sighed, *You're right, as usual.*

Of course, I'm right, he responded, *Now, get some rest. You'll be training tomorrow, too.*

As he was heading off the field to go get some sleep, he detoured over to Xharia, who was loading her supplies to head off herself, "Hey, can I ask you something?"

"Orion," she said in surprise, looking up. After a pause, she said, "Of course. What is it?"

He opened his mouth to ask her his question, but stopped himself. After a moment, he said, "I've never known anyone able to sneak up on an elf. How is it I surprised you?"

"I apologize," she said, "I'm not myself today. I'm afraid my head is in the clouds, and I wasn't paying any attention to my surroundings."

"Your head is in the clouds?" he asked, "What's on your mind?"

She smiled, "It's nothing. Nothing to concern yourself with."

He looked at her curiously, wondering if perhaps she was thinking of him the way he was thinking of her. After another pause, he said, "You're the elven warrior from her second quest, aren't you?"

Xharia looked up, "Yes. I'm the daughter of the previous king, Boreas, and sister to our current queen, Gizella."

Orion's eyes grew wide, "So, you're a princess?"

"I'm a warrior," she snapped.

"I'm sorry," he said, "I didn't mean to offend you."

"It's alright," she said, "I'm not offended. I just never really liked the title of 'princess.' I'm a warrior at heart. That is my passion. That is who I am."

"Well, that's certainly respectable," he said, "As a rider, I've naturally always admired warriors."

Xharia smiled.

"So, what happened to her?"

"It's not my place to say," she replied, "It's not my story."

Orion looked down, "So, what is your story?"

She shot him a wry smile, "No more questions today, rider. If you train with me tomorrow, I shall tell you."

He nodded, "Very well."

"Keep up, rider," Xharia shouted, "If that's as fast as you can go, you'll never beat Dredon."

Orion swung his sword up to meet her blow, but she changed her swing at the last second, hitting his side.

"How many times have I killed you today?" she asked, "Eight?"

He lunged forward, stabbing his practice sword toward her, and she pivoted to block him, but he managed to connect before she could stop him.

She looked at him, impressed, "Touché. Well done."

They turned to the sideline as they heard clapping. "Well done, indeed," Callisto said.

Orion smiled as his mentor nodded to him. He couldn't believe she was the great princess of legend, Celestia. He'd heard so many stories of her, and of all her incredible deeds. Yet, the whole time she'd been training him, he hadn't known who she was. He wondered for the millionth time what had happened to her that she wanted to be someone else.

"Let's take a break," Xharia said, lifting her canteen to her lips.

"Alright," he agreed, grabbing his own canteen. Once he'd quenched his thirst, he walked to where she'd taken a seat beside Callisto, sitting on her other side. "So, will you tell me your story, now?" he asked.

Xharia smiled, shaking her head, "My story is not that interesting. I grew up here in Garellis. My father kept us hidden from the outside world, and I spent my life training, dreaming of nothing more than becoming an elven warrior. When Celestia and her warriors came here to ask my father for an elven warrior and weapon to fulfill their quest, I longed to lose my in-training status, and prove myself. My dear friend, Aurano, had perished on their first quest, and he would have lost his life for nothing if they failed the second. They needed a warrior. My father refused them one, because he was afraid of losing another of our warriors. So, I volunteered in secret to accompany them. The rest of that story, I'm sure you've heard."

He nodded, "You're all quite famous."

She continued, ignoring his comment, "After we completed our quest, I returned home, bringing the weapon back. My father finally came around, and decided to allow us to be seen by the outside world. He named me an official elven warrior. Everything changed thanks to our quest. My dreams came true: I became a famous warrior, *earning* a high rank, rather than simply being handed one because of my royal status. But, over the years, things have grown stagnant. Though I'm a full-fledged elven warrior, I've never seen battle. The hundred years of peace meant no wars. I've had nothing to do with my status since I received it. But now, the hundred years is up, and there's to be a war for the ages. I'm determined to be a part of it any way I can."

Orion was silent, looking down, *There is to be a war for the ages. And, I think we shall all be a part of it.*

He felt Saphron's agreement from across the elven city.

"Let's get back to training," Xharia said, getting up.

He nodded, rising with her, and they headed back onto the practice field.

Digging up the Past

8

The next morning, Orion and Celestia received a summons from Queen Gizella. They were ready with their decision. The two of them headed to the throne room, and he felt his stomach doing flip flops the whole way there. When they reached it, they saw that Boreas was there as well, and so was Xharia.

"We have discussed your request," Queen Gizella began, "And, we have come to a decision."

There was a long pause as everyone exchanged glances with one another, anxiously awaiting what that decision would be.

"The elves will fight," she said, "We will send messengers to the other kingdoms of Gliken, asking them to join us."

"This is wonderful!" Celestia said.

Did you hear that? Orion thought excitedly, *We have the elves on our side!*

Yes, Saphron replied, *We are one step closer to victory!*

"Furthermore," Gizella continued, "We shall send a representative to accompany you forward. You could use the extra warrior, and the added diplomacy. Though I must admit, Orion, you have a way with words yourself. The argument you presented, coupled with your ancestry, were the main reasons we agreed to fight."

"Your words humble me," Orion said, bowing his head and blushing.

"The best part," Xharia piped up, "and the reason I'm here is . . . I'm the one who shall be accompanying you!"

"Really?" Callisto said excitedly.

Orion tried to contain his own excitement at the prospect of traveling with the elven beauty for an extended period.

Xharia nodded, hugging her, "It's just like old times, Celestia! How I've missed our adventures!"

She smiled as they moved apart.

"You set out at dawn," Boreas said.

"Rest today," Queen Gizella added, "Enjoy the feast tonight, and make haste on your journey tomorrow."

Orion and Celestia nodded as they left the room. When they got down the hall, he said, "Another feast?"

"Yes," Callisto laughed, "The first was to celebrate our arrival. This one is to see us off. We must fill our bellies before departing on a long journey, for food is sparse on the road."

He nodded, understanding. After a pause, he said, "Are we really going to spend the day resting? Or shall we train some more before we leave?"

"It's always good to rest before departing on a journey," Celestia said, "You never know when you'll see a bed again. Besides, there'll be plenty of time to train on the road."

Orion sighed.

She smiled, "Get some rest. It's only tomorrow, after all."

As the sunlight began to stream in through the trees of the sparkling elven kingdom, Orion met up with Celestia and Xharia in the royal stable. Unfortunately, Saphron would not be able to carry all three of them, so Xharia would have to join them on horseback. She guided her white steed from the stable and leaped upon its back, riding off.

Callisto followed Orion to Saphron, and they climbed upon his back. The shiny-scaled dragon leapt out of the forest and into the morning breeze, unfurling his wings. They soared north, toward Korga—the land of the dwarves.

It was slow-going, as they had to crawl through the skies so Xharia could keep up. When they stopped to make camp that night, Orion was disappointed they were still in Gliken. If they could fly normally, they would already be in Korga.

Is there any way you could carry three? Orion thought.

I'm afraid not, Saphron sighed, *It would slow us down.*

We're already being slowed down, he retorted, *Plus, it would give you some strength training, which would help in the battle.*

If the elves sent an ambassador, the dwarves almost certainly will, too, he said, *I certainly couldn't carry four. Then Xharia wouldn't have a horse with her, and it wouldn't make sense for three of you to ride upon me, and one member of our company to ride a pony. No, she must keep her horse.*

He sighed.

"So, what's your story, Orion?" Xharia asked, shaking him from his thoughts, "You seem so interested in everyone else's." She and Celestia were seated by the fire, eating.

"I . . . uh . . . I moved to Abyumo when I was eleven, and Saphron here hatched for me. I've been training to be a rider ever since. But, I must say, I've learned more from you and Callisto here than I ever did back home."

Xharia smiled, "Well, the riders don't exactly have a training program. Still, it's surprising you didn't have a better teacher."

"Indeed," he said. After a pause, he added, "Well, I've told both of you my story, and Xharia has told me hers. What of you, *Celestia*?"

The silver-haired witch turned to face him, "I already told you my story."

"No, you didn't," he countered, "You only told me about your time as The Oracle's keeper, not anything before that, other than that you were from Duwazo. I know the stories of your quests, as everyone does, but what about the rest of your story? A lot of time has passed between your last quest and now."

She sighed, "What is it you want to know so badly?"

"What happened? What changed from then to now?"

Celestia sighed again, looking off into the darkened forest.

Xharia's hazel eyes twinkled with concern. She knew her old friend was feeling pressured, and perhaps overwhelmed by thoughts of the past. But, Orion needed to know what happened. He had to understand who she was now, and why. She was a part of this quest, and if she couldn't be who she once was, he needed to know.

"Life happened," she replied finally, "I returned home to my children. My husband, Bridgot, and I raised them together. Our son, Aurano, and our daughter, Nastazya."

Orion started in surprise at the names.

Celestia looked at him, "Yes. We named them for our friends who perished on the first quest. Our daughter was named after a rider."

He nodded, understanding.

"They grew up, as children do, and became a man and a woman. Bridgot and I served our time as king and queen of Ivétoiless. When our son was old enough, he took over the throne, becoming king. He married and had children of his own. Our daughter married the king of Chemsson, and became a queen, having children of her own as well. We were there for the births of all our grandchildren. We watched them grow. When our great-grandchildren were born, we realized we had done our duty. We had served our time as king and queen. Our grandchildren were on the throne. We had raised our kids. Their kids had kids. My mother had passed away. We had no duties to anyone anymore. We realized it was finally time to think of ourselves again." She paused, looking pained.

"You don't have to—" Xharia began, but Celestia cut her off.

"We thought after our second quest that we'd quenched our thirst for adventure for a hundred years, at least. But, it had only been about thirty, and we were ready for more. This time, the fate of the world wasn't at risk. We were free to do as we pleased—to travel for leisure. We went every-where. We stayed with the riders for a while. We stayed with Nastazya's brothers in Cardeas for a time. We stayed with the dwarves until our dear friend, Kgansten, passed away. Then, we stayed with the elves for a period."

"That's how you know so much about their customs," Orion said.

She nodded.

"I was thrilled when they came to stay," Xharia said, smiling at her friend, "It was always so good to see them."

"We stayed in the village of Kataran in Katangalo with Bridgot's family. We even ventured to the far-off land of Tomainda, where my grandmother was from. When Bridgot got sick, we made the journey back home. After he died . . . " she paused, choking back tears, "After he died, there was noth-ing left for me. Not because I had nothing without my love, and not because women can't live without their man, or any such nonsense, but because I had no duty to anyone, no one to care for, nothing to do, and no one to share my life with anymore." She paused again, letting a tear stream down.

Xharia touched her arm sympathetically.

"So, I finally decided to follow my mentor, Thaandor's suggestion, and move to Abyumo. I felt lost, and moving there gave me a new sense of purpose, and life. I finally had something to do with my time. In light of my new life, and so no one in my family could find me, I changed my name to Callisto. I was no longer a retired queen, wife, mother, and grandmother. I was a witch—a full-time witch. I knew I had a lot of years left in me. My human life was over. But, my time wasn't done. I just needed to figure out what to do with it. Thaandor finished my training, and when he died, I took over his post as keeper of The Oracle."

He paused, taking in what she'd told him. After a moment, he asked, "Why did you not want your family to find you?"

She sighed, "I wasn't me anymore. I didn't want them to see me that way. I wanted to preserve their memory of me alongside my husband's. I didn't want to watch generation after generation of my family grow old and die while I lived on. My old life was done. I had to let go of it. I started a new life that day, with a new identity. And, I've been lost ever since. Being The Oracle's keeper fills my time, but I don't know who I am anymore. I just . . . " She trailed off, looking away.

"It's alright," Xharia said, patting her arm.

Orion finally understood what had happened to her. Growing old, watching your loved ones die, but not dying yourself . . . is that what it would be like for him as he got older? Other than those with magical blood, humans didn't live that long. He looked at her, "I'm sorry. Thank you for telling me that." He tried to project his gratitude and his understanding in his voice.

She gave him a nod through her tears, offering a half-smile.

He got up, unable to look at her tear-soaked face, as everything she had experienced was exactly what he feared for his own future.

You're a rider, Saphron said, *It is your destiny. It is your gift and your curse. It is your burden and your power.*

I know, he thought, *But what about everyone I care about?*

You have many friends among the riders, he thought, *They will live as long as you. And you will always have me.*

Orion smiled, feeling the warmth and love that radiated from his dragon, *Thank you. I will always have you. And you'll always have me. The blessing of being a rider is that I'll never be truly alone.*

No, he thought, *You won't.*

The next day, Celestia rode with Xharia, and had Orion and Saphron do drills as they flew to keep their senses sharp, increase their strength and speed, and maintain their synchronization. When they stopped to make camp that night, Xharia did some drills with him as well, continuing his sword training.

"You're doing well, rider," she said, "I'm impressed by how quickly you're improving."

"Thank you," he replied as he twirled around, dodging her swing. Truth be told, he was just as surprised at how fast he'd been able to learn. If he'd had a teacher amongst the riders, maybe he would've actually been somebody. If he could match the physical dexterity of an elf, maybe he actually stood a chance against Dredon.

We'll have to get you trained, too, somehow, he thought, *if you are to beat Obsidian.*

Don't worry about me, Saphron thought, *I'm a dragon.*

So is he. And, he's much bigger than you. You'll need a strategy to win that fight. You can't rely solely on your instincts.

And how am I to find a trainer? he asked, *I won't be able to find another dragon until we return to Abyumo. By then, it will be too late.*

There must be some way, he thought.

"Orion, focus," Celestia was saying.

Xharia shot him a questioning look as she brought her sword down upon him.

He blocked it at the last second. Normally, it required his full focus to fight her. So, he knew he was improving. At least she hadn't killed him this fight. Yet.

"Where's your head?" she asked, stepping back.

"Sorry," he replied, "I was just thinking . . . all this training I've undergone, and how the both of you have been working with me to prepare me to face Dredon . . . well, I was thinking that Saphron needs training, too. How is he to beat Obsidian?"

Xharia paused, unsure, and looked back at Celestia. She shared her look of uncertainty.

"I'm afraid we're short on dragons around here," Xharia said finally.

"Indeed," Callisto added, "I'm not entirely sure how to train a dragon."

Orion sighed, disheartened. How could they expect Saphron to face Obsidian with no training? There was no way they could win. Not to mention, it would put his dragon in danger.

"I know Kogatsa is a dangerous place," Celestia said, "I know better than anyone. But, it's also a place full of magical creatures. Perhaps someone there could train him."

"*Dark* magical creatures," Xharia said, "They would not help us."

"We have to try," Orion said, "Or else, we're doomed."

Mithrel

9

Orion watched as the elven forest disappeared below, going from leaves with a bluish tint and trees with a silvery sheen to their bark, to the normal greens and browns of all other forests. The drills Callisto had them work on each day were increasing their strength, speed, and agility, and he was finally able to move perfectly with his dragon without difficulty. He knew exactly when he was going to turn, shift, or dive. It had become as second-nature as his own movements. She was proud of the progress they'd made.

He was also finally able to beat Xharia more often, as evidenced by his fight with her when he wasn't completely focused, but had still managed to hold her off. His combat techniques had continued to improve as she'd worked with him. Celestia continued to help him with his magic as well, as they made their way through the forest of the elves. And, when Saphron went on his daily hunt, Orion would shoot or run his sword through his prey, giving him the chance to practice fighting from his back. In only a few days' time, there had been noticeable improvement.

They reached the land of the dwarves the following day, meeting a line of terrified dwarven warriors who reluctantly led them to the entrance of their tunnels. Celestia spoke with them, attempting to calm them down, as they stared wide-eyed at Saphron. They opened the doors with obvious hesitance, and the three warriors entered with their horse and dragon. The dwarves built things so large that Saphron could easily fit inside. Orion guessed they might regret that now.

A couple of red-bearded dwarves greeted them, "Right this way." They appeared nervous, but tried to hide it as they led them into the massive tunnels. They went up for miles, and were covered in ornate, intricately carved designs embedded with jewels. The floors were made of marble, and there were points along the tunnels with skylights, allowing the sun inside.

They were led into the massive throne room of the dwarf king, which was nearly the size of Lorena's. The king sat upon his golden throne, garbed in a too-tall crown and a too-long robe. His beard was a mixture of blonde and red, giving off an almost pinkish hue.

"Welcome to Dirthix," he said, "I am King Tunxst. What brings you and your . . . dragon . . . here?" He looked up at Saphron anxiously.

"We've come to ask for your help," Celestia said.

"Oh? I see . . . " he replied uncertainly.

She went on to explain the situation, telling him that Dredon was Vidar the Conqueror's heir, and that Orion was descended from Derekkian. She told him of the imminent war, and how they needed the dwarven army on their side.

King Tunxst's eyes grew wider as she spoke, looking at each of them in turn. His face moved through a variety of emotions, but mostly appeared anxious and fearful.

"Sir," Orion said finally, "If I might interject . . . I can see you're fearful for what this all means. I am, too. But, the bravery and fighting skill of the dwarves is legendary. Your warriors can help good triumph. And, you'll go down in history when they do, as a great king, who led his people to victory. The war will find you no matter what you do. If you do nothing, you will all be slaughtered. If you join Dredon, you will be aiding the side of darkness and despair. But, if you join us, you'll be part of the world's efforts to remain free of darkness. You will be leading your people into the light, and saving them from a reign of terror. The choice is yours."

The dwarf king stroked his strawberry beard, looking at Orion curiously. After a long pause, he said, "I will consult with our war leaders, and get back to you with my decision. A good king knows the fate of our people cannot be decided by a single dwarf."

The three of them bowed respectfully, giving a nod.

"Curtis and Isaac will show you to your rooms," he nodded to the red-bearded dwarves, "You are our honored guests, and we shall feast in your honor tonight."

They followed the two dwarves from the throne room, and they brought them to a giant cushion in the center square, which the dwarves had proudly fashioned for Saphron in a matter of an hour. He snorted with content, nestling into it. Orion smiled, glad they were willing to accommodate their fearsome guest.

Once he was settled in, and Xharia's horse, Shadow, put in the royal stable, they were led across the hall to a few guest suites. They were spacious enough, with large, comfortable beds, and Orion instantly felt right at home. He decided to let the ladies wash up first, and sank down into the bed. It was extremely comfortable, and he dozed off before Xharia came to let him know the washroom was free. Her dark hair was wet, and it dripped down her ebony skin, making the golden band around her head shine more starkly.

As he walked out the door, he said, "I hope you don't find this improprietous, but I think you're very beautiful."

She lowered her head, blushing, "I'm flattered, young rider."

He turned to head to the washroom, not knowing what else to say. Before he could change his mind, he spun back around, taking her hand and kissing it. His heart pounded in his chest the whole time, and he wasn't sure how she would react.

She sucked in a breath, pulling her hand away and giving him a gracious nod.

He swallowed, quickly scurrying off to the washroom.

At the feast that night, Orion sat beside Xharia nervously, hardly daring to breathe. Celestia kept shooting him questioning looks, but he ignored them.

It was *very improprietous,* Saphron thought from the square. He was enjoying the meal the dwarves had brought before him of roasted boar. He was even provided with a tank of mead, which he gladly gulped down.

Shut up, Orion retorted, *That's enough from you.*

You should not try to romance her, he said, *She is far too old for you. She is wise, brave, and skilled in combat. She's the daughter of the elf king. And, she's a friend of Callisto. She's out of your league.*

That shows how highly you think of me, he snapped.

It's not only about you, he replied, *It will distract you from this quest. Not to mention, if things go wrong, it will make things extremely awkward for everyone.*

Orion sighed.

After a pause, Saphron said, *I see you will not waiver.* He sighed, too, adding, *Your feelings are genuine. I suppose there's nothing further for me to say, then. Just don't let it distract you. And, keep in mind, she may not feel the same.*

That's all that's on my mind, he replied.

I know, he said, *I can hear your thoughts, remember?*

"So, Xharia," he said, "I suppose dwarven cuisine must be difficult for you, being an elf and all."

Smooth, Saphron thought.

Shut up, he snapped, mentally kicking himself for sounding stupid.

She looked at him questioningly, "Yes, it is. We elves dine on fruits, vegetables, breads, and juices. Dwarven cuisine consists of meats, cheeses, breads, and mead."

"Um . . . here," he said, pulling some elven vegetables from his bag.

She looked at it in surprise, "Thank you. That's very thoughtful." She added it to her plate of bread, eating.

Orion beamed.

When everyone was done eating, and the drinking and dancing started, he offered her his hand, "Care for a dance?"

Xharia looked at his hand with a strange expression. When she looked up at him, she said, "Sorry. We elves don't usually dance right after a meal. It's bad for digestion."

He mentally kicked himself again, realizing he'd carelessly disregarded her culture, "Right. Of course. My apologies. Perhaps later."

"I think I shall get some rest," she said, hurrying to her room.

He swung his fist through the air, realizing he blew it.

"Something wrong, Orion?" Celestia asked, coming up behind him.

He shook his head, not wanting to tell her how he felt.

"Come on," she said, "Let's take a walk."

He reluctantly followed her, as they strolled along one of the corridors.

"What do you think of Xharia?" she asked.

His eyes widened as he looked at her, "What do you mean?"

Celestia smiled, "I'm an old woman, Orion. I've seen a lot of things. One thing I've seen time and again is love."

His mind raced, looking for a way to deny it.

"It's okay," she said, "I'm not going to say anything. I'm happy for you. Xharia is an amazing woman. She's been my friend for years, and I'd love to see her find someone."

"Really?" was all he could manage to say.

She laughed, nodding, "I wish you well, Orion. I just wanted you to know you don't have to hide it from me. I support you."

He let out a sigh of relief, "Well . . . thanks."

Her face turned serious, "But, know this: if you hurt her, you'll have me to deal with. As you said, I can wield raw power. Don't test me."

"I would never . . . I'm not that kind of guy . . . I couldn't . . . " he sputtered.

"Good," she replied, smile returning, "No worries, then."

With Celestia's blessing, Orion bought some flowers from the dwarves' marketplace—as none grew wild in the gilded tunnels—and knocked on Xharia's door.

She answered, mossy green robes falling over her shoulders, "Yes?" After a half-second pause, she said with surprise, "Orion?" She looked at the flowers in his hand, understanding. Then, she looked up at him, "Oh."

Orion felt like she had punched him in the stomach. His throat was dry, and he couldn't formulate words. He dropped the flowers, turning around and hurrying away.

"Orion! Orion, wait!" she called.

He ran into the next corridor over, stopping to catch his breath. It wasn't the running that had caused his breathing to become difficult. He slammed his fist into the wall, thinking, *How could I be such an idiot?*

Perhaps not as much as you think, Saphron thought.

"Orion," Xharia said, coming up behind him.

When he looked back, he saw she was holding the flowers, "What?" She looked at him steadily, "Why did you run?"

"Because it was obvious you don't feel the way I do," he replied.

"Is that why you brought me these flowers?" she asked, "You feel something for me?"

He looked away, drowning in humiliation.

"Look," she said, fiddling with the bouquet nervously, "I . . . uh . . . I've never had time for love. I'm a warrior, and that's all I know. I just never thought about it. I don't really know how it goes." She pulled a petal off of a flower, dropping it to the floor, "Perhaps I'm afraid of it. I've never felt it before. Or, maybe I have, but I didn't know." She paused again, "It's admirable that you are able to love. But, I am not. I know it sounds like a bad line when I say this, but it's true . . . It's not you. It's me."

He looked up at her, trying to keep his cool, unsure how to respond.

She held up the bouquet, "They're lovely. I'm sorry."

He held up a shaky hand, taking it from her. As she turned to walk away, he said, "Do you think you ever could have loved me?"

She turned back toward him, "I don't know. Maybe."

"Then, maybe you still could. Perhaps it will just take time. Perhaps . . . you're just not ready, yet. I may have rushed it. I can slow down."

Xharia gave him a half-smile, "Perhaps."

He held the bouquet out to her, "These are for you."

Her smile grew as she took it, "They're lovely."

Orion nodded, his confidence returning.

"Goodnight, rider," she said.

"Goodnight . . . Xharia."

When morning came, they received a summons to appear before King Tunxst. The three of them, along with Saphron, entered his throne room, ready to hear the decision of the dwarves. He stood at the top of the stairs that led to his throne, arms behind his back.

"I have spoken with the war leaders, and we have reached a decision," he said once they were all inside the room, "The dwarves will fight with you. We are not a race known to back down from a challenge. I have dispatched several of them to speak with the leaders of the other dwarven kingdoms, and we shall send an ambassador with you as you continue on your journey."

Orion felt relieved, joyous, and anxious, all at the same time. Relieved and overjoyed that the dwarves were on their side, but anxious for the fight to come.

"This is your appointed dwarven warrior," King Tunxst said, gesturing as a black-bearded dwarf with tawny brown skin entered the throne room, "Mithrel."

The dwarf nodded to them in acknowledgment.

"Mithrel," Xharia said, "Pleasure to meet you."

He looked up at her in awe as he said, "I never knew elves could be so beautiful. Truly, the pleasure is mine, milady."

Xharia blushed.

Orion cleared his throat, stepping forward and hastily trying to break up the moment, "We shall set out at dawn, then. Thank you, your majesty."

King Tunxst gave him a deep nod, and they all headed out of the throne room. Orion kept a close eye on Xharia and Mithrel, making sure they didn't have a chance to talk.

Jealousy does not become you, Saphron thought.

I don't care, he replied, *There's no way I'm going to lose her to a dwarf.*

Don't forget, she had the same reaction when you paid her the very same compliment. Just because he thinks she's pretty doesn't mean he's going to pursue her, and just because she blushed doesn't mean she likes him.

Orion sighed, *Thanks, Saphron. That may be the kindest and most helpful thing you've said about it.*

But, you must remember, no matter what happens, you can't let this become a distraction for you.

I know, he said, looking down, *But what if she* does *like him?*

That's her choice, Saphron replied, *How she feels is not up to you.*

Orion sighed again, *I know you're right. But, I don't think I can admit it just yet.*

You don't know anything yet, he said, *Just wait and see.*

Orion, wake up, Saphron thought, *It's time to set out. I can see the light of dawn coming through the skylight.*

He groaned, stretching and yawning, and rolled out of bed. As he was heading out the door, he saw that Xharia and Celestia were already up and ready, heading for the royal stable to get Xharia's white stallion, Shadow. He hurried to the square to meet Saphron, and they all joined up in the main hallway, ready to head out of Dirthix.

When they assembled, he saw that Mithrel was with them as they came from the stable. He led a black pony behind him. He was talking to

Xharia, and she was laughing. Orion's eyes darkened at the sight, and he felt jealousy creep up on him once more.

He glared at Mithrel, "Shall we set out?"

Mithrel looked at him questioningly, "That's what we're here for."

"Can your pony keep up?" he asked snidely.

"He's as fast as any horse," he answered, beaming with pride, "Helado here is the pride of dwarven war horses." He smiled, patting his pony.

"Saphron here is the pride of war *dragons*," Orion said, "At least he will be, if we succeed in this quest."

"Congratulations," he said, obviously oblivious to his anger.

"Alright," Celestia chimed in, "I think we've all had enough chit-chat. Let's get a move on."

Xharia leaped upon Shadow's back, and Celestia pulled Orion over to Saphron so they could mount him. Mithrel clambered onto Helado's back, and they all set out through the dwarven tunnels. It was easier for Saphron to keep up with the horses, as he couldn't fly very fast through the tunnels.

How long will it take to reach Kogatsa? Orion thought.

It will be three weeks before we get through Korga, Saphron replied, *Then, another week to reach Kogatsa.*

He groaned internally with frustration, *Isn't there a faster way?*

If we had another dragon.

He sighed, *No chance of that.*

Saphron sent him a wave of agreement.

There's no guarantee we'll find anything helpful there, either, Orion inserted.

True, he replied, *But, it's better that we try.*

As they rode through the intricately designed tunnels of the dwarves, Orion watched from above as Xharia and Mithrel rode side-by-side, talking. He knew he had to think of something to win her affections before this dwarven warrior did. But, he wasn't sure what he could do. He'd made the first move, and she'd rejected him.

Well, you have made a proper ass of yourself lately, Saphron thought.

Thank you for that, he sarcastically replied, *That's very helpful.*

Come now, Orion, he said, *Do you think the way you've behaved is what a woman wants? Would you find it attractive?*

He sighed, thinking back over what he'd done. He'd called her beautiful, gotten to know her a little bit, and tried to make a move. It didn't seem wrong, but he knew he'd rushed and overwhelmed her with the flowers. And, instead of accepting her rejection, he'd pathetically begged for her to give him a chance. Then, he'd treated their new dwarven companion terribly, growing jealous when he'd complimented her and tried to talk to her.

I can see why you're upset, Saphron said, *But, you're letting it distract you. She's been nothing but kind and considerate with your advances. But, you have to let her make her own mind up, and stop treating Mithrel that way. It will get you nowhere. We need as many friends and allies in this as we can get.*

He looked down at Mithrel once more. This time, he wasn't looking to make sure he stayed away from Xharia. He was looking at him as their dwarven ambassador. And, he knew they needed to be friends, or at the very least, allies, *You're right, Saphron, as usual.*

I know, he replied.

"Orion," Celestia said from behind him.

"Yes?" he looked over his shoulder at her.

"I understand that you view Mithrel as competition for Xharia, but this quest is bigger than that. We need him. We're all warriors here. And, we need to get our minds right for battle. Love can be placed on the back burner until it's over."

"I know," he answered, "Saphron and I were just discussing that very thing."

"Oh," she said, "Well, good. It's important that we all stay focused. I'm glad he understands that."

"Of course," Orion said, "He's a dragon. He's a wise, ancient creature, with the magic and intelligence of his ancestors."

Saphron beamed, coasting through the air.

"Indeed," she replied, "His wisdom has helped us on numerous occasions already."

Orion nodded.

"Listen," she continued, "I know how important love is. I also know how uncontrollable it is. I know that when I was your age, nobody could tell me anything about Bridgot. I knew we couldn't be together. I was a princess and he was a peasant. Our friend, Aurano, tried to talk to both of us, to tell us to ignore our feelings. He wanted to save us from heartbreak. But, we couldn't control the way we felt. In the end, it worked out for us. My mother allowed us to marry, after she knighted him. Before that, I thought I would have to give him up. It was the hardest thing I ever had to do. But, I had a duty to my kingdom and my people. So, too, do you have a duty, Orion. And, above all else, it must be fulfilled, regardless of how you feel."

He looked back at her again, "Your situation was different. Your love was reciprocated. It made you stronger on your quest. You were willing to give it up to fulfill your duty, but you didn't have to. You wound up together. For me, she does not reciprocate my feelings. She may even like someone else. I don't get the luxury of waiting for this quest to be over to deal with heartbreak. I have to fight through the pain. But, the worst part is not knowing."

She sighed, "I know. But, this quest is too important to let anything distract you from it. Try to win her affections if you can, but be willing to accept it if you can't."

"I can't promise anything," he replied, "But, I'll try. I do understand the gravity of this quest."

They continued the next few days through the tunnels, focused on their mission. Orion tried his best not to get distracted by all the talking Mithrel and Xharia were doing as they rode below. When they stopped to make camp, he'd find a way to sit beside her, waiting for a chance to prove himself better than Mithrel.

"I know the foods of the dwarves aren't exactly to your liking, as an elf," Mithrel said, "I hope the elves packed you enough for the journey."

"Yes, thank you," Xharia replied, "I've never met a dwarf so understanding of elf culture. Well, besides my friend, Kgansten."

"Yes, dwarven cuisine is *far* different from that of the elves," Orion inserted, "Elves don't kill animals for their meat or cloud their senses with mead. *They* care greatly for the earth."

Mithrel shot him a look of surprise, with a flash of anger.

"We do consider ourselves caretakers of the earth and the forest, it's true," Xharia said, "But, we also understand that other cultures and other races view things differently. It's not our place to lay down judgment."

He smiled, "Elves and dwarves have always had their differences, but I think our races could get along, if only we gave each other the chance."

"Well, I don't know about *that*," Orion said, "There might be too many differences to overcome just by talking it out."

"Orion, I'm surprised at you!" Xharia said, "You should know the stories of Celestia's first quest. Kgansten and Aurano hated each other at the start. They were the epitomes of elf and dwarf culture. But, by the end of the quest, they had become best friends. I think that shows that it *is* possible for our two races to ally themselves."

Orion sighed, looking down. He could see Mithrel chuckling to himself out of the corner of his eye, and he felt his anger rise. Every effort he made to sabotage the dwarf warrior backfired. He needed to simply woo Xharia, instead of trying to undermine Mithrel.

"You're right, of course," he said, "My apologies. Kgansten was a great dwarf. *Friendship* between elves and dwarves is a beautiful thing. As are friendships of all other races."

She smiled, "Thank you, Orion. That was beautiful. I'm glad you can understand."

"Of course," he replied, "I'm a very understanding person."

Mithrel stopped chuckling long enough to glare at him, "Well, I'm glad that's settled, because I think we'll be *very* good friends."

"I think so, too," she replied, smiling.

"Yes, we shall *all* be very good friends," Orion said.

"Wonderful," Xharia said, "Now if you'll excuse me, I just need to go take care of some business." She got up, heading to one of the restrooms the dwarves had placed along the long stretches of hallway for travelers to relieve themselves.

As soon as she'd walked away, Mithrel said, "What is your problem, rider?"

"I don't have a problem," he retorted.

"Oh yeah? Then why do you keep making passive-aggressive comments? If you want aggressive, there's no need to be passive about it," he said, lifting his axe.

"Then let's do this," Orion said, drawing his sword.

"That's enough!" Celestia shouted, "Look at you two. Why don't you work out your disagreements now so we can *all* focus on this quest? Our mission is far more important than your little scrap. You both like Xharia. There, it's out in the open. Now, fix it." With that, she headed off to the restroom as well.

"You like Xharia?" Mithrel asked in surprise.

Orion looked away, "I thought that was obvious."

"Now it is," he replied, "That explains so much. No wonder you've hated me from the beginning."

"What of it?" he asked defensively, "So, you like her, too?"

"Of course!" he replied, "She's beautiful, smart, strong, and graceful. What's not to like?"

Orion let out a frustrated sigh, "Well, what do we *do* about it?"

He dropped his axe, extending his hand, "We let her decide. May the best man win."

He looked at his hand a moment before shaking it, "Friends?"

Mithrel pursed his lips, "Allies. No matter who she chooses, we shall remain so for sake of the quest. Though, I can't promise no hard feelings."

He nodded in agreement, feeling some relief that the tension between them could break, "Nor can I." Though they would still both pursue Xharia, at least they had laid out their intentions beforehand, and they could still remain cordial in spite of the awkward situation.

Well, I suppose this is better than nothing, Saphron thought.

As the ladies returned from the restroom, they all went back to their meals, each of them lost in their own thoughts.

Now, the playing field is level, and it's any man's game, Orion thought.

It's not a game, Saphron replied.

I know, he said, *It's a figure of speech.*

I never understood that, he said, *Human dialect is so strange.*

He laughed, sarcastically adding, *Because dragon dialect is so easy to understand.*

To the trained ear, it is, he replied indignantly.

Goodnight, Saphron, he thought, *I hope you never change.*

His dragon wiggled with happy surprise at his comment, curling his warm body around his rider, *Goodnight, Orion.*

Friendly Feud

10

They journeyed through the dwarven tunnels, making their way out of Dirthix, and into the outer reaches of Korga. It was painfully slow for Orion, who was used to being able to fly quickly upon his dragon.

We're never going to make it in time, he thought, *If we could fly, we'd already be in Kogatsa.*

Patience, Saphron replied, *Our companions are important to this quest. They are not riders, so this is how we must do things.*

He groaned internally.

It will all work out, he thought, *Wait and see.*

"Everything alright, Orion?" Xharia asked, coming over to sit beside him. They'd spread their things out on the floor of the dwarven tunnels to make their campsite. They had a fire in the middle to cook their meals, and they were seated around it.

"Yeah, I'm fine," he said.

She looked at him doubtfully, "You can tell me . . . "

He looked at her, seeing how she was leaning toward him with an earnest expression, "It's just . . . I feel like we're going so slow. I'm used to flying somewhere quickly, and having to keep up with horses worries me. I'm afraid we won't have enough time."

She nodded, "I can understand that. But, don't forget that Celestia traveled by horseback for two of her quests, and she still completed them in time. There was only one leg of one of her quests she traveled by dragon-back. We'll make it."

He looked down, still uncertain.

She took his hand in one of her hands, patting his back with the other, "We will. You'll see."

Orion looked up at her, feeling the warmth of her hand around his own. Their faces were inches apart. His breath caught, and he wasn't sure whether he should lean in for a kiss.

Before he could, she kissed his cheek, "Don't worry." With that, she got up, heading over to check on Shadow.

When he looked up, he saw that Mithrel was staring at him with an expression of hurt, anger, worry, and jealousy. He felt a little guilty and bad for him, knowing just how he felt, but not bad enough to stop him from smiling. He'd finally had a real moment with her, and that was enough for right now.

He grinned from ear to ear the rest of the night, even as he drifted off to sleep . . .

The next day, as they were traveling, Orion felt like he was floating as he flew upon Saphron. He slid his black gloves over his dragon's neck, patting him. Mithrel was glaring silently as he rode below, his terracotta skin flushed red with anger. Xharia looked worried that she may have upset him, a concerned expression forming on her ebony face, but Orion didn't care. Celestia sat behind him calmly, enjoying the feeling of flying, and waiting for the end of the dwarven tunnels. Her blue and silver robes shimmered in the lantern-light.

It seemed like it had been forever since they'd seen the sun, and the tunnels continued to stretch out for miles ahead. They still had a fortnight to reach their end. Traveling was so monotonous, especially when they went at the speed of a horse.

They stopped when they came upon a dwarven village, and decided to stop for the night. When the villagers saw them coming, they scattered, fleeing in fear at the sight of Saphron.

"Wait, stop!" Mithrel shouted, "Brothers! Sisters! It's alright! We mean you no harm!"

They continued running, grabbing their children and sprinting for their bunkers.

"Sie es frugs! Sie haill i Dirthix, u zatrage i King Tunxst!" Mithrel called.

They stopped, looking over at him. After a pause, one of the men shouted, "Ie draigyhr? Yaug in vraden sie?"

"In!" he replied, "Yaug es frug!"

The villagers looked at each other uncertainly, hesitating. After another long pause, the man shouted, "What is it that you seek?"

"We seek accommodations!" Mithrel answered, "For us and our horses! The dragon can sleep in the corridor, but we do need food for him! He would require a boar or a goat!"

When they still hesitated, he added, "Yaug in vraden gyo! Yatren bie!"

"Alright!" he replied finally, waving them over, "Come on!"

As they dismounted, leaving Saphron in the hall and heading over, Orion asked, "What did you say to them?"

"Just that we mean them no harm. They were fearful of your dragon."

"Thank you," Xharia said, "That was wonderful!"

As Orion glared and Mithrel beamed, Celestia added, "Yes. I see it was a good idea for the dwarves to send us an ambassador, after all."

Indeed it was, Saphron thought, *If they hadn't, I may well have starved. These tunnels aren't very good for hunting, and the meat supplied by the dwarves does nothing to sate my hunger. It's been over a week, and I've had nothing but scraps.*

He grimaced, realizing his dragon was right, but hating to admit that Mithrel had saved them.

Whether you care for him or not is irrelevant, he said, *You must only accept that we need him.*

Unfortunately, he said, *You are right. He has proved his worth.*

"Come on, Orion," Celestia said as he lagged behind.

The four of them entered the village, following the man to the town's inn. They put Shadow and Helado in a corral and led them inside. They headed upstairs and to two rooms.

"We cannot give out more than two rooms for a single party," the inn-keeper said.

"That's alright," Celestia replied, "We shall be fine."

"I'll prepare a meal for you all, and wash your clothes for you. If you pay us, we shall bring a boar for your dragon, but you must take it to him."

"Here," Orion said, tossing him a small bag of coins, "Bring three."

When the innkeeper hesitated, staring at him wide-eyed, he added, "He's hungry." At that, his eyes bulged out of his head, and he hurried off to fetch the boars.

"I'll room with Xharia," Mithrel said, "For her protection, of course."

"I'm perfectly alright," Xharia said, "I do not require protection."

As Orion opened his mouth to interject, Celestia said, "Before you two start fighting over sharing a room with Xharia, let me just say, *I'll* room with her. Then, we do not have to worry about impropriety. Girls in this room, boys in that room." She gestured to each door in turn.

The two of them sighed, looking at each other.

Xharia headed down the hall to wash up, and Celestia stood there, shaking her head.

"I'll go feed Saphron," Orion said, heading down the stairs.

There were three dead boars waiting at the door of the inn, and he quickly took them out to his dragon, who hungrily devoured them, satisfying his growling belly. Once he was taken care of, he headed back inside to take his turn washing up. When he reached the top of the stairs, Celestia was just coming out of the washroom, so he knew the ladies were done. He entered, washing quickly, and using magic to clean his bodysuit, as he always did.

When he looked in the mirror to trim his hair, he gasped. He'd changed a lot since the beginning of his training. He hadn't yet realized how much. But, he had muscle now. He looked like a warrior. His milk chocolate skin looked hard, and his black, coiled hair was disheveled. His facial hair was disheveled to match, growing out at odd angles. He quickly trimmed it, making sure he looked fresh, before leaving the washroom to Mithrel.

Orion awoke in the middle of the night, looking over at Mithrel, who was asleep beside him. They'd made a wall of pillows between them, so they could sleep without rolling into each other in the night. His black beard was smushed into the pillows, and a line of drool was flowing from his open mouth.

What is it? Saphron thought, feeling Orion's consciousness.

I'm not sure, he thought, getting up. He peeked into the hallway, seeing nothing in the darkened inn. He quickly slipped across the hall into the girls' room to check on them. He could see the both of them, sound asleep, with a pillow wall between them as well. Nothing seemed out of the ordinary, *I guess it's nothing.*

Just then, they heard what sounded like a distant *crash,* and the inn shook beneath their feet.

"Orion, what is it?" Xharia asked, waking up in a panic.

He hurried over to her, "I'm not sure. Let's get out of here." He wrapped an arm around Xharia protectively, as she was readying herself to get up so they could head out.

"It's alright," Celestia said, sitting up, "I know what it was."

They stopped at her comment, looking at her expectantly, worry in their eyes.

"Two more stars collided," she said, not even looking at them.

They moved apart, unsure how to react.

Mithrel ran into the room then, madly yelling, "What's happening?"

"It's alright, Mithrel," Orion said, calming down, "Go back to sleep. It's nothing."

"Nothing?" he said, swinging his axe, "That *nothing* shook the whole village!"

"It was two stars falling outside the tunnels," Xharia said, "There's nothing that will harm us, but our time for completing this quest is lessened."

He lowered his axe then, looking deflated.

"There's nothing we can do but keep going," Celestia said, "Get some rest, all of you. We must continue through the tunnels tomorrow."

When morning came, Orion bought three large goats for Saphron, letting him feast before they set out again, knowing his food supply was significantly less on the road. He could feel his dragon's hunger when his stomach was empty, and he wanted to make sure he was taken care of.

They kept going through the tunnels at what felt like a snail's pace to Orion. The next couple of weeks were long and monotonous, as they made their way through the rest of the tunnels. Mithrel helped them talk to two more villages along the way, ensuring them access to food, baths, and beds.

"Here we are, at last, friends," Mithrel said, gesturing grandly ahead from the back of his black pony, "The end of the dwarven tunnels."

Orion could see that he was right. Up ahead, there were two large doors. The terrified dwarven guards opened them at the sight of Saphron, glad to let the great dragon exit their tunnels. As soon as they were outside, and Saphron could fully stretch his wings, he landed, letting Orion and Celestia slide off, and he took off to hunt. After three weeks of travel with only a few villages along the way, and nowhere to hunt, Saphron was starving. His stomach growled as he soared through the skies, searching for his prey.

Eat as much as you want, Orion thought, climbing onto the back of Mithrel's pony, *I can feel your hunger. You need to eat.*

I plan to, was all he said.

Celestia leaped onto the back of Xharia's horse, and they rode into Kuttub. They had one more week before they'd reach Kogatsa, and hopefully find a creature capable of training Saphron. Either way, Orion was relieved to leave Korga behind.

When they stopped to make camp that night, everyone gathered round the fire to eat, and Saphron finally returned from his all-day hunt.

"Such amazing creatures, dragons," Xharia said, marveling at Saphron.

"Yes, they are," Orion agreed, "They're even more amazing when you get to fly upon them."

"I bet," she said, looking as though she were daydreaming of the experience.

After a pause, he said, "Would you like to?"

She looked at him in surprise, "What?"

He stood, offering his hand, "Fly with me."

Her eyes widened, but she took his hand. He helped her up, and led her over to Saphron.

You think a midnight flight will win her heart? he asked.

It's worth a shot, he replied.

The sapphire dragon shook his head as Orion leaped upon his back, and reached down to help Xharia into the saddle behind him.

"Ready?" he asked.

She answered by wrapping her arms around him tightly, bracing herself.

He smiled, enjoying the feeling. *Alright, let's go,* he thought.

Saphron launched himself into the sky, and Xharia let out a shout as he did, clinging on tighter. Both Orion and Saphron enjoyed her reaction. Orion, because she clung tightly to him, wrapping her arms around his chest, and pressing herself against him. And Saphron, because she showed the proper fear of riding upon his back.

They soared higher into the night sky, leveling out. The night was crisp and clear, and they could see the moon and stars with perfect clarity. Xharia began to loosen her grip, looking around her, "It's so beautiful . . . "

Orion nodded, not wanting to disturb the moment. Though the night was beautiful, and the feeling of flying with Xharia was magical, he could see the row of stars moving closer with perfect clarity, and it dampened the mood. There were three more pairs of stars that would collide before their quest was over.

They flew through the darkened sky, enjoying the feeling of peace and serenity. It truly was beautiful, and, in spite of the bleak situation, Orion was able to enjoy himself. When they came in for a landing, Xharia let out a scream. Saphron laughed, and Orion smiled.

As they dismounted, she said, "Wow, that was incredible! Thank you, Orion." When Saphron snorted, she added, "And thank you, Saphron."

"You're welcome," Orion said, "I'm glad you enjoyed it."

"I did," she said, "I see why you riders love it so much." She turned toward Celestia, "I also see what I missed out on on your first quest."

Callisto smiled, "Indeed."

As they all settled down to sleep, he felt in his heart that he would be with Xharia. Mithrel seemed to have a permanent frown these days, and he glared at him as he took his post for the first watch. But, to Orion, it didn't matter. All that mattered was he'd had a magical evening with the woman he wanted to be with.

Congratulations, Saphron thought, *You finally learned to behave like a gentleman.*

I'm going to ignore your snarkiness in light of this incredible evening, he replied.

I mean it, he said, *You showed her a good time, and were able to get closer to her without pressuring or pushing her. I'm proud of you.*

Oh, he thought, *Well . . . thanks.*

The blue dragon gave his rider a nod, nestling into the ground to sleep. *I love you, Orion,* he thought warmly.

I love you, too, you great big lug, he replied, curling up beside him.

Tanzanite

11

The next day, they continued through Kuttub, making their way slowly to Kogatsa. Celestia rode with Xharia again, having Saphron and Orion do more drills to keep up their training. He could feel his strength increasing, and his speed and reflexes improving. He was beginning to get cocky, knowing how skilled he'd become. His dragon was getting just as cocky, despite his lack of training, and they both felt ready to take on whatever opponent dared to face them.

When they landed that night to make camp, Saphron took off to go hunting, and the rest of them got their fire going so they could eat. Orion sat beside Xharia, "The fire's beautiful, isn't it?"

She smiled, "Yes, it is."

"But, not as beautiful as the night sky from above . . . "

She looked at him coyly, "No, it's not."

"Well, the night sky looks pretty beautiful from this angle, too," Mithrel inserted, sitting on her other side.

"The moon and stars are beautiful from any angle, it's true," she agreed.

"I've never thought so," Celestia said.

The three of them looked at her in surprise. "What do you mean?" Xharia asked.

"I mean, I suppose I did once," she continued, "But, after two quests with the stars as our timer, and now a third, they just don't hold the same meaning for me. I see a sparkling hourglass, nothing more."

They all looked down silently, none of them sure what to say.

She wordlessly rose, wandering off.

There was a long pause before any of them could say anything. Finally, Xharia broke the silence, "I'm going to go check on her."

As she headed toward the forest where Callisto had gone, they heard a scream. Xharia looked back at the guys, and they quickly armed themselves, rushing toward the sound. They heard another scream, and a *thud*, before they reached a clearing. They saw Celestia, wand drawn, fighting off a horde of kodrizans. The dark creatures resembled men, but with pointed ears on top of their heads, fangs, and claws. Their skin had a grayish tint— the mark of evil.

As they watched, Celestia erupted in blue magic, the sparkle of her raw power lining her entire body. "They caught me by surprise," she yelled, "I hardly had time to grab my wand!"

The three of them charged into the midst of the ambush as they began turning toward them. *Saphron!* Orion thought, panicked, *We need you!* But, his dragon was out of mental range on his hunt.

"I thought these creatures never ventured outside of Kogatsa!" Xharia yelled.

"Me, too!" Celestia said, "But, here we are!"

Orion was awed by the sight of raw power. He'd never seen a witch or wizard's power form a visible ring around them before. He had to keep his head, however, as the kodrizans continued to attack them. He swung his sword, killing them off with ease. He was glad for his training now more than ever.

As he fought them, he wondered who had created them. Kodrizans were creatures created through dark magic and ritual sacrifice. They were bred to serve as pons for a dark wizard. Typically, they existed solely in Kogatsa, as that land was a breeding ground for dark wizards. Yet, they were only a couple days into Kuttub.

A group converged on him, getting close enough for him to see the black blood oozing from their lips where their fangs cut into them. He blasted them back with a ball of blue magic, swinging his sword through their midst, and cutting more of them down. Celestia had an easy time blasting them away, with her use of raw power. Mithrel cut through them with his axe, shouting dwarven battle cries all the while.

Xharia looked as though she were in heaven, finally getting to see battle. Her dreams were coming true, facing real opponents for the first time in a century. She was satisfying her bloodlust on these creatures of darkness, slicing her sword through them with ease. Her elven reflexes were truly impressive, as was her speed. They had no hope of keeping up with her.

The battle wore on, more and more of them streaming in steadily. Orion looked worriedly at the others, "There are too many of them! We need to get out of here!"

"Get back to the campsite!" Callisto yelled, "We'll take the horses! Saphron will catch up!"

They pulled back, the two of them trying to blast back the horde with magic to give them an exit. When the smoke cleared, he could see Mithrel behind them, but Xharia hadn't pulled back, "Xharia! Come on!"

"No!" she yelled, "We can take them!" She continued swinging her sword, fighting them off with glee.

He looked to the other two in a panic, starting to run toward her. He knew he had to get her out of there. As he did, a large group of them sprang up in front of him, blocking his path. He blasted some of them back, slicing his sword through the others.

"Orion!" Celestia shouted, "I can't hold them! My energy is draining too low!"

He looked between her and Xharia, unsure what to do. As he did, he saw a mass of them approaching through the trees. They were headed straight toward Xharia. He quickly blasted the group around him, running toward her. Before he could reach her, she was knocked down by the swarm, and one of the kodrizans grinned at him with glee, raising his axe to slice through her.

As he brought it down, he was blocked by another axe, and they turned to see Mithrel standing there. He quickly cut down the kodrizan, reaching down and pulling Xharia up. He swung his axe in a half-circle, cutting down the ones behind them as he pulled her along, running back toward the campsite.

Orion sent magic blasts through them, trying to give them some cover. He met up with Celestia, and they sent out waves of magic as they ran, keeping the horde at bay. They made it to the campsite, the mass of kodrizans pouring out through the trees. Mithrel made sure Xharia made it onto Shadow's back, and then he leaped upon Helado's. Celestia leaped behind Xharia, and they took off, riding away hard.

"Come on!" Mithrel yelled, looking back as he waited for Orion, "Let's go!"

He sent one final blast back as he jumped onto the black pony behind Mithrel. They rode off as quick as they could, trying to put distance between them and the ambush. Finally, as they rode away, Orion felt a familiar consciousness come in contact with his own. *Saphron!* he thought, *There you are!*

On feeling his rider in danger, he quickened his pace, flying at full speed back to them, *Orion!* His emotions were a mixture of fear, surprise, confusion, worry, and a deeply burning rage that anyone would dare to harm his rider. He arrived in seconds, tearing through the horde of kodrizans, and ripping their heads off. He breathed a jet of flame across them, burning them to a crisp. He clutched several of them in his claws, flying upwards, and dropping them.

It didn't take long before Saphron had destroyed most of them, and the rest had fled in fear. With a mighty roar, he flew over to his rider, landing in front of the horses. They quickly pulled them to a stop, looking back at the empty woods behind them.

They dismounted, Celestia saying, "Well done, Saphron." After a pause, she looked at Xharia and added, "Imagine how much easier the second quest would have been if the dragon riders had actually granted us a warrior."

Xharia wasn't focused on her, however, "Mithrel! You saved my life!" She rushed over to the dwarf, embracing him.

He started with surprise, and then warmly accepted the embrace, "I couldn't just let you die."

As she pulled away, she kissed his cheek, "Thank you."

His light brown skin flushed red, and he cleared his throat, "It's nothing."

Orion looked on, unsure how to react. If he'd only been a little quicker, it would have been him. On one hand, he was glad Mithrel had saved her. He was glad she was still alive. On the other, he was upset with himself for not reaching her faster, and jealous of the attention she was giving to Mithrel.

"It's not nothing," Celestia said, almost angrily, "It shouldn't have been necessary. Why did you not come when we called you, Xharia?"

"I'm sorry," she replied, hanging her head, "I was too caught up in the battle to stop myself."

"You could have been killed," she snapped, "You could have gotten the rest of us killed, too. You should be ashamed of yourself."

"I am," she said, "I made a foolish mistake. But, believe me when I say, it won't ever happen again."

"It better not," Callisto chastised. After a pause, she sighed, softening her tone, "I'm glad you're alright. I was worried about you."

The two girls hugged, and Xharia said, "I'm sorry."

When they moved apart, Celestia said, "Well, now that Saphron's back, and has dispatched the kodrizans, I think we'll be safe enough setting up camp again. Come on."

They all trudged slowly, unpacking their things to try to get some sleep once more.

I'm alright, Orion thought, feeling his dragon's worry. He shared his memories with him, allowing him to see what happened.

You should not be jealous just because she thanked him for saving her life, he said, *If that's the most harm that came to you, you should be grateful. It could have been a lot worse.*

It could have been, he agreed, *But, it wasn't. I am grateful to be alive. I'm just . . . what good am I if I can't protect her? I was right there, but I couldn't be there when she needed me. I failed her. She'd be dead if it were up to me.*

But she's not dead. It's not up to you alone. We have a team. We all share some responsibility in this quest.

Still . . .

It's not your fault. Sometimes, you just can't get to her, he paused, *We all make choices—some good, some bad. She made a stupid one. You at least tried to save her, and that's commendable. But, keeping her alive is not up to you. It's up to her. You can't blame yourself. She's still alive, and that's what matters.*

Orion sighed.

Get some rest, he thought, *We must continue our journey, and make it to Kogatsa.*

They continued the next few days through Kuttub, finally reaching the border of Kogatsa. They could feel the darkness of the land growing the closer they got. The days grew longer, and the nights grew darker. At last, the city of Khanjgi was in their sights.

"Khanjgi," Celestia said with disgust, "I have many memories of this place; none of them pleasant."

"Let's just get this over with," Xharia said, looking around, "I have no desire to linger in this place."

"Agreed," she replied.

They rode past the city, and up the nearby hill to the woods. Orion got an ominous feeling as they did so, and he scanned the treeline, unsure why. Suddenly, he got a sense of rage and malcontent from Saphron. *What is it?* he asked.

These woods are cursed, he replied, *A dragon was killed here.*

How do you know?

I can sense it, he said, *I don't like this.*

"We should go," Orion said, "These woods are cursed."

Celestia shot him a strange look from her place behind Xharia on Shadow's back.

"Saphron says a dragon was killed here," he explained.

Her eyes widened, and her mouth opened and shut as though she were about to say something.

"What?" he asked.

She knows, Saphron thought.

"You know what happened here?" Orion said.

She nodded. After a long pause, she said, "This is where Nastazya and Ezmyra were killed."

It was Orion's turn for his eyes to grow wide. He could feel that Saphron was feeling the same as he. He wasn't sure how to describe his emotions. Shock, rage, sadness, and wonder were a few of the feelings flowing through the both of them.

Xharia bowed her head. It was obvious she'd known as well. Mithrel looked as surprised and awed as they were. Celestia's eyes showed her great sadness and reverence of this place. The horses stirred nervously in the shadow of the trees.

"Let's go," Orion said finally, "We shall find no help here."

"Wait," Callisto said. Everyone stopped as she dismounted, standing upon the hill. After a moment, she pulled out her wand, casting a spell over the hillside. As they watched, little white flowers started to pop out of the ground, covering the hill. Once it was covered, she gave a little nod, hopping back upon Shadow's back.

They rode further into the woods, searching for a worthy mentor for Saphron. *Seems strange, looking for a dark creature to teach you,* Orion thought, *Even if we find one capable, why would they?*

And if they were willing, would they be the best choice? he agreed, *Yet, what other option do we have?*

Orion sighed. He knew his dragon was right, as usual. But still, how could they expect a creature of darkness to train a dragon?

"There!" Mithrel shouted, pointing ahead.

Up in the sky in front of them, they could see two long, slender, dragon-like creatures flying through the air.

"Vekkens!" Xharia yelled.

"Would they not be the perfect trainers?" Callisto asked, "They are the closest things to dragons we'll find."

Orion projected thoughts of doubt, which he could feel Saphron agreed with.

I share your doubt, the blue dragon thought, *But, what choice have we? We should at least give it a shot. Prepare yourself. This will probably result in a fight.*

He braced himself, squeezing the saddle between his legs and drawing his sword.

They flew closer, approaching the reptilian creatures. *Ho there!* Saphron thought, *We mean you no harm. Can we talk?*

The vekkens hissed and screeched, causing Orion to cover his ears. *Dragon!* they thought, *What do you want?*

I have come to ask for your help. I'm in need of a mentor. I'm training for a battle, you see.

Battle? they thought. Orion could feel the dark, slippery tentacles of their consciousness through Saphron. Though he could not communicate with the creatures on his own, his dragon could, and so he could tune in. *Yes,* they continued, *We know of what you speak. You will all burn . . . a fitting end for a dragon, don't you think?*

Saphron growled, giving them a warning.

They backed up, catching an air current with their wings. After a pause, they said, *Why would you ask us for help? You must be desperate . . . it's laughable.* They let out a few screeches of laughter, twisting through the air in amusement.

He breathed a jet of flame across them, roaring in anger.

They screeched and hissed again, quickly darting out of the path of his fire. When they were clear of it, they said, *You shall receive no aid here, dragon!*

They started to fly away, but Saphron followed, snapping his jaws on their tails.

The vekkens turned then, and they locked into a fight. The others watched helplessly below, a safe distance away. Orion flailed about, trying to hang on as his dragon fought. One of the vekkens snaked its head around Saphron, trying to reach Orion. He swung his sword at it, scratching its nose. It backed up, shaking its head, and went back to fighting Saphron.

As the fight wore on, Orion knew he needed to do something to help his dragon. He grabbed hold of the top of the saddle, removing his feet from the stirrups, and allowing himself to dangle.

"Orion!" Xharia yelled, "Be careful!"

He couldn't help a quick smile of satisfaction that she was worried about him. But, he didn't have time to dwell on it. He pulled himself up, climbing onto Saphron's shoulders. As he did so, he could see the two vekkens in front of him clearly—a mess of teeth and claws ripping flesh below him. He swung his sword down into their midst, slicing at the vekkens.

They screeched in surprise, turning on him. Saphron wasn't having it, though, and the momentary distraction allowed him to tear into the vekkens freely. They backed up, trying to retreat. The sapphire dragon followed, Orion balancing back on his shoulders as he turned to keep from falling. He was impressed with himself for successfully maneuvering, and he looked back at the others to see their reactions. As he did, Saphron turned up again, locking back into battle with the vekkens, and he fell.

His dragon swooped down to catch him quickly, and he climbed back up to help him fight. The cold, slimy creatures saw their opening, dive-bombing them. Orion swung his sword in defense, but he couldn't keep up with both of them at once. Saphron flipped upside down, and Orion had to clutch the saddle quickly, hanging on for dear life. The sapphire dragon breathed a jet of flame upwards, sending the vekkens scurrying away.

Orion could tell that Saphron was using this battle as training for himself, and he was learning as it wore on, but without a teacher, he knew it was not enough. Not to mention, they were losing. He knew he had to do something, or the vekkens would tear through his dragon. He tried to climb around to his underbelly to help him, but he was dangling from the saddle on his back, unable to get a leg up.

He began swinging, trying to get the leverage to make the jump, but Saphron twisted at the same time, and he nearly lost his grip. Suddenly, there was a jet of flame searing across the vekkens, but it wasn't coming from Saphron. Orion looked up in time to see an indigo dragon flying over them, and tearing into the dark creatures.

Saphron rolled back over, and Orion landed in the saddle. They joined the dragon's efforts, fighting off the vekkens, and sending them flying away, screeching through the forest.

The indigo dragon, Saphron thought.

Orion shared the same thought as they looked at the dragon in wonder.

I'm Saphron, he thought, projecting it to the other dragon, *Who are you?*

Tanzanite, she said, sizing him up.

Are you the dragon who got away when Dredon and Obsidian slaughtered Cabri's mountain leaders? Orion projected through Saphron.

How do you know about that? she demanded, snarling.

We saw it, he replied, *There was nothing we could do. I'm sorry.*

How did you see it? she asked gruffly, *You weren't even there.*

We were a ways away, up in the clouds, Saphron said, *I wanted Orion to see the practices, and benefit from second-hand training. He had no hope of making it to the training mountain. We never expected to see what we saw . . .*

Tanzanite looked away, her face contorted with pain.

I'm sorry, he said, *Truly. We tried to tell Lorena, but Kirstiana didn't believe us. She sent investigators to the mountain, but somehow they had cleaned the scene. We thought she would believe us if we found you, but you were long gone. We never expected to run into you here.*

What are *you doing here?* she asked suspiciously.

We could ask you the same thing, Orion projected.

We're searching for someone to train me, Saphron said, *so I can face Obsidian.*

Face Obsidian? Tanzanite thought in shock, *You're either stupid or you're crazy. If you face him, you'll die! He killed off all the other leaders! You're an untrained newbie. What makes you think that's a good idea?*

Not all the leaders, he thought.

She started in surprise, looking at him.

So, what are you doing here? he asked.

She bristled, looking carefully from Saphron to Orion. After a long pause, she said, *I didn't know where to go when they were slaughtering us. My rider had already been killed.* She paused again, her grief tangible even without being able to feel her emotions, *I just flew and flew. I got away through the mountains, and I started out south. I realized there was nowhere to go that way, so I circled widely around the mountains, and journeyed to the northern reaches of Abyumo, trying to get help from the wizards. But, they couldn't understand me without my rider. When they decided to contact the riders about me, I knew I couldn't stay there, so I just tried to get as far away as I could. Kogatsa seemed like a good place to hide. It's the last thing he'd expect.*

Well, that's true, Orion thought.

That's terrible, Saphron thought, *Are you alright?*

I'm not sure, Tanzanite replied, *I'm not sure of anything anymore.*

We're going to make this right, he thought, *But, we need your help.*

What happened that day? Orion asked, *Why did he do it?*

She paused again, looking at the both of them, *He called a meeting of the leaders. He told us of his plan—his plan to take over the lands of this world. He wanted us to join him. Some did.* She looked away in disappointment, *When the rest of us refused, he asked our riders to come forth, to form a truce. They did, and he killed them. His followers helped, ready to see his plans come to fruition. Then, Obsidian and his dragon minions launched their attack on the rest of us. He didn't want any witnesses to his treachery. He wanted more followers. And, if we refused, he wanted us out of his way.* She paused again, *How many of us got away?*

They were silent, looking at her.

So . . . it is just me, then, she thought.

After a long pause, Orion said, *Yes. You're the sole survivor . . . which means you're the only one who can help us. Please. If you want to make Obsidian and Dredon pay for what they did, we need your help.*

Tanzanite scoffed, *And just how are the two of you going to do that? You honestly think you're a match for them? Even if I did train you, it wouldn't be enough. Our only hope is getting the army of Cabri on our side.*

Yes, exactly, Orion thought, *And to do that, we need a plan, a lot of back-up, and a dragon and rider pair capable of facing the two of them alone.*

Oh? she said, *Like it's so easy? Maybe you have a hair-brained plan, maybe you even found back-up, but where do you expect to find a pair capable of facing them? I see none. You couldn't even take a couple of vekkens alone.*

You're right, Saphron thought, *That's why we need your help.*

I'll not train you to go to your deaths, she thought.

We spoke with The Oracle, he said, *She has foreseen this. She said we are the only ones who can defeat him. Dredon is the descendant of Vidar the Conqueror. Orion is the descendant of Derekkian—the one who defeated Vidar.*

She looked at them in surprise, *Truly? You are the descendant of Derekkian?*

Orion nodded.

Tanzanite paused again, deliberating. After a while, she said, *Alright. I'll train you.*

You're amazing, Saphron said.

She turned her indigo head away, almost looking as though she were blushing.

"Everything alright?" Celestia called.

"What's going on?" Mithrel asked.

"This is Tanzanite," Orion said, "She's the indigo dragon we saw escape. She's going to train us."

The War has Begun

12

"What a horrible thing to escape from," Xharia said as they sat around their campfire in the forest of Kogatsa, "I'm so sorry that happened to you."

Tanzanite nudged her with her snout, appreciating her care and concern.

Xharia gave her a pat as Celestia said, "Yes, it truly must have been."

"We shall avenge your rider!" Orion said, rising and drawing his sword, "And all the other leaders as well!"

I admire your bravery, young rider, Tanzanite thought, *But it can cause as much harm as good. We would not want you charging blindly into battle. You need to be prepared, and remain level-headed in the face of conflict with evil.*

"Orion," Celestia reprimanded, "Sit down. Do not be so eager to charge into battle."

He sat back down, looking from Tanzanite to Celestia, *Well, at least our mentors are on the same page.*

Saphron chuckled, *Indeed. They are both very wise, and we are lucky to have them.*

"Well," Mithrel said, "I, for one, admire your courage."

"It's not that I don't admire his courage," Callisto said, "It's that I worry for his prudence."

"Prudence can be taught," Xharia inserted, "Courage cannot."

Orion shot her a smile, glad she was on his side.

"And so, we shall teach you," Celestia said.

And so, we shall teach you, Tanzanite thought.

Right, left, right, dodge! Tanzanite thought quickly.

Saphron did as she said, moving swiftly through the air, and trying to keep up with her instruction. She had been training him all day, guiding him through various combat maneuvers. He was keeping up fairly well, but they could see he had a ways to go before he would reach even her level.

How are those instincts working out for you? Orion thought.

Saphron growled, *Focus on your own training.*

And let our synchronization sink? he chided.

They'll train us together later, he thought in irritation, *For now, we need to improve individually.*

"Orion, focus!" Celestia shouted.

"Sorry!" he yelled, getting back to his spar with Xharia.

He knew he was blessed to have two skilled mentors to train him, and now Saphron finally had one as well. As long as they kept training and drilling, he had faith they could face more powerful adversaries. *I wonder if we could find those vekkens for another test run,* he thought.

Just focus on your training, Saphron thought, *We'll search for worthy adversaries later.*

"Orion!" Celestia yelled.

"Sorry!" he shouted again, focusing. But, it was too late, and Xharia swept his feet, knocking him down.

"So, I'm not a challenge for you anymore?" she said, "Perhaps I've been too easy on you. Care to try again?"

He jumped up, straightening his black bodysuit with blue accent lines. Its sapphire belt shone in the sunlight like Xharia's hazel eyes. As he marveled at the gold flecks they captured with the light in them, they narrowed in a challenge. He raised his sword, taking his stance, and indicating he was ready to go again. She smiled, charging forward.

They locked into battle again, and this time it took his full focus, as she moved far faster than normal, and he struggled to keep up with her. Before he knew it, she'd swept his feet again, and he was looking at the world from the ground.

"Where did that come from?" he asked, rising, "Have you been holding back on me?"

She smiled cockily, "I didn't think you could keep up otherwise."

"Oh?" he said, both impressed and annoyed, "Well, holding back on me will do me no favors against Dredon. Why don't you show me what you've *really* got?"

Xharia smirked, "Very well, rider. As you wish."

With that, they engaged again, and she completely overwhelmed him, knocking him down very quickly. He barely got a couple of swings in before he was on his back once more.

"So, now the real training begins," he said as he rose, "I have to start from zero again, and learn to beat you for real."

She smiled, "Maybe tomorrow. For now, it's time to work on your magic. I'll be taking a break."

As Xharia sat beside Mithrel, and they began chatting, Celestia drew her wand, readying herself to face him in magical combat.

Orion took a breath, barely able to focus as he took his stance, summoning his powers.

"Perhaps I should turn it up a notch, too," she said, erupting in raw power.

His eyes grew wide as they began their fight, not sure how he could battle such incredible power. No one could beat raw power. As he thought that, he wondered, *Why does* she *not face Dredon? She can wield far greater power than I could ever hope to match. He couldn't match it, either. She'd be a far greater adversary than I would.*

Stamina matters as much as strength, Saphron thought, *Though she's more powerful, age will have slowed her reserves of energy. She may have stores built up, but they cannot equal that of a dragon—particularly a dragon of Obsidian's size.*

So, you're saying I could beat her by dodging and waiting for her energy to drain before attacking?

I'd say that would be your best bet, he thought, *But, you may not be equipped to wait her out, yet. Not to mention, it would be useless to employ that tactic against Dredon. And, since that's what this training is for, I wouldn't recommend it.*

Some help you are, Orion thought, *What should I do, then?*

Experiment with different strategies, he thought, *I have to focus on my own battle.*

He sighed, *This will end badly.*

As soon as he'd thought it, Callisto cast a spell at him, blasting him across the field they were practicing in. His body ached as he rose, from the number of times he'd been knocked down in his training, coupled with his soreness from the strength, speed, and agility drills they'd been doing.

"Looks like we've still got a long way to go," she said.

He nodded in agreement, panting, "Perhaps we should take a break."

She smirked, "Very well. Be ready to start fresh tomorrow."

Orion had a tough time sleeping that night, just thinking of how far they had come with their training, and how far they still had to go. Just when he'd thought he was really doing something, his delusions were ripped out from under him. He could see the stars above growing closer, and he knew they didn't have much time to complete their training. He tried to quelch his thoughts, not wanting to disturb Saphron, but it was difficult for him.

"Can't sleep?" he heard Mithrel say.

As he was rolling over to answer, he heard Xharia's voice, "My mind is too full."

"Aye," he said, "Me, too."

"What are you thinking about?" she asked.

He let out a short, humorless laugh, "You."

After a pause, she said, "I think about you all the time as well."

"Then why can't we do anything about it?" he asked, "If you feel the same as I, there's no reason we shouldn't."

"You already know why," she said.

He sighed, "Orion." After a pause, he said, "You may feel like you're doing the right thing, waiting to tell him so he doesn't get distracted, but leading him on might be worse for him in the long-run."

"I'm not leading him on," she said defensively.

"Then, what are you doing?" Mithrel asked.

"I'm protecting his feelings," Xharia said softly, "Heartbreak would be detrimental to his mind-set. If he's to face Dredon, his mind needs to be right."

"You're trying to be kind," he replied, "But, I'm afraid you might not be *being* kind."

She sighed. After another pause, she said, "I told him when he tried to give me flowers that I didn't think I *could* love . . . that I had never felt love before. He asked me if I ever might, and I said it was possible. I should never have said that. It gave him false hope. But, it was true . . . at the time. After I met you, I finally felt what I never thought I could. But, after what I had said . . . I just couldn't bring myself to hurt him. I didn't know what to do. Now, I feel I've done the wrong thing." She groaned, "I don't know what to do now."

"Xharia," Mithrel said softly, "Listen to me. I'm a guy. You have to tell him. It's far worse to feel like you've been led on. You feel like you've been played for a fool. Yes, it will be hard for him to deal with in the face of this quest, but not knowing is worse. False hope is worse."

She sighed again, "Perhaps you're right."

Orion felt that feeling again—the feeling that he'd been punched in the stomach. There was no air left in his lungs. His ears were ringing so loud, he could no longer hear their conversation. *She's been leading me on to avoid distracting me with heartbreak? She's been in love with Mithrel the whole time? I never had a chance with her? Of course, I never had a chance with her. How could I be stupid enough to think I did?*

Orion, Saphron thought, waking at the feelings emanating from his rider, *You can't blame yourself. You can't control the way another person feels. I know it's hard for you, and I know it hurts right now—I can feel it. But, it was nothing you did. There was nothing you could have done. Mithrel's right: it was worse for you, not knowing. Now, you know. I know it's not what you wanted to hear, but we can't always get what we want. I know how hard it is for you—I know better than anyone. But, you have to let it go and focus on the quest. That is the most important thing right now.*

Spare me your lectures, he thought, *I have no need of them.*

Saphron paused, and Orion could sense the pain he had caused his dragon.

I'm sorry, Saphron, he thought, *I just need to be alone with my thoughts right now.*

Very well, he replied, *I'll be here if you need me . . . always.*

Thank you, he thought, *I'm glad at least I can always count on you . . .*

"Orion, I know it's impossible to best raw power, but you need to actually try!" Callisto said.

He felt as though he were in a daze, unable to focus. His thoughts were still dwelling on the conversation he'd overheard the night before.

When she saw his face, she looked at him with concern, "Is everything alright?"

"I'm fine," he said, "Let's just keep going."

"Is there a point in that when you aren't fighting back?"

He looked up, bracing himself, "You're right. I'm ready."

She sighed, "Very well." With that, she began her assault again, casting magical blasts his way.

He tried to dodge and block them, but it was far more difficult than normal. Saphron was struggling above him just as much, as he felt his rider's pain. Tanzanite was feeling the same frustration and concern as Celestia, trying to keep Saphron focused.

"Maybe you would do better on your sword training, and we'll continue magic later," she said finally.

He opened his mouth to object, but couldn't think of an argument he could use.

"Are you ready, rider?" Xharia asked, walking up.

Orion didn't say anything, but raised his sword, bracing for a battle he wasn't mentally prepared to fight.

She swung her sword, easily able to knock him down. As she looked down at him, she said, "You can't very well best me if you don't fight back." She held out her hand to help him up.

He silently got up, brushing her hand away.

As she looked at him, she realized he was upset, "What's wrong?"

"Nothing," he said, raising his sword.

Xharia lowered her sword, looking at him intently, "Obviously, *something* is wrong."

"Nothing that could be considered 'detrimental to my mind-set.'"

She started in surprise, looking at him, and then the realization set in, "You overheard us."

He remained silent, crossing his arms.

"I'm so sorry, Orion," she said, "I never meant for you to find out that way."

"I know," he replied, "You meant to lead me on until this quest was over, and then tell me you've been in love with Mithrel the whole time."

Xharia stared at him, sympathy and guilt in her eyes, unable to say anything.

He was disgusted that anyone should feel sympathy for him. He turned away, standing with his back to her. He could feel as she reached out, trying to comfort him, but there was nothing she could say, and they both knew it. Finally, she turned and hurried away, tears streaming down. He continued to stand there—unable to move, unable to breathe.

I know there's nothing I can say to ease your pain, Saphron thought, *But, just remember: I'm still here.*

This affects you, too, Orion thought, *For that, I'm sorry.*

Don't be, he replied, *You have nothing to be sorry for.*

"Orion," Callisto said softly, walking up.

"What?" he snapped.

She paused, unsure if she should say anything more. "I just wanted to check on you," she said finally.

"I'm fine," he snapped again.

She sighed, "I'm sure you're too proud to want my sympathy, but just know, I'm here if you need me."

He sighed, lowering his arms, "Thanks." After a pause, he said, "I just need to be alone for a while. I'm going to take a walk."

Celestia nodded, understanding.

With that, Orion headed into the trees, seeking solitude.

Orion spent the rest of the day wandering through the forest, lost in his thoughts. Though it was dangerous to do so in Kogatsa, he didn't care. The way he was feeling, he wouldn't care if he was ambushed and killed.

By the time it grew dark, he felt at least ready to go back. He arrived at the campsite after everyone was already asleep. Everyone except Celestia, as it was her watch.

"Orion," she whispered, "Is that you?"

"It's me," he said solemnly.

"Come," she said, "Sit."

He sighed, reluctantly sitting beside her.

"You've had time to clear your head. I'm afraid we have no more time to spare. Tomorrow, you must focus on your training again. We are running out of time to prepare you to face Dredon. This quest is bigger than just you. You can't afford to let your emotions rule you. The world is counting on you. I know it will be hard for you, but you must put everything else aside, and focus."

Orion looked off into the trees, "I'm not sure I can."

"You don't have a choice," she replied, "You didn't want sympathy, and you shall receive none. Do you think if you were to face Dredon tomorrow that he would take it easy on you? Therefore, I can't take it easy on you, either. If you must learn the hard way, so be it."

He looked at her in surprise.

"It's not that I don't care. But, this quest is more important than how you feel right now. Those destined for greatness can't afford to dwell on their emotions. This shall pass. But, don't be so selfish to think any of this is about you. It's not. It's about everyone in the world who's relying on you to save them. It's about your family. It's about your friends. It's about your allies. It's about Tanzanite, me, Saphron. You must go on for all of us."

He sighed, "You're right."

"Get some rest," Celestia said, "You're going to need it."

When morning came, Orion was ready to train. He focused all of his heartbreak into rage, increasing his power. He fought Celestia back and forth, offering her more of a challenge than he yet had. She actually had to try against him. Though, eventually, her raw power overwhelmed him.

"I'm impressed, Orion," she said, "Truly. Well done."

"Thank you," he replied, catching his breath.

They dueled until lunchtime, and he felt better than he had before about the upcoming conflict, knowing he was able to challenge someone who could wield raw power. Saphron was doing better as well, at his training with Tanzanite. Orion's emotions weren't throwing him off as much as the previous day, since they were concentrated on the training.

After lunch, he had to work on his sword training with Xharia. As much as he tried to maintain his concentration and focus on the training, seeing her again threw him off. Up until then, he'd been able to avoid her. Now, he had to face her, and fight her.

She seemed to be as thrown off as he, and she wasn't doing her best against him. Her elf-like reflexes were off-kilter. She was slower and more clumsy than normal. It was very unusual to see an elf lose their poise.

Neither of them said anything to the other, continuing to battle each other in awkward silence. They went on until dinner, stopping to eat. He was relieved to be able to go back to avoiding her, leaning against Saphron and eating. He kept his eyes averted from her and Mithrel. He could see how awkward everyone was feeling, whether they were involved or not.

At the end of the day, he felt good about his training, and he was all too glad—much more so than he thought he'd be—to be able to focus on that. It allowed him to avoid his feelings and keep his mind occupied with thoughts of their quest.

It would be better to deal with your feelings than to avoid them, Saphron thought, *If you don't, they could come out at the wrong time, and jeopardize our mission anyway.*

I don't have the luxury of dealing with them now, he retorted, *We have no time to spare.*

You should talk it out with Xharia, he said.

What? Orion screamed in his head, *Now, you're being ridiculous. I have nothing to say to her.*

Saphron sighed, *I can't force you. But, that's my advice.*

Noted, he snipped, *Goodnight, Saphron.*

The great blue dragon snorted in frustration, curling up to sleep. Orion could feel that he just wanted to help his rider, but there was no way he was going to talk to Xharia. As far as he was concerned, she and Mithrel could go be happy together somewhere far away from him.

He curled up against his dragon, trying to sleep. Just lying there allowed his mind to wander too much, and he couldn't keep it busy focused on other things. So, he forced himself to picture his home in Cardeas, allowing the vision to fill him up as he faded out of consciousness . . .

The next day, Orion continued to focus on his training, avoiding conversation with Xharia. She looked as though she wanted to say something, but couldn't find the words. For that, he was glad. He didn't want her to make excuses or apologies.

You'll have to face her eventually, Saphron thought from above.

You may be right, he replied, *But, right now, I don't care.*

Just then, they heard a dragon screech. It wasn't Saphron, and it wasn't Tanzanite. They all looked in the direction of the sound, and saw a familiar white dragon approaching.

Moonstone? Saphron thought.

"Epsilon?" Orion called, "What are you doing here?"

"Orion!" he called, sounding panicked.

"What? What is it?" he asked worriedly.

Moonstone landed, and Epsilon dismounted, hurrying toward his friend, "You were right. You were right about everything!"

"Slow down. What are you talking about?" he asked.

"Dredon and Obsidian! They've declared war on Cabri! They killed off the trainees who refused to join them!"

"What?" Orion cried, a shocked expression forming on his face.

The others seemed to be sharing his shock, gathering round as Epsilon spoke, "I narrowly got away. I didn't know where to go, but I knew I had to find you!"

Tanzanite emanated feelings of horror as she relived her own experience, *At least you still have each other . . .*

"Who's that?" Epsilon asked.

"This is Tanzanite," he replied, "She's the sole survivor of the mountain leaders I told you about."

He turned his ebony face toward her in awe.

"How did you find us?" Orion asked.

"I used magic to search for you," he replied, "I could see you. I could see the area around you. I just had to figure out where it was. The screech of vekkens in the distance gave it away."

"Then . . . it has begun," Celestia said solemnly.

"Yes," Epsilon replied, "The war has begun."

An Unexpected Turn

13

"What can you tell us about what he's planning?" Xharia asked when they were all seated around the fire, eating.

Epsilon looked around at each person in turn, taking in their party, "Well, he plans to take over all lands of this world, and destroy anyone who gets in his way."

"No kidding," Celestia said sarcastically, "We know that already. We were hoping you'd have some *real* information."

His eyes darkened as he looked at her, "It was a little hard to pay attention while I was escaping with my life."

"We understand that," Xharia said quickly, "But still, you must remember *something* of his plans."

Epsilon sighed, "He said he was going to wage war on Cabri, destroy their army, and slaughter their people. At the same time, he's sending groups of his followers to other lands, launching campaigns to gain followers and eliminate any resistance."

They all gasped.

"So, he's recruiting followers and planting seeds of war throughout the land," Mithrel said.

"Now, *that's* useful," Celestia said, "Did he say where he was starting?"

Epsilon looked at the old witch steadily, "Everywhere."

Everyone looked back at him questioningly. After a pause, she said, "What do you mean . . . everywhere?"

He sighed again, "He has more followers than any of you realize. He's been planning this for a long time. He's dispatched groups of them to Cardeas, Gachichken, Duwazo, Fluorasti, Millhaymae, and Katangalo. He's even dispatched groups as far as Kuttub, Mashang, Korga, Gliken, and here in Kogatsa."

They all stared at him, wide-eyed. Orion could feel that the sense of horror within him was imprinted on his face, and it matched the expressions worn by everyone else.

"This is beyond anything I feared," Celestia said.

"What do we do now?" Xharia asked.

"There's no telling who will join him," Mithrel said, "We already beat him to Korga and Gliken, and got the dwarves and the elves on our side."

"Yes, but we didn't try Katangalo when we were there, we slid straight through Kuttub, and we will surely find no aid here in Kogatsa," Callisto countered, "And, it may be too late by now to gather forces from Fluorasti, Gachichken, and Cardeas. Mashang and Millhaymae would be lost causes. I can call upon some old contacts from Duwazo; I am certain they would be on our side. But, other than that, he may well have already amassed a force beyond what we'll be able to."

"We have to try," Orion said, "What else can we do?"

"Orion's right," Xharia said, "We have to try."

"We're going to train for three more days," Callisto said, as she worked with Orion on his magical combat, "Then, we have to set out to recruit as many as possible. We don't have time enough to dwell on our training here. Since you and Xharia can train on the road, as sword fighting doesn't attract as much attention as magic and flying, your training these next few days will be solely with me and Tanzanite."

Orion let out a sigh of relief, glad to not have to work with Xharia again until they set out. He was able to keep his head clear and focus on his training with Callisto. She held nothing back, destroying him with raw power. But, the fact he was even able to hold his own for a short time showed just how far he'd come.

Epsilon stared wide-eyed at Celestia, awed by her use of raw power. He had never before seen anyone wield such might. He watched Orion and Saphron's training from the sidelines, relaxing with Moonstone safely away from Abyumo.

Orion trained all day with Celestia, and Saphron trained with Tanzanite. By the end of it, they were exhausted, and ready to get some sleep. But first, they wanted to catch up with Epsilon and Moonstone.

"How have you been?" he asked, sitting beside his old friend, "It seems ages since I've seen you."

Epsilon sighed, "I've been fine. I've just been working hard on the training mountain, learning all I can. I was too focused to pay attention to the warning signs . . . "

He looked at his friend with concern, "You're safe now; that's what matters."

"But, for how long?" he said in frustration, "It's only a matter of time before his plan comes to fruition, and his reign reaches the outer limits of this world."

Orion looked off into the night, "Not if I have anything to say about it."

Epsilon looked at him then, "You? What do you think you can do against the might of Dredon?"

"It's what I've been training for," he replied, "I'm a warrior now. I've been preparing to face him."

He let out a humorless laugh, "Face him? Even you aren't that stupid, Orion." When he met his gaze steadily, he said, "You can't be serious. You'll die!"

"You've never had faith in me, Epsilon," he said.

"And you've put a blindfold over your concept of reality," he retorted, "You're no match for him. No one is . . . "

"We'll see," he said confidently.

"Orion, listen to me," he said, "You. Will. Die."

"*You* listen to *me*," he replied, "I am the descen—"

"Orion," Callisto said, interrupting, "Why don't you get some rest? You have a big day of training tomorrow."

"You people are supporting this madness?" Epsilon yelled, rising.

"We have our reasons," she replied calmly.

"Your reasons?" he looked at each of them in turn, "What reasons could you possibly have?"

"That's our business," Celestia said.

Calm yourself, rider, Tanzanite thought, *In this war, much doesn't make sense.*

Doesn't make sense? he replied, *This is beyond not making sense.*

Do you have a better suggestion? she asked.

Epsilon, Saphron thought quickly, *Why don't we all just get some rest for now, and we can discuss the particulars later. It's late, and we're not all thinking clearly.*

Obviously! he thought.

Epsilon, Moonstone thought, *Let us wait.*

Fine, he snarled, *But we're not done with this conversation.*

The next day, Orion and Saphron trained together, combining the instruction they'd received on their own to synchronize their efforts. Saphron was impressed with Orion's development in magical combat, and Orion was both impressed and thrown off by Saphron's new maneuvers through the air. Tanzanite coached them, teaching them more about the bond between dragon and rider, and how to use that to their advantage in a fight.

She taught Orion several new maneuvers as well, including how to fight from different parts of Saphron's body besides only the saddle. It was difficult for him at first, figuring out how to balance from his dragon's various moving parts, but Tanzanite was a good teacher. She was patient and wise. She explained that if he was truly in perfect synchronization with his dragon's movements, then he could anticipate them from anywhere.

They drilled and drilled, and Orion began to anticipate Saphron's movements more easily. He climbed onto his tail, leapt onto his back, swung beneath him, and hoisted himself upon his head. The tail was the hardest for him, as it was the least steady, and moved the most.

You're doing well, Tanzanite thought, *My only regret is not having more time to work with you. I just hope the time we have will be enough.*

I hope so, too, Saphron agreed.

Perhaps tomorrow, you could practice battling a real opponent, she thought, *Your friends may be willing to practice with you.*

I'm not so sure they will be, Orion thought, *They aren't very supportive of what we're doing.*

They fear for our safety, Saphron said.

I can understand that, Tanzanite thought, *But, if they are true friends, they will understand, and want to help you. If they really don't want you to get hurt, they'll help you prepare.*

I hope so, Orion thought.

Me, too, Saphron agreed.

They finished up their training, readying themselves to talk things out with Moonstone and Epsilon. As the three dragons, two riders, two horses, dwarf, elf, and witch gathered around the fire to eat, their official council began.

"According to The Oracle," Xharia began, "We must gather forces and stop Dredon and Obsidian. Only Orion can. Therefore, the rest of us will train him and support him in his efforts to do so."

"So, The Oracle said Orion can beat Dredon?" Epsilon asked.

"Why do you believe he cannot?" Celestia countered.

"Because," he said, "No one can. You did not see what I've seen. He is far too powerful. Orion and Saphron couldn't even make it to the training mountain. Dredon and Obsidian are its kings."

I have seen what you've seen, Tanzanite thought, *I know why you would think the way you do. But, I believe in them. That's why I'm training them.*

"The Oracle's never been wrong before," Callisto said, "I should know. I'm her keeper."

"If you are her keeper," Epsilon said, "Why are you not with her?"

"The position of keeper of The Oracle comes with many tasks. Not all of them have me by her side."

"I know you fear for our safety," Orion said, "But, we have no choice. We have to do this. We need you by our side. You can help us train tomorrow, as practice partners once more."

"No," he replied, "We cannot."

"Why not?" he pleaded, "You're our friends. We need your help."

We're all scared of what's to come, Saphron thought, *But, we all must do our parts. We cannot let them win.*

"They're just cowards," Mithrel said, "They came here fleeing in fear. They did not come to help us."

"Mithrel," Xharia snapped.

You have no idea what's coming, Moonstone thought.

What do you mean? Saphron asked.

"He means that you will all be crushed by the might of Dredon and Obsidian," Epsilon said, "There is nothing any of us can do against him."

"What would *you* have us do?" Celestia asked.

His white eyes looked at each of them in turn, lingering on Callisto, "There's nothing we can do. We have no other choice. Don't you see? We must join him."

"What?" she asked in disgust.

"Join him or die," he said.

"Traitor!" Mithrel yelled, raising his axe.

Xharia held him back, "No, wait!"

"How can you say that?" Orion asked quietly. His blue eyes reflected his disgust with his old friend.

Everyone grew silent after he spoke.

"It's the only logical solution," he said, "He *will* kill us all. It's only a matter of time. Only his followers shall be spared. We can't beat him. So, we must join him."

"You're a coward," Orion said, rising and spitting, "A coward and a traitor."

"You don't understand," he said.

"You're right. I don't," he replied.

Epsilon was silent.

"Get out," Orion said, not even able to bring himself to look at his old friend. He crossed his arms, gritting his teeth, and looking out into the darkened woods.

"It's too late," Epsilon said, "That was your last chance."

"What do you mean?" Xharia asked.

Epsilon grinned, saying nothing.

"What have you done?" Celestia demanded.

"He's betrayed us!" Mithrel shouted, "Don't you see? He's been working for the enemy the whole time!"

Orion gawked at his friend in shock and horror, unable to believe his oldest friend could betray him, "Is that true? Have you been working for Dredon this whole time?"

Epsilon rolled his eyes, "You've been blind, Orion. While you were caught up in prophecies and training, the rest of us have been accomplishing something in this war. We won before you even got started."

"So, all those times you didn't believe me about Dredon . . . you knew the whole time? You were spying on us?"

"Hard to believe, I know," he replied, "You're so naive, Orion. I was embarrassed to be called your friend. You were going nowhere fast. I was ready to be someone. Now, you've pulled your head out of the sand long enough to see what I've become . . . before you die."

"If you want to kill him, you'll have to go through us," Xharia said, stepping in front of him.

"And we won't make it easy for you," Mithrel added, joining her.

You lying, manipulative, cowardly, traitorous weasel! Tanzanite thought angrily. She lifted her wings, preparing to launch an attack on them, when they heard a sound. It was a loud rustling in the brush.

"Ah," Epsilon said, leaping upon Moonstone's back, "Right on time."

As the rest of them looked at each other, unsure, a horde of kodrizans came running out from the forest, with a couple of vekkens flying above them.

"Quickly!" Celestia shouted, "Arm yourselves!"

She drew her wand as Mithrel charged axe-first into the ambush, giving Xharia time to draw her sword and join him. Tanzanite leaped into the air, going straight for the vekkens. Orion jumped onto Saphron's back, still in shock at his friend's betrayal.

How can they do this? he thought.

I don't know, Saphron thought, *But, we can't think about that right now. Right now, they're a threat. They're a threat to us, and to our friends.* He paused, *We have to fight them.*

He sucked in a breath, not wanting to fight his friends. But, as he looked around, seeing Tanzanite battling two vekkens, Mithrel and Xharia bravely fighting the horde of kodrizans, and Celestia trying to help them by blasting them back with magic, he knew his dragon was right: they had to fight them. They had no choice. No one else could. And, like it or not, they were now on opposing sides of this war.

Okay, he thought, *Let's do it.*

With that, Saphron launched himself up, heading straight for Moonstone and Epsilon. Moonstone maneuvered out of the way, avoiding Saphron's jaws. He spun, attacking again, and the two dragons locked into battle. Orion leaped upon his blue dragon's head, drawing his sword. Epsilon grinned, meeting him atop the head of his white dragon, sword drawn.

The two riders locked into a fight, swinging their swords. Metal clashed with metal in their balancing act upon the heads of their dragons. It was a precarious dance, but one Orion had at least practiced. Despite the fact he would not gain Epsilon as a practice partner, their fight now could prove just as useful to his training. Though, he did not truly wish it to happen this way.

The dragons shifted, causing their riders to step apart to catch their balance. In the pause in their battle, Orion said, "Why are you doing this?"

"Because," Epsilon said, "I can learn a lot from Dredon! Don't you see? This is my chance at greatness! I would never have achieved anything on your side of this war! You're weak! All of you are weak! You're afraid to pursue power! Well, I'm not!"

With that, he moved forward again, swinging his sword. Orion blocked it, and they engaged again, pushing each other back and forth on the relatively small surfaces of only the tops of their heads. They were evenly matched—the first time that had ever happened.

For the first time, Orion realized just what he was going up against with Dredon. He had trained Epsilon as Orion had been training. If he was evenly matched with his old friend, then Dredon would be a far more formidable foe.

"I thought you were my friend!" he shouted, "You care more about power than friendship or justice?"

"What have those things ever gotten me?" he said, "Nothing! Power . . . power will get me everything I want!"

"That can't truly be what you want!"

Epsilon let out a yell, swinging his sword.

Orion blocked it as he said, "You created the kodrizan army, didn't you?"

"Obviously," he replied, grinning, "You like it?"

"And it was you in Kuttub, too, wasn't it? You've been following us since Katangalo!"

"No," Epsilon answered, "Sadly, it wasn't me. But, Dredon has followers everywhere. One of his other riders must have created them. I returned to Abyumo after Katangalo, and Dredon worked harder on my training when he discovered that you were able to beat me in our practice fight. Then, when he believed I was ready, he sent me to find you and destroy you. He knows of The Oracle's prophecy already, and he doesn't want you getting in his way!"

"So . . . he considers me a threat, then?" he asked in amazement.

"Of course not!" he shouted, "Don't be ridiculous! He just doesn't want to deal with the annoyance of a half-assed attempt at stopping him!"

"So, you'd really kill your friends?" Orion asked solemnly.

"With pleasure," Epsilon answered, taking his stance, "Nothing personal, you understand. But, I need to prove my worth to Dredon. Then, I'll be given my own kingdom in his new world. The higher you rank in his eyes, the better position you'll receive when our mission is complete!"

With that, he swung his sword once more, continuing their fight. Orion battled him back and forth, but he knew something had to give. They couldn't just keep fighting and fighting, with no end in sight. The members of their group on the ground were obviously struggling against the sheer number of kodrizans, and he knew they couldn't hold them off forever.

He leaped into Saphron's saddle suddenly, unlocking from his battle with Moonstone, and forcing the white dragon to move as Saphron breathed a jet of flame across him. It made it difficult for Epsilon to hang on as he struggled to reach the saddle. Orion gave him no respite, however, Saphron keeping Moonstone moving as Orion swung his sword at Epsilon.

Finally, he caused him to lose his grip, falling toward the earth. Moonstone dove to catch his rider, and Saphron pursued him, breathing flames across him the whole way. As he caught him, Saphron bit his tail, swinging him around, and launching him higher into the sky.

As they gained the upper hand, Tanzanite killed one of the vekkens, tossing its body into the trees and making the second one easier to kill. Celestia looked hopeful as she caught sight of their battles, eager to gain some back-up as she blasted through the kodrizans. Xharia and Mithrel were watching each other's backs as they fought with axe and sword against the ambush.

Saphron pursued Moonstone, giving him no respite. As he did, Orion readied himself to attack Epsilon. He saw him coming and tried to prepare himself, but it was difficult as his dragon was spinning out. The second they got their bearings was the second Saphron and Orion attacked. Moonstone and Epsilon were disoriented, but they fought back, a blur of teeth, talons, and swords in the sky.

Tanzanite killed the second vekken, diving down to help the others with the kodrizans. They were in need of her aid, as there were too many for them to hold off any longer on their own. With a dragon on their side, they began to gain some ground.

Epsilon swung his sword, nicking Orion's bodysuit on his arm. It wasn't quite enough to reach his skin, but it tore through the magical black material. He moved quickly, striking back, and gashing Epsilon's leg. He cried out in pain, and Moonstone faltered, concerned for his rider. Saphron took his opportunity, clenching his jaws around his neck and tossing him again.

This time, Epsilon fell when Moonstone was tossed. For a moment, they weren't sure if the white dragon would gather his bearings quickly enough to reach his rider before he hit the earth. But, he managed it, swooping down, obviously dizzy, and catching Epsilon just before he would have been too low to dive beneath.

As they tried to gather their strength to launch a counter-attack, there was a *crash*, and the very sky seemed to shake. They turned in time to see two stars falling toward the earth, dust and debris left in their wake. They landed a ways away, but the waves from their impact reached the battlefield, knocking many kodrizans over.

Moonstone and Epsilon used the distraction to their advantage, flying away as quickly as they could. Saphron and Orion turned just in time to see them fade away in the darkness of the night. The kodrizans also retreated, following the example of their leader. The good dragon and his rider landed, as the others gathered around.

Are you alright? Tanzanite asked.

As well as I can be, Orion said.

Agreed, Saphron added.

You fought well, she replied, *I'm proud of you.*

Thank you, Saphron said.

"Is everyone alright?" Orion asked, looking around at the other three.

They nodded, catching their breath. After a pause, Celestia said, "We can't afford to delay another day. We must set out at dawn. Everyone get some rest; I'll take the first watch."

To Befriend or Not to Befriend

14

*W*e need to travel faster, Orion thought, *Horses are too slow. This quest requires speed.*

Perhaps I could be of assistance, Tanzanite offered.

What about the horses? Saphron thought, *Mithrel loves Helado, and Xharia loves Shadow. There's no way they would just let them go.*

Let me see what could be done, Orion thought.

The two dragons nodded.

"Everyone," Orion announced, "Tanzanite has kindly offered to allow the two of you to ride upon her back. If we ride dragons rather than horses, we'll be able to cover more ground much more quickly. Now, that does present a problem. What do we do with the horses?"

"Shadow knows his way back home," Xharia said, "He was wild before; he chooses to stay. No one will bother a riderless horse."

Mithrel looked at Helado sadly, "For sake of this quest, I suppose I must let him go. He's a noble pony, but I don't know if he would make it home on his own."

"Shadow will show him the way," Xharia said, putting her hand on his shoulder comfortingly.

He nodded.

She went over to the horses, packing up their saddles and reins, and letting them go, "Take care of Helado, boy. Show him the way home."

Shadow whinnied, and the two horses made their way south together, back toward the lands of the dwarves and the elves. Xharia and Mithrel watched them walk away, wrapping their arms around each other.

Orion grimaced, "Alright, let's go."

He leapt upon Saphron's back, and Celestia climbed up behind him. Xharia and Mithrel cautiously walked to Tanzanite's side. Her previous rider's saddle was still upon her back. Xharia gingerly hoisted herself up into it, extending her hand to Mithrel. He had to clamber up her scales just to reach Xharia's hand. When he did, she pulled him up, and he climbed into the saddle behind her.

"Everyone ready?" Orion asked.

They all nodded, Mithrel looking petrified as he clung to Xharia. Saphron took to the sky, soaring over the forests of Kogatsa. Tanzanite followed, launching herself into the air. Xharia was somewhat prepared to fly upon her, as she had ridden upon Saphron already. So, she was fairly calm. But, Mithrel's face was very pale compared to his usual tawny brown complexion. Orion could tell he was trying not to scream, and it made him smile.

They flew west, making their way through Mashang. They already knew they would find no allies there. They were closely allied with Kogatsa. They planned to stop once they reached Fluorasti, finding its royalty, and gaining its alliance.

When they landed to make camp that night upon the plains of Mashang, the time Orion had been dreading finally arrived. He had to train with Xharia again. The two of them grabbed their swords, meeting a short distance from the campsite. Neither one said a word. They began fighting, swinging their swords, as Orion attempted to match her speed.

The brief reprieve he'd gotten had helped ease the awkwardness of training with her, but not by much. He still found it hard to focus, and his mind kept picturing her with Mithrel. He'd actually thought he had a chance. He'd seen a future with her, but she'd never liked him that way.

Xharia could see he wasn't focused, and she paused, saying, "Are you alright, Orion?"

He ignored her, swinging his sword.

She blocked him easily, knocking him to the ground, "You aren't focused." She paused, sighing, "I still care about you."

Orion rose, starting to walk away.

"Are you going to ignore me forever?" Xharia called after him.

He stopped, turning around, and shrugging.

She let out a frustrated sigh, "I suppose if you must hate me, then that's what you must do. But, you can't let it cloud your judgment. This is exactly why I didn't say anything. I was afraid for how it would interfere with this quest. It's far too important for you to throw it away because I made you lose focus. I'm sorry, Orion. I know you wanted us to be together, but I just don't feel the same. I'm sorry I didn't tell you, and I'm sorry for how you found out. But, this quest isn't about me or you. So, however you feel now, you just have to suck it up and fight."

He threw down his sword, walking away. As he did, an arrow grazed his ear. He turned quickly, arming himself with magic. When he did, he saw that it was Xharia.

"You could be ambushed at any second if you're not on your guard," she said, "You don't want to train with me, fine. But let's see how you defend yourself!" With that, she lifted her sword, running at him.

Orion's eyes grew wide, and he had to react quickly, diving out of the way of her swing. He somersaulted over to where he'd dropped his sword, picking it up and turning just in time to see her coming down on him. He scrambled back, narrowly avoiding her blade. The split second it took for her to dislodge her sword from the earth gave him time to get up and brace himself.

She charged straight for him, and he had to use his full focus to keep up with her. He swung, blocked, and parried as fast as he physically could, and still, he struggled against her. They moved back and forth, and all the way around the campsite, fighting. Finally, he was able to knock the sword from her hand, holding his own blade against her throat.

"If you can't kill me," Xharia said, "You don't really hate me."

Orion's eyes grew wide again, and he backed up, dropping his sword, "You would gamble your life so willingly?"

She stood straight, meeting his eyes, "It wasn't a gamble."

He looked back at her, unable to say anything.

"Let your anger go, Orion," she said, "We have no quarrel here. I'm on your side. I would give my life to defend you. Even if I can't reciprocate your romantic feelings, I still care greatly for you. I value you as an ally, as a person, and . . . as a friend."

He looked down, unsure. *You've been awfully quiet this whole time, Saphron,* he thought.

It wasn't my place to say anything, he replied, *I was letting you work things out your way.*

I'm not sure how to feel right now, he said.

I know, he answered, *But, don't ask me how you should feel. I'm here for you always, but this is something you have to figure out for yourself.*

Orion sighed, "I just don't know, Xharia. I don't know how to feel."

"That's okay," she said, "You don't have to know right now. Just let me know when you decide. All I ask is that we can at least remain allies, and continue training together. I want to help you. Even if you don't feel we can still be friends . . . "

She did step in front of you when Epsilon threatened to kill you, Saphron said, *And so did Mithrel.*

I suppose that's true . . .

That sounds like loyal warriors to me, he said, *We could definitely use those right about now.*

He stood there for a while, contemplating his response. Finally, he said, "I will have to think on it. I'm not sure yet whether we can be friends. But, I suppose, for sake of this quest, we can be allies."

Xharia nodded, accepting his response. As she turned to walk away, she paused, saying, "By the way, you did well in our fight today. I was impressed with how far you've come."

Orion smiled to himself as she walked away. Through all of his mixed-up emotions, his pride shone through in that moment, and he allowed himself to indulge in it.

Even if we don't keep in contact when this quest is over, Saphron thought, *I think they will prove useful to our mission.*

He sent his dragon waves of agreement.

We'd best get some rest, the blue dragon thought, *We've got a big day of flying and training tomorrow.*

His rider nodded, and they joined the rest of their party around the fire, curling up to sleep.

They flew through the day, making it the rest of the way through Mashang by nightfall. When they landed, Orion continued working with Xharia on his sword training. This time, he was able to focus and keep up with her as they fought. She tried several new maneuvers, thinking she could slip him up, but he managed to overcome them all.

"Well done, rider," she said, "You continue to impress me."

He gave her a deep nod, "Thank you."

She returned his nod, and they joined the others by the fire to eat and get some rest.

You're making great progress, Saphron thought.

I just hope it will be enough, Orion replied.

The great dragon snorted, *Me, too.*

As he settled down to sleep, he curled up against his dragon. His mind was full, as it often was these days, of thoughts of their quest. He knew they needed to complete his training and gather as many allies as possible, but he wasn't sure how many they could get on their side. They were running out of time, with only two more pairs of stars left to collide. They had to be back in Abyumo before the final pair, or they'd be too late to save their queen.

"You're still awake?" he heard Xharia ask.

"I just wanted a moment alone with you," Mithrel replied, "We hardly have the chance to talk anymore."

"The wind does prevent much conversation as we're flying," she agreed. After a long pause, she said, "What's on your mind?"

He sighed, "We're finally able to be together, and yet still not openly. I feel terribly for how it was revealed." He paused, "Perhaps I should've just told him myself."

"No," she said, "That would've been worse. He needed to hear it from me. It was my mistake, and I must bear its consequences. It's not your fault."

He sighed again, "I still feel I bear some blame."

She paused, "I'm not sure if he'll ever forgive me."

"He already hated me," Mithrel said, "So, there's not much change on that front."

She chuckled, "You two fought more than elves and dwarves." When she spoke again, her voice was serious once more, "Maybe I'm not the right warrior for this quest."

"No," he said, "You are."

"I'm screwing it up," she replied, "I can't seem to do anything right. From the battle I should've retreated from to this mess with Orion . . . I'm an embarrassment to the elves."

There was a pause before he said, "You're no embarrassment. You've fought bravely in every battle we've faced. You've brought him so far on his sword training, he may actually stand a chance. You've stood up for him and tried to protect him at every turn. You'd even be willing to lay down your life for him. You're the most dedicated and loyal warrior I've ever had the pleasure to know. You bring honor to the elves. I daresay, you'd give dwarven warriors a run for their money, and that's saying something."

There was another long pause before she said, "Thanks, Mithrel."

It seems Xharia's torturing herself over what she did, Saphron thought.

Yes, Orion agreed, *It does.*

She really does care, he said, *I can see it. I know how bad she hurt you—I can feel your pain. But, I think she brought just as much pain to herself, in the form of remorse and regret.*

He sent a wave of agreement, *I still don't know how to feel just yet. But, despite the pain she caused me, and the fact that she doesn't feel the way I do, I still don't like to see her suffer.*

It will take a while for your feelings to fade, he said softly, *But, when they do, you may find different feelings in their place.*

What different feelings? he asked.

Friendship, he replied, *When you care about someone in a non-romantic way.*

His response took Orion by surprise, and he wasn't sure what to say. He hadn't really thought about what his feelings would be toward her when the old ones faded away.

Goodnight, Saphron thought.

Orion gave him a thought of acknowledgment, still trying to sort through all of the feelings that had been flowing through him the last few days. There were just too many to deal with at once. He couldn't wrap his brain around them long enough to process fully. Finally, he gave up, drifting off to sleep.

They flew into Fluorasti the next day, and Tanzanite led them to the royal palace of their most powerful kingdom: Batosque. Orion had never been to a human castle before. Even before he became a rider, his family had been poor, and he'd never seen the likes of a castle. It wasn't nearly as impressive as the palace of Lorena, or even those of the elves and dwarves. But, it was still far larger than his childhood home. It was made of gray stone, with simple towers and wooden doors. The two dragons landed, and Orion and his warriors dismounted, heading up to the drawbridge. The terrified guards were trying to close it, staring up at the dragons in fear.

"Wait!" Orion shouted, "Stop! It's alright; we're not here to hurt you!"

The guards ignored them, continuing to raise the bridge.

"We need to speak with your king and queen on an urgent issue!" Celestia added.

As the drawbridge nearly closed, Saphron flew over, placing his claw upon it, and pushing it back down. The guards didn't stand a chance against the might of a dragon, and they all lost their grip as it came tumbling back open.

Thanks, Saphron, Orion thought as the four of them entered the city.

He snorted, flying back over to Tanzanite.

"Halt!" the guards yelled, pointing their spears at them.

Callisto drew her wand, casting a spell of protection around them, and they continued running through the town, up the hill, through the courtyard, and into the castle.

They threw their spears, chasing them, but they all glanced off Celestia's shield, leaving them unharmed.

They burst into the throne room, closing it behind them to prevent the guards from following them and causing more unnecessary panic.

"What's the meaning of this?" the king demanded, his queen moving behind him, and the servants hiding behind the pillars.

"We mean you no harm," Celestia said, "We've come to ask for your help."

They all stopped a few feet from the thrones, kneeling.

The king straightened, clearing his throat and calming himself, "What would a witch, a dwarf, an elf, and a dragon rider need from a human—even a king?"

She explained everything to him about Dredon, their quest, and how they needed their army to help save the world.

He stood there, listening, the queen standing beside him, listening as well. Their faces showed their surprise as they did—looking at each other, unsure. When she was finished, he said, "What can mere humans do against an army of dragon riders?"

"Our army will have dragon riders, too," Orion said, "He will have humans on his side. We need human armies to fight them."

"So, you're deciding which humans should fight each other? You want to compromise our alliances to choose a side in *your* war?"

"Of course not," he replied quickly, "*You're* making the choice. Just know, everyone must choose a side in this war. Whether you think you should be involved or not, it will affect you, and your people. He will spread his reign everywhere, and you can decide whether you will help him do that, or join us and stop him."

He looked back at his wife, contemplating. It took a long pause before he said, "Who is on his side?"

"We can't be sure," Orion said, "He's sent followers everywhere to try and recruit forces. No doubt he'll have Kogatsa and Mashang on his side. Parts of Gachichken, perhaps. He may even get some elven and dwarven kingdoms. We have several good ones on our side. We recruited Dirthix and Garellis, and they sent ambassadors to the other kingdoms of Gliken and Korga to recruit them as well. We cannot say what the results will be. We are hoping to gain Cardeas, Duwazo, and parts of Gachichken for our side. Hopefully, we can gain the kingdoms of Fluorasti as well." On his last statement, he shot the king a pointed look.

Before he could say anything, Celestia chimed in, "That's why we came here, to Batosque. This is the most powerful kingdom in Fluorasti. If anyone could help us gain the aid of the other kingdoms of this land, it's you."

"So, you not only hope to gain my army, but you wish me to send ambassadors to the other kingdoms of this land as well," the king said, growing angry.

"Yes," she replied firmly, "Because I know this land and this kingdom to be the home of good people. I knew one of them, long ago . . . a lady of your court." She smiled to herself for a moment, growing serious as she continued, "And, those people deserve the chance to fight. You're fighting for your freedom. If Dredon wins, you will all be slaves. He will take your kingdom for his own, along with every other kingdom in this world. Give yourself and your people a chance. Fight with us."

He cleared his throat, "We must think on this decision. Come back tomorrow. We shall grant you a place in our inn, and food for you and your dragons."

As Orion was wondering how he knew about their dragons, he saw that there was a high window in the throne room, through which he could see Saphron and Tanzanite.

"Thank you," Callisto said, "Your hospitality is appreciated."

The king gave a nod, and a couple of servants escorted them out. The guards eyed them carefully as they exited the throne room, angry at being so easily surpassed, but unable to do anything about it. The four of them were led to the inn, and their rooms were paid for by the king. Several deer were tossed over the city wall for Saphron and Tanzanite. Orion could feel his dragon's appetite being sated by the beasts.

They stuck to their previous room arrangements, Celestia and Xharia taking one, and Orion bunking with Mithrel. He was not looking forward to sharing a room with the dwarf, but it was better than letting him room with Xharia.

As the two of them set up their wall of pillows, settling in for the night, Orion looked over at him. Thoughts of killing him in his sleep drifted through his mind, but he repressed them. He shook his head as he lay down, clearing his mind. He was angry with Mithrel, but, like Xharia, he didn't hate him enough to kill him. Besides, they needed him on this quest.

Suddenly, Mithrel's voice cut through the silence, "I thought of killing you at first, too, when we met, and I discovered you liked Xharia. I know how you feel. I was threatened by you. I didn't think I had a chance. She's a tall, beautiful elf. You're a tall, powerful dragon rider. I'm a mere dwarf. I thought my only shot was if I killed you. But, that wouldn't have helped anything. First off, we need you. This quest depends on you. Second, Xharia would never have forgiven me."

"It doesn't matter," Orion replied, "She doesn't like me. She likes you." After a moment, he added, "How did you know I was thinking of killing you?"

"You were staring at me with crazy eyes," he said, "I thought the blood vessels in your head would burst."

He sighed, looking away, ashamed, "I'm sorry."

"Don't be," he replied, "I'm not. You have every right to be angry." After a pause, he said, "The sad thing is, if it weren't for us liking the same girl, we might have been friends."

His comment took him by surprise, but after a moment's thought, he realized he was right. The only reason they didn't get along was because of their feud over Xharia.

"Goodnight, Orion," he said.

Orion was unable to reply as thoughts filled his head. Maybe Mithrel wasn't *such* a bad guy . . .

Opposing Forces

15

"We will fight with you," King Silus said when the four of them were gathered back in his throne room, "This war is important for all of us, and some of our allies have been taken over by followers of this 'Dredon.' They are eager for the opportunity to fight back, but they know they are not strong enough."

"How did you so quickly discover that your allies had been taken over?" Celestia asked.

He smiled, "You're not the only one who can wield magic, witch. We have wizards in our company, as do many kingdoms. They prove very useful in times like these."

"So, you will also inform your allies, then?" she asked.

King Silus nodded, "Indeed."

"And, who *are* your allies?" Orion interjected.

"Other kingdoms of this land," he replied.

Well, at least Fluorasti is covered, Orion thought.

Yes, Saphron replied, *That is very good. The more area we can cover in a short amount of time, the better.*

So, where to now?

Gachichken, Tanzanite thought.

"Thank you," Callisto said, "We appreciate your help in this."

He nodded, "Gather as many as you can."

They headed south, toward Gachichken, making their way to one of their most prominent kingdoms in hopes that they would join them as well. They didn't have much time remaining to gather their forces.

"Duwazo will fight with us," Callisto said as they sat around the fire, "I contacted some of my allies there, and they are recruiting for us."

"How do you know for certain they will join us?" Orion asked.

"I just know," she replied, "Trust me."

After a pause, he asked, "Who was your old contact? The one you knew from Batosque . . . "

She sighed, brushing her silver hair behind her ear and looking around at the faces of everyone there. Orion's milk chocolate skin shone in the light of the fire, Xharia's silky black hair fell over the shoulders of her mossy green robes, and Mithrel's rough, black beard gave off unusual shadows in the darkness.

"Her name was Irene," she replied finally, "I met her on my first quest. She was one of the slaves we liberated from that village in Millhaymae. But, she was *from* Batosque. She was a lady of their court."

He nodded, running his hand over the tight coils of his hair, "I see."

"So, if the king is gathering followers for us in the rest of Fluorasti, and Celestia has gotten Duwazo on our side, who else are we going to ask?" Mithrel questioned.

"Gachichken is next," Orion replied, "And then, Cardeas."

They flew through the following day, reaching Gachichken by nightfall. The next day, they planned on visiting the kingdom of Chichka, and asking its royalty to join their cause. They all settled in for the night, Mithrel taking the first watch.

Orion lied awake, wondering how many followers they would be able to gain, and if it would be enough to best Dredon's forces.

"You should get some rest," he heard Mithrel say.

There was a pause, before Xharia said, "What's your home like?"

"I . . . uh . . . " he stammered, taking a breath, "It's beautiful. You saw the tunnels. They go up for miles, with intricate dwarven carvings embedded with jewels."

"I know what it *looks* like," she said, "I was just curious what life was like for you."

"Oh," he replied, "Well . . . it's not very interesting. Dwarves are hard workers, and spend their days dedicated to their craft. Warriors, architects, miners, carvers, blacksmiths, hunters . . . they all work hard. We each do our part to ensure life is good within our tunnels. Our people are safe and cared for. We have strong ties to our families and our people. I think more so than the other races." He paused, "No offense."

"None taken," she said.

"We're stubborn, loyal, and diligent," he said proudly.

"I know all that," she said, "I wanted to know about you specifically."

"Well, I've spent my life training as a warrior, ready to serve my kingdom at a moment's notice. My father, Ghabriel, was a warrior as well."

"Was?"

"He's retired now," he said.

"Oh," she replied.

He chuckled, "Don't worry; he's still alive."

"I'm glad," she said.

"My mother, Ljourdes, is a seamstress, and so are my two older sisters, Crastanza and Zimera. My three younger brothers will likely become warriors as well. Ljuis is in training currently. Crarstos and Diethro are too young."

"So, you really are a typical dwarf, then," she laughed, "Hard-working and dedicated to your family."

"Yes," Mithrel replied, "I'm afraid I'm not very interesting."

"No," Xharia said, "You are."

After a pause, he said, "Well, what about you?"

"You already know my story," she replied, "It's famous."

"I know the story, yes," he said, "But, not the deeper parts of *you*."

She paused, "What makes you think I go deeper?"

He didn't answer.

Xharia sighed, "I suppose . . . sometimes it feels like a burden, being an elf. A certain manner is expected of you at all times. Now that my father has finally allowed us to be seen, we must act with even more discretion. It's exhausting. The only time I feel free to let myself go is when I'm in battle. I've been training my whole life. I guess that's why I was so eager to see conflict."

"Makes sense," he replied, "I feel the same . . . just perhaps not to that extent."

She laughed, "Well, you haven't been waiting as long as I have."

"That's true," he said, "I suppose if I had to wait a hundred years to see battle, I'd be bloodthirsty, too."

There was another pause before she said, "The life of an elf is often full of waiting. We're expected to have a wellspring of patience. And, for the most part, we do. But, a life this long is harder to find meaning in." She paused again, "I watch humans and dwarves go through their lives so quickly in comparison. They know what little time they have, and they try to make the most of it. They learn quickly, they search hard to find love, they reproduce young so they can see their offspring grow . . . "

"Sounds like the life of an elf might be lonely . . . "

"Yes, well, it does include long stretches of solitude," she agreed, "I guess my point is that you all find meaning in your lives in the little time you're here. You make your time count."

"We try to," Mithrel replied, "I suppose we just want to make our mark on the world, leave something behind, not be forgotten . . . "

Another pause, "A life lived with purpose is a life lived well."

"I suppose one benefit to a long life is that you have more time to make an impact," he replied.

"We do," Xharia said, "But most of us do nothing with it."

"You have," he said softly, "You will be remembered."

"So will you."

To Orion's horror, he heard the sounds of them kissing. Though he knew it was meant to be a private moment, he couldn't help but overhear. But, to his surprise, he wasn't as upset as he had been before. It still bothered him, just not as much.

I think you're starting to get over her, Saphron thought gently.

I think you're right, he replied. He felt light, like he could actually breathe through the pain, now.

Time heals all wounds, the great dragon thought.

It only took half a day to reach Chichka. They spoke with its king and queen, gaining its alliance. Their allies covered a good portion of the land, but Gachichken was huge. They had to go to a couple more of their kingdoms to gain additional allies. As they traveled, they continued to train, increasing Orion and Saphron's skills further. Tanzanite proved an excellent teacher, and Xharia and Callisto continued to prove their worth. Orion was soon able to best his mentors, and Saphron even began to offer Tanzanite a challenge. They flew west to the kingdom of Gachich, gaining its alliance as well, and then they made their way to Kiken.

It was as close as they dared fly to Abyumo. When they arrived, there was no one in sight. The city was abandoned. Dust and debris blew around in the wind, dancing over the dirt roads. The buildings had doors and windows left open, and they could see possessions scattered inside, as though the residents left in a hurry. They ventured into the castle, and there was no one there, either. No servants, no guards, no royals.

"Where is everybody?" Xharia wondered.

"I don't like this," Celestia said, "Something doesn't feel right. I think we should go."

Just then, they heard a rustling sound.

"What was that?" Mithrel asked. He pulled out his axe, brown eyes wide.

Xharia notched an arrow to her bow, pulling it taught along her ebony cheek.

Celestia's blue and silver robes illuminated in blue as she employed her raw power.

Orion drew his sword, his sapphire eyes reflecting in its shiny blade. They backed into each other, readying themselves to face whatever had made the sound.

"Welcome, Orion," a familiar voice said, "Is your recruiting going well?" They all turned to see Epsilon stepping out from the shadows. His dark skin blended into the darkness, and his milky white eyes stood out against it.

"Where are the people?" Orion demanded.

He smirked, "Is that any way to greet your old friend?"

"You . . . you are *not* my *friend*," he snarled.

Epsilon grinned, "They had to leave in a bit of a hurry. You see, they were called into service. No hard feelings, you understand. But we couldn't let you recruit *everyone*."

"What have you done?"

He rolled his eyes, "They're not hurt . . . yet. They're preparing for battle. On *our* side."

"Is that by choice?" he growled.

"Does it matter?" he said, "The point is we got here first, and there's no one here for you to recruit."

"So what, then? He has the rest of Gachichken under his thumb already?" he asked.

Epsilon gave a slight nod, "Indeed. It seems your efforts have been in vain."

Good question, Saphron thought, *You're getting information from him.*

I know, he replied, *That's the idea.*

Suddenly, his dragon's thoughts changed, *Orion, you need to get out of there right now!*

What is it? he questioned worriedly.

It's an ambush! There are other dragons approaching, which means their riders must be in there!

"Talking to your dragon?" Epsilon asked, "Let me guess, he's letting you know what's happening outside, and telling you to get out of here?"

Orion remained silent as the other three looked to him nervously.

"Too late," he grinned. With that, three other riders emerged from the shadows, standing beside the rider with white lines through his black bodysuit. He drew his sword, circling Orion.

"What are you waiting for?" Orion asked.

As soon as he'd said it, Epsilon swung his sword, engaging him. The other three sized up the other riders to determine who should face whom. Though it was a cut to his pride, Mithrel had to face the weakest one, as a mere dwarven warrior was no match for a rider. The girls could hold their own against them. Xharia, with her elven reflexes, could easily offer a challenge in hand-to-hand combat with a sword. Celestia, with her ability to wield raw power, would be untouchable even by a rider.

Outside, Orion could feel Saphron and Tanzanite struggling against their dragons—each of them having to face two. It was still hard for Saphron to face Moonstone, as they had been friends their whole lives. But, he had no choice. He and his mentor had to stay focused to win this fight.

They all had to use their full focus, their opponents skilled enough to demand it. Mithrel struggled in his battle against a rider, his tawny brown skin beaded with sweat as he swung his axe. Xharia was evenly matched against her opponent, twirling and swinging her sword. Her silky black hair flew around her as she tried to gain an advantage. Celestia was easily able to hold off her opponent, smirking all the way to her twinkling blue eyes as he struggled against her raw power.

Orion's bodysuit stuck to his muscles as he swung his sword, offering a challenge Epsilon did not expect. They narrowed their eyes at each other, and Epsilon snarled, charging him. Orion dodged easily, slamming his elbow into his old friend's back, and knocking him forward. It gave him time to twirl and bring his sword down as he tried to get back to his feet. He had to dive out of the way of his blow, and Orion could see he had the advantage as Epsilon struggled to gain his footing.

As Orion saw his opening, he felt Saphron's pain as Moonstone's teeth tore into him. He yelled out, trying to get back to his fight, but the distraction had allowed Epsilon to reach his feet. He charged him again, and they locked back into their battle. His training was evident, as his old friend was no longer a match for him. He could see that he would win.

Again, his dragon's thoughts distracted him, as he worriedly rushed to Tanzanite's aid. He hadn't felt his dragon fear that much for anyone besides him before. He realized while he had been preoccupied with Xharia, he hadn't been paying attention to his dragon. He had feelings for Tanzanite. *You have a crush on your mentor?* he thought.

Now's not the time, Orion! he replied, struggling in his fight with the other dragons, *Just take Epsilon down and get out here!*

The dark-skinned rider of the white dragon charged him in anger, sword raised.

Orion snapped back to his fight quickly, lifting his sword just in time. When he looked down, he could see it had pierced straight through Epsilon's gut. His old friend stumbled back, clutching at the blood that was soaking through his bodysuit.

As Epsilon collapsed to the ground, dropping his sword, Orion rushed to his side, tears forming in his eyes, "I'm so sorry."

"I'm sorry, too," he said, barely able to get the words out. Epsilon looked him in the eyes, and he watched as his white eyes faded back to brown, the connection between rider and dragon lost forever. With that, his old friend died in his arms.

The sorrow Orion and Saphron felt were nothing compared to the cries of mourning Moonstone emitted. They were so loud and agonized that the rest of the dragons and riders stopped fighting for a moment, and everyone just stood there, unsure.

Callisto used the opening, blasting the other riders back, "Let's get out of here! Go!"

Xharia and Mithrel grabbed each other's hands, running toward the exit. Orion couldn't move from beside Epsilon's body. Celestia yanked him up, pulling him along. He felt like he wasn't present in his own body as he ran, ears ringing. The four of them fled the city, meeting up with Saphron and Tanzanite, who were hovering with the other dragons over Moonstone.

We have to go! Orion thought, feeling the crushing weight of his emotions catching up with him. Tanzanite landed, allowing Xharia to toss Mithrel into her saddle, catapulting herself up in front of him. She took off as the other dragons regained their senses. Saphron swooped down, and Orion leaped into his saddle, Callisto using her magic to lift herself off the ground and into the saddle behind him.

They raced through the night sky, trying to put as much distance between them and the other dragons as quickly as possible. They headed north toward Cardeas—the last place they had to try recruiting before making their way to Abyumo for the final battle.

While they flew, the other dragons falling back for their riders, the sky shook, and they could see two more stars colliding. As they fell to the earth below, Orion knew they were out of time. There was only one pair left, and they had to be back in Abyumo before they collided, or they would be too late to save Lorena and Kirstiana.

We don't have time to go to Cardeas, he thought.

We have no choice, Saphron replied, *If we don't recruit their armies, we won't have enough warriors to face Dredon's army . . .*

Moonstone

16

"Hold still, Saphron," Callisto said as she healed his wounds. Orion was amazed by her healing skill and her power. Healing a dragon took far greater reserves than any other creature, due to their massive size. Her raw power coursed through her, sending glowing blue magic into each of the sapphire dragon's wounds. He had several deep lacerations from Moonstone's teeth. Each one was as wide as Orion's forearm in both width and length. Seeing the red blood of his dragon spilling onto his sapphire scales angered him.

He wasn't making it easy for her to heal him, squirming at each touch. *It stings, and it tickles,* he said, both laughing and in obvious pain.

You need to hold still so she can heal you.

I know, he replied, still squirming.

Orion shook his head, hoping Callisto would have enough energy to heal all of his gashes.

She finally finished the last one. She was obviously tired, collapsing down, and saying, "I need to rest."

He nodded, helping her get comfortable, "Thank you."

She smiled, "Of course."

Saphron nudged her with his snout in appreciation.

Celestia patted him as she drifted off, falling asleep very quickly.

How do you feel? Orion asked.

I'm alright, Saphron replied. When he kept picking up on waves of worry from his rider, he added, *She's a powerful healer. I feel good as new.*

He nodded uncertainly. After a pause, he said, *So, how long have you had a crush on Tanzanite?*

He growled, *Hush! I don't need her to hear you!*

Relax, he replied, *I'm not projecting my thoughts.*

They looked over at the indigo dragon. She was curled up, falling asleep, seemingly unaware of their conversation. Then they looked over at Mithrel and Xharia. They had wound down as well, and were curled up together, his head resting against her bosom as they slept.

Looks like we have the first watch, Orion thought.

I guess so, he agreed.

After another pause, he said, *Why do you not wish her to know your feelings? Are you afraid she won't feel the same, like Xharia with me?*

Saphron didn't answer, looking away. A long moment went by before he replied, *She's much older, wiser, and stronger than I am. I'm her student. There's no way she would be interested.*

You won't know unless you try, he responded, *Like you said, it was worse for me not knowing with Xharia. Yes, when I found out, it was hard, but now I'm able to start healing.*

Dragons are different, he snapped, *You wouldn't understand. It's not about how we might feel. It's improprietous, inappropriate, and wrong.*

What's so wrong about it?

With the age gap and the student-teacher relationship, it would be frowned upon by our fellow dragons. I couldn't put her in that position. I respect her too much.

Orion sighed, feeling the indignation emanating from his dragon.

It will never amount to anything more than a crush, he said with finality.

Then I'm sorry for you, he replied.

The sapphire dragon turned his great, scaled head away, blinking slowly. Orion could feel his pain, and the ache in his heart, yearning for someone he knew he could never have. It made it harder for him to cope with his own pain, and he was unable to stop himself from thinking about

Xharia. The two of them sat for a while, not saying anything, drowning in their misery, before Orion woke Tanzanite for her shift, and they curled up together to try and sleep.

Traitor! Murderer! Moonstone's voice projected through Orion's mind, *How could you?*

I'm sorry! he thought, his guilt and remorse strong over killing his friend.

You will burn for what you've done! he replied.

He could feel the pain and rage emanating from the white dragon.

Orion! Saphron thought.

I'm sorry! he thought again.

Orion! his dragon's voice insisted, *Wake up!*

He shot up, covered in a cold sweat, looking around him in a panic. They were still at their campsite, his dragon looking at him worriedly. It appeared to be Xharia's shift, as she was the only other one awake.

She hurried over with a canteen, kneeling beside him, "Here. Drink this."

He took a long swallow, trying to slow his breathing back to normal.

"That's it," she said, "Just relax." She took the canteen, "What happened?"

"Bad dream," he replied.

"I know that," Xharia said, "But, what happened?" She looked at him earnestly, hazel eyes burning in the starlight.

Orion looked up at her, longing to tell her everything. Finally, he shook his head, snapping out of it, "Nothing. It was just a dream."

She sighed, "Look, Orion, I'm trying to help you. I can't do that if you don't tell me what happened."

He scooted away, unanswering.

She sighed again, "I'm truly sorry for everything that's happened. I wish things weren't so awkward between us. But, I know it's my fault. I hate seeing what I've put you through. I wish every day that I could take it back, but I can't. I know you haven't decided whether we can even be friends. But, as your ally, I still want to help you. If your dream relates to this quest, it might have a hidden message. On Celestia's second quest, she had dreams of facing Zandor before we ever reached Khanjgi. Dreams should never be taken lightly."

Orion looked over at her, the gold band around her head gleaming in the moonlight, "I saw Moonstone. He called me a traitor and a murderer, and told me I'd burn for what I did."

She looked at him solemnly, not saying anything.

He scoffed, "What help or 'hidden message' can you offer me?"

Xharia continued to look at him, finally saying, "This is serious. It could mean he's out for vengeance."

He let out a humorless laugh, sarcastically saying, "You think? *I* could've told you that!"

"I mean, maybe he's after us *now*," she added.

"What's all this about?" Celestia asked, sitting up groggily.

Orion sighed, feeling guilty for shouting, "Nothing. Sorry to wake you."

Orion! Moonstone's voice echoed through his head.

It won't go away! he thought, *I can still hear him, even now that I'm awake!*

No, Saphron said, *I heard it, too.* Suddenly, realization hit, and he thought in a panic, *He's here!*

Orion jumped up, shouting, "Everyone, get up! Arm yourselves! We have to go, now!"

Xharia scrambled back, shaking Mithrel to wake him. Celestia drew her wand, using magic to pack up their campsite. Saphron woke Tanzanite, and Orion drew his sword, checking every direction for signs of the white dragon.

As Mithrel and Xharia mounted Tanzanite, he appeared, breathing a jet of flame across them. Orion and Celestia ducked, avoiding the fire. It glanced off the blue and indigo dragons' scales harmlessly, the elf and dwarf just out of range upon her back.

Go! Orion shouted to Tanzanite, *Get out of here! We'll meet you at the border!*

The indigo dragon launched herself into the air, taking off. Orion let out a quick sigh of relief that the three of them were out of harm's way. But, he didn't have long to feel relieved, as Moonstone circled back, heading straight for him.

Orion! Saphron thought, panicked. As the other dragon opened his mouth to burn Orion to a crisp, Saphron flew over, blocking the path of his flame.

Get out of the way, Saphron! Moonstone thought angrily, *This doesn't concern you!*

Doesn't concern me? he replied in disbelief, *He's my rider!*

"Get out of here!" Orion shouted to Celestia, "Take cover!"

She looked at him, obviously not wanting to leave him to face an angry dragon. But, she finally darted away, hiding among the trees of the surrounding forest.

Then you'll burn with him! Moonstone snarled, breathing a jet of flame across Saphron.

The two dragons locked into a fight, and Orion watched helplessly as Moonstone reopened some of Saphron's wounds that Celestia had healed. "Hey!" he yelled, "Moonstone!"

The white and blue dragons paused, looking over at him.

Your quarrel is with me, he thought, *Leave him out of this.*

After a pause, he said, *You know, I've thought about it, and I think the best way to make you pay for what you did isn't to kill you.*

He shot him a confused look, *It's not?*

No. It's to kill your dragon! With that, he resumed his fight with Saphron, a blur of teeth and talons in the sky.

Saphron! he thought, panicked. He looked around, trying to figure out a way to help his dragon. But, there was nothing he could use. Finally, in desperation, he launched a blue ball of magic at the white dragon.

Moonstone looked over at him in irritation, giving Saphron a small window to redouble his efforts, but it was not enough. He had to do something bigger. He ran to the treeline so he wouldn't see it coming. *Bring him closer,* he thought.

His dragon followed his instruction, slowly moving the fight through the sky toward the trees. Orion notched an arrow on his crossbow, taking aim. He waited as patiently as he could for him to get close enough. Finally, he fired, the arrow lodging itself between Moonstone's scales.

He roared, but more in anger than pain. He hadn't been close enough to gain the force necessary to pierce a dragon's hide. He'd nicked him, but that was all. He cursed under his breath, running to the other side to try again.

The white dragon wouldn't be fooled twice. He moved the fight away from the treeline, too far for Orion to hit him. *Saphron, fly low to the ground so I can leap on your back,* he thought.

No! he replied, *I'll not risk it! Leave this fight to me!*

We're stronger together, he said, *He's too angry and hurt for you to fight him alone. That's a dangerous combination.*

I know, he said, *But, he's only doing this to hurt* you.

Yes, but you heard him! He's not interested in harming me anymore. He wants to kill you!

He didn't say anything as he continued to fight.

Saphron, listen to me! he pleaded, *We're destined to defeat Dredon and Obsidian. I can't do that alone. I need you! The world needs you.*

You are *destined to defeat him. It has nothing to do with me. Tanzanite's a better fighter than me, anyway. She can go with you and face Obsidian.*

You want to put her in that situation? he asked.

He winced, both from the bite Moonstone was giving him, and from the thought of Tanzanite in danger. But finally, he said, *Whatever it takes to protect* you.

Orion continued to watch helplessly as the two dragons battled, blood raining down on the grass below. As he looked up, he knew what he had to do. He notched another arrow, taking aim. Then, he had to keep his aim as he ran out from the trees to get close enough. As soon as he was in range, he let his magic flow through him and add extra power to the arrow.

Before Moonstone could react, he'd released it, and it streaked across the night sky like a blue shooting star, plunging into the white dragon's hide between his scales. He screeched, clutching at his chest with his claws.

They watched as he fell from the sky, landing with a reverberating *thud* in the clearing below. It took a long while before they could react. Saphron landed, limping over to his old friend. Orion walked up to him, looking into his blank, white eyes.

"Moonstone," he whispered sadly.

Callisto had been inching her way over as they'd been standing there, and now she was only a short distance away. "Is he . . . dead?" she called.

Orion nodded, tearing up, "I killed him. I killed both of them." He looked away, trying to prevent her from seeing his tears.

They were traitors, Orion, Saphron said, *They're the ones that betrayed us. You did nothing wrong.*

Then why do I feel so guilty? he asked, dropping to his knees.

"I'm sorry, Orion," Celestia said from beside him. She placed her hand comfortingly on his back.

He leaned into her, allowing the strange mixture of emotions within him to spill out. Though he knew his dragon was right, it was still hard for him to accept that his oldest friends were traitors. Despite what they had done, their deaths still affected him.

Saphron nuzzled him with his snout, offering his comfort to him as well. Orion reached out and patted him, glad he was there.

After a long while, he stopped, getting up and walking around to Moonstone's head. He gingerly reached out, closing his eyes. Then, he looked up at the other two. Finally, he realized the terrible shape his dragon was in. He was bleeding profusely from multiple wounds, and one of his wings was torn.

Saphron! he thought, rushing back to his side.

"I might need your help this time," Celestia said.

He nodded, and the two of them began muttering the healing spell and placing their hands over the various gashes on his dragon's body. They were able to heal all of the wounds that were bleeding, but neither of them had the strength to get to his wing.

"I'm sorry," Callisto said, "We may have to wait until morning to set out. I don't think any of us are in any shape to travel tonight."

The dragon and his rider nodded, each of them as exhausted as she. They moved into the trees for some cover, hoping they wouldn't be followed that night by anyone who might be looking for Moonstone, or for any other reason. The three of them curled up, using Saphron for warmth, as they fell asleep almost instantly.

When the morning sun peeked through the trees, Orion awoke, shielding his eyes. He had a headache, and his whole body ached as well. He looked over at Celestia, who was still asleep. He knew she had used more energy than him, and healed more of Saphron's wounds with her use of raw power. His sapphire dragon was still asleep as well, and he could see him better in the daylight. He was covered in dried blood, but there were no open wounds on his body. His wing was badly torn, however. He knew he didn't have the capability for such advanced healing, so he'd have to wait until Callisto awoke so she could do it.

While he was waiting for the two of them to wake, he got up, stretching, and walked out of the forest into the clearing. There lay Moonstone, his white scales stained red with blood. His arrow was still sticking out of his chest. He looked away quickly, fresh sorrow and guilt flowing through him.

"Orion?" Celestia asked, stepping out from the treeline, "Are you alright?"

He turned to face her, "I'm fine."

She gestured back to the forest with her head, "We should get out of here."

He nodded, and they went back to where Saphron was lying. Orion could see his wing was good as new, "You already healed him?"

Callisto nodded, yawning, "Yes."

"The others will be worried about us," he said, "And, you never know if any more of Dredon's followers will show up. You're right. We should go."

She nodded again, obviously still tired. The two of them climbed upon Saphron's back.

Good morning, big guy, Orion thought, waking him.

He snorted, shaking his head to clear the sleep from his eyes. Then, he stretched, letting out a massive yawn. The two of them had to hang on tight to avoid being thrown off.

Ready to set out? Orion asked.

He could feel Saphron's disjointed thoughts as he came into awareness. Finally, he woke fully, raising his wing to look at it. Waves of relief and happiness emanated from him as he saw that it was healed. He began flapping it joyfully, and he launched himself into the sky, heading north to Cardeas.

Haaka

17

When they reached the border, Tanzanite, Mithrel, and Xharia were waiting for them. Tanzanite's indigo scales gleamed in the sunlight. Xharia's mossy robes gave off various shades of green as she waved frantically. Mithrel waved just as frantically, the sun bringing out the reddish-brown hue of his skin between his helmet and his beard.

Saphron! Tanzanite thought as soon as they were in range, *You're alright!*

Yes, we're all fine, he replied, and Orion could feel his glee at her having been worried about him.

They landed, and were immediately embraced by their friends. "I wanted to go back for you, but Tanzanite refused!" Xharia said.

You told me to get them out of there, Tanzanite said, *I knew I would only endanger the three of us by going back. Besides, I had faith that we'd trained you well enough to win that fight. If you couldn't defeat your old friends, you'd have no hope of defeating Obsidian and Dredon.*

"I know," Orion responded to Xharia, "I told her not to. There was no sense endangering the rest of you when he was only after me."

"What took you so long to get back?" Mithrel asked.

Orion looked back at Saphron and Celestia, "Saphron was badly injured in the fight. Callisto and I healed his wounds, but we couldn't get all of them at once, as it drained our energy too low. He was still too hurt to fly, and we were too exhausted to do anything more. So, we went to sleep. In the morning, she finished healing him, and we all felt well enough to finally catch up with you."

"What happened?" Xharia asked worriedly.

He faltered, unable to say what he'd done.

"Moonstone is dead," Celestia said.

She nodded solemnly, "Then, your training served you well."

"Orion's, yes," Celestia said, "But, not Saphron's."

What is she talking about? Tanzanite asked.

Saphron was ashamed and horrified at her proclamation.

"Orion was able to duel Epsilon effectively and defeat him. He got everyone else to safety when Moonstone attacked, and did his best to help his dragon in their fight. He strategized as the fight wore on, and finally figured out a brilliant way to win it: he got close enough, and fired an arrow right between two of his scales, using magic to propel it with enough force to pierce his hide."

Everyone cheered and applauded Orion's skill and quick thinking, Xharia and Mithrel patting him on the back, and Tanzanite nodding in approval.

Callisto waited for everyone to calm down before she continued, "Saphron attempted to fight Moonstone alone. I, of course, couldn't hear their thoughts, but it looked like Orion was doing everything in his power to help him, but Saphron wouldn't let him. I can only assume he was trying to defend him and keep his rider safe. But, he couldn't handle the fight alone. He was losing. Moonstone would've killed him if it weren't for Orion."

Saphron, is this true? Tanzanite asked.

The blue dragon looked away, unable to face his mentor.

"You're right," Orion said, "He messed up. But, he's not the only one of us to have messed up on this quest. Though he needs to work harder on his training if he's to face Obsidian, and though he should've listened to me and let me help, we can't be too hard on him. He was only doing it to protect me, as she correctly assumed. He fought bravely, and got in some good practice. He's harder on himself than any of us, and I think he learned his lesson."

Regardless, Tanzanite said, *What you did was irresponsible. I know you desire to keep your rider alive, but do you not think he also wishes the same for you? You're stronger together. You must never do that again. You have to trust him the way he trusts you.*

He didn't answer, but gave a slight nod of understanding.

If you don't, she added, *You will never defeat Obsidian.*

You're right, Saphron said, *I'm sorry.*

Tanzanite nodded, *It's alright. Now, we need to train harder before we reach Abyumo.*

"I know I learned from my mistakes," Xharia said solemnly.

Mithrel cleared his throat, "We'd better get going. There's no time to spare on a quest like this."

"Mithrel's right," Callisto said, "Let's go."

They all hopped back onto the dragons' backs, taking off into Cardeas.

The next day, they reached the kingdom of Cartouche, the most powerful kingdom in Cardeas, where Orion was born. They knew they wouldn't be able to venture into any of their other kingdoms. They couldn't spend very long there as it was. They just had to hope and pray that they would be on their side.

They landed outside the royal castle, and Orion felt strange walking up to the wooden doors. Knowing these had been the rulers when he was a child, and now he was returning to this city as a dragon rider, he wasn't sure how to feel. He had never actually been to the castle or met the rulers, but it was still strange.

The four of them entered, the servants announcing their arrival to the king and queen. Callisto did the talking, explaining the situation to them, as Orion looked around, feeling as though he were having an out-of-body experience. None of it seemed real. The king had dark skin, long dreadlocks, and a beard. The queen had dark skin and a large afro. Her golden eyes shone in contrast. He was captivated by her beauty for a moment.

"You want us to drop everything and go to war with you?" King Thabiti was saying, "Are you crazy?"

"No," Celestia replied, "But you'd be crazy not to."

"I was born here!" Orion cried suddenly. Everyone stared silently at him for a moment, "I'm a dragon rider, now. Many of our people follow the same path. We are a nation of warriors. It would be a shame if we were left behind. Derekkian was a native here. He defeated the legendary Vidar the Conqueror. What would've happened if he'd gone before the king and queen of Cartouche and been denied?"

Everyone remained silent.

"I am the descendant of Derekkian. I am a native of Cardeas. And, I am proud."

King Thabiti smiled at him.

"Will Cardeas fight? Or will they fall short of the history books?"

"I knew a few Cardeans," Celestia added, "Long ago. Your ancestors, in fact. Nastazya was my dear friend. I also had the pleasure to know her brothers: Jacobi, Theodonis, Ajala, Chiumbo . . . and Thabiti."

There was a long, tense pause as the king contemplated everything. The four of them stood there, uncertain what his response would be. Finally, he said, "We will fight. Get to Abyumo, and trust the armies of your homeland to follow."

The four of them gave the king and queen a bow, heading out of the throne room. Orion wanted to stop by his childhood home and visit his parents, but they had no time to spare. They had to get to Abyumo before the last stars collided, otherwise Kirstiana and Lorena would be killed.

They flew through the rest of the day, west toward Abyumo. When they landed to make camp, they were a mere half-day's flight away. They huddled close together, using the two dragons' body heat for warmth, as they couldn't risk attracting attention to themselves with a fire.

"We'll reach the realm of the wizards tomorrow," Celestia said, "I've been in contact with them, and they're all on our side. They've been acting as a base for the kingdoms we've recruited, communicating with them, and organizing our troops. We'll make a quick stop to get information from them, and then head into the dragon rider realm."

Orion nodded, glad they would be able to coordinate their attack. "We'll enter in the north," he said, "Maybe we can get a couple of dragon rider kingdoms to join us on our way south to Cabri. The more dragon riders we have on our side, the better."

"Excellent," she said, "Now, we have a plan."

"Maybe some of the other riders could help train you further on the way down," Xharia said, "If you only narrowly defeated Moonstone and Epsilon, you'll need the extra training."

Orion nodded. He hated to admit it, but she was right.

"Not to mention the added number of riders," Mithrel said.

"Yes," Orion agreed, "The more riders, the better chance we have against his forces. But, in the end, it will be up to me and Saphron to defeat him."

Everyone was silent as the true gravity of their quest sank in. Orion was beginning to realize the likelihood they wouldn't survive this conflict. Thoughts of imminent death invaded his mind, but he had no choice. He had to keep going. If he didn't, he and Saphron wouldn't be the only ones to die.

They flew into Abyumo, landing outside the office of the wizard council. It was a long, tall, rectangular building made of white stone. Celestia led the way, as they went up the steps that led to the entrance.

When they reached the door, it opened, and an old wizard was standing there. After a pause, he said, "Right this way."

The four of them followed him inside and down a short corridor to the council meeting room. The rest of the wizard council was seated around it. They all looked the same: old, pale-skinned men with gray robes and long, gray beards. The one leading them showed them to four vacant seats, and they took their places at the table.

"Mirin," Celestia said, nodding to the wizard at the head of the table.

"Callisto," he replied, nodding back to her.

There was a long pause before she said, "We have recruited several kingdoms, and can only hope they've communicated with you, and that they've recruited more of their allies to join us."

"Indeed they have," he said, "On your side, you have all six kingdoms of Duwazo, all four kingdoms of Cardeas, six of the eight kingdoms of Fluorasti, five of the twelve kingdoms of Gachichken, nine of the eleven kingdoms of Korga, three of the six kingdoms of Gliken, and two of the four kingdoms of Katangalo."

"We didn't even recruit in Katangalo," Xharia said in amazement.

Mirin smiled, "I know. A few of your allies did it for you."

"This is more than we could have hoped for," Celestia said.

His smile faded, "On his side, he has two of the eight kingdoms of Fluorasti, seven of the twelve kingdoms of Gachichken, two of the eleven kingdoms of Korga, three of the six kingdoms of Gliken, two of the four kingdoms of Katangalo, all five kingdoms of Mashang, all three kingdoms of Kuttub, all eight kingdoms of Millhaymae, and all six kingdoms of Kogatsa."

They looked at each other hopelessly.

"As for Abyumo," he continued, "all three kingdoms of the wizard realm are on your side, and—"

"Yes!" Mithrel shouted. When everyone stopped to stare at him, he said, "We have all the wizards. That's got to count for something."

"You have the light wizards, yes," Mirin said, "The dark wizards reside in Kogatsa."

Mithrel looked down, trying to hide his embarrassment.

"That means we're tied with him," Xharia said.

"Yes," Mirin continued, "The thing that will tip the scales is the dragon riders. Though I must add, while you have the same number of kingdoms, he has several that are larger. So, in total, he does have more troops."

Everyone was silent once more. Orion felt his stomach sink to his shoes. Finally, he said, "So what's the plan?"

"The plan is for the troops to march on Cabri in two days' time. You have until then to recruit in the dragon rider realm. Hopefully, you're prepared to face him."

He gulped, looking around at all the faces staring at him. They were pinning all their hopes on him being able to defeat Dredon. Suddenly, he felt hot, and he could feel his sweat as it formed and started trickling down his body. He pulled on the collar of his bodysuit, finding it hard to breathe.

"He is," Celestia said confidently, "Well prepared."

He was relieved as they all turned their attention away from him.

"We will set out for the dragon rider realm at dawn," she added, "Thank you for the information, councilmen."

They nodded, and the four of them rose, heading out of the meeting hall.

They spent the rest of the day training with Tanzanite. She drilled them on their synchronization, and worked extra hard on Saphron. She wanted to make sure he was as prepared as she could make him. She focused on his defensive maneuvers, how to keep himself out of the line of attack, and do the most damage the quickest.

When she felt satisfied with his progress, Celestia leaped upon her back and offered them a practice duel. They didn't take it easy on them, Tanzanite offering her best to Saphron, and Callisto firing the full force of her raw power against Orion.

Orion felt like he'd learned a lot in a short amount of time, and he was as ready as he'd ever be to face Dredon. He worried for Saphron, going up against Obsidian, but they were out of time. They couldn't delay this inevitable battle any longer. The last pair of stars could collide and fall at any second, and they still had two more days until the battle.

Perhaps what Xharia said will come true, Saphron thought.

Which part? Orion asked.

When she said that perhaps some of the other riders we recruit could help us train further. Let's face it: Tanzanite, Xharia, and Callisto have taught us all they can.

He sent waves of agreement, pondering. After a pause, he said, *Let's just hope they're more skilled than our current mentors, otherwise their aid will not prove useful.*

Indeed, Saphron agreed.

They finished up their training for the day, settling in to sleep. They were to leave at dawn to the realm of the dragon riders, hopefully gaining some more powerful allies in this war . . .

At dawn, they took to the skies, crossing the border between the realm of the wizards and the realm of the dragon riders. The world changed from grassy plains to desert, expanding before them into the vast dragon rider city of Haaka. It was a relief to Orion, seeing other riders again. He felt like he was coming home after a long journey, which he was. But it wasn't all relief. His stomach was still in knots thinking of the battle that awaited him before he could *really* go home.

They flew into the city, all the way to the royal palace, which was made of black diamonds and stones. This was the city of their realm responsible for growing most of the food. It was near a span of active volcanoes, which helped produce fertile soil, enabling them to grow a large number of delicious items.

When they landed, the guards of the castle escorted them inside. It was a relief to Saphron to be able to actually fit inside a building again. Everywhere but the dragon rider realm was too small for him, and he was sick of being left outside.

The king, Michaël, was tall, with brown hair and pale skin. He wore red armor; his red dragon, Sardonyx sitting beside his throne. His red eyes were a bit unnerving, but he wore a great smile. "Welcome," he said, rising, "What brings you to Haaka?"

"The war," Orion said.

His smile faded, "The war in Cabri?"

"It's not only in Cabri," he replied, "It's everywhere. Obsidian and Dredon are taking over, and they need to be stopped. They've killed their fellow dragons and riders. Their crimes need to be punished."

"Please, sir," Xharia said, "You know the story of Vidar the Conqueror, do you not?"

"Of course," he responded, "What kind of question is that?"

"Then you know that Dredon is Vidar's heir," she said.

He started in surprise, looking at them carefully.

"Orion is the descendant of Derekkian," Mithrel said, "The Oracle has seen that only he can defeat Dredon. But, he can't do it alone."

"Enough," Celestia said, waving her hand to quiet them. She stepped forward, looking at the king, "Give me your hand."

Everyone stared at her in confusion, including Michaël. Finally, he descended the steps to his throne, standing before her, and holding out his hand. Sardonyx bristled, obviously nervous for his rider. Celestia took his hand, and the two of them closed their eyes. Orion wasn't sure what was happening, but they were silent for a few moments, just standing like that. Finally, the king stepped back, eyes wide.

After another pause, he shouted for one of his servants, "Keil! Ready the troops. We leave for battle in the morn."

The man nodded, scurrying from the room.

"Also, we would like your best rider to come with us," Orion said.

Everyone turned to stare at him, but he maintained his composure, looking at Michaël steadily.

Finally, he nodded, "Very well. Himey! Fetch Kendreil. Have her and Citrine ready to leave in an hour."

"Thank you," Orion said.

Yes, thank you, Saphron added, projecting to Sardonyx.

The red dragon nodded, and the king had another servant show them where they could wait for Kendreil. They followed him down a long corridor to a large room with an opening in the ceiling, through which dragons could come and go.

"What did you do to him?" Orion asked once they were alone.

"I shared The Oracle's vision with him," she said.

"What?" he marveled, "How?"

"It's a spell I invented that allows you to share thoughts, memories, experiences with someone else. I could see he wasn't going to listen, but I knew if he saw what would happen to his kingdom, he would."

Orion paused for a moment, "If you had the ability to do that, why didn't you use it on the other kings and queens we were trying to recruit?"

"It only works on those with magical ability themselves."

He nodded, understanding.

Just then, a golden yellow dragon came through the door on the opposite side of the room. From beside him stepped a young woman with golden eyes, garbed in yellow armor. She had pale skin and golden blonde hair.

"You must be Kendreil," Celestia said, "And Citrine. Pleasure to meet you."

The rider nodded, "So, why did you request for me to accompany you?"

"I'm Callisto, keeper of The Oracle. This is Xharia, our elven warrior, and Mithrel, our dwarven warrior."

The two of them waved and nodded.

"This is Tanzanite. Her rider was killed by Dredon. And, this is Saphron and Orion. They are the dragon and rider pair who will have to face Obsidian and Dredon in the final battle. Dredon is the descendant of Vidar the Conqueror, and Orion is the descendant of Derekkian."

"I requested Haaka's best dragon and rider," Orion said, "because we need another mentor to help us prepare. Callisto and Xharia have taught me all they can, and Tanzanite has taught Saphron."

Kendreil scoffed, "The great rider and dragon who are supposed to be the keys to winning this war want *me* to train them? If you can't beat me already, how do you expect to win a battle in two days against a greater foe?"

"I don't know," he admitted, "But I have to try. Every little bit of training helps."

"We're sending the troops of Haaka to their deaths," she said solemnly, "Never trust the word of an oracle."

"You may be right," he replied, "But it's better than doing nothing."

"We will lead the armies of many kingdoms into battle," Callisto said, "We will not go down without a fight. If you're truly the best this kingdom has to offer, then you should be with us at the helm."

Kendreil looked at each of them in turn, and then over to Citrine. After a long pause, she said, "Very well. Let's go."

Chyia

18

On their way to the kingdom of Chyia, Orion and Saphron trained with Kendreil and Citrine. They learned several new maneuvers, and were able to offer a challenge to Haaka's best. It helped them gain confidence that they were able to beat them. Citrine did know several maneuvers that Tanzanite did not, so he was able to help Saphron add to his knowledge base. Kendreil was a skilled fighter, but there was not much more Orion could learn about sword fighting or magical combat.

She did teach him several new ways to move along his dragon, including how to evade your opponent by swinging around to the underbelly. She showed him that he could fight from that position, which he had always struggled with. She was well-versed in the maneuver, educating him on how to hang on and still be able to swing his sword.

"I'm impressed," Kendreil said as they all sat around their campsite, "I did not think you would offer much of a challenge when you asked me to train you, but you did. Use that to your advantage. The likelihood of them underestimating you is high. They will not expect it."

Orion nodded, "Thank you."

Just remember the evasive maneuvers I taught you, Citrine thought, *They might save your life.*

Saphron gave him a deep nod of appreciation.

Remember all I've taught you as well, Tanzanite thought, *Every maneuver will count in your fight.*

He shot her a confused look, saying, *Of course.*

Did I detect a tone of jealousy? Orion thought.

Hush, Saphron snapped, *She's not jealous.*

Orion chuckled, *Whatever you say.*

"Let's all get some rest," Celestia said, "We'll make it to Chyia tomorrow, and we need to be prepared to recruit their army."

"I'll take the first watch," Kendreil said.

They all nodded, settling in for the night.

When Celestia woke Orion for his shift, she sat beside him.

"Aren't you going to get some sleep?" he asked, confused.

She nodded, "But first, I wanted to give you something. The closer we get to Cabri, the less likely it is I'll have another chance." With that, she grabbed his hand, slipping something into it.

When he opened his hand to see what it was, he saw that it was a ring. It had a silver band with a sparkling diamond atop it. He looked up at her in sheer confusion, "What's this?"

"It's my wedding ring," she said solemnly.

He stared blankly at her.

"On my second quest, I learned how to store energy within it. Over the years, I've developed quite a massive reserve. And I want you to have it. It may help you in your battle with Dredon."

His eyes grew wide, and he clutched the ring tightly, "Thank you."

She nodded, "Anyway, it will do you more good than it will me."

He gave her a half-smile, "Let's hope so."

She patted his hands, "Goodnight."

He nodded as she got up and went to lie down.

I stand by what I said before, Saphron thought, *We're lucky to have her as a mentor.*

Orion sent him waves of agreement. He looked down at the ring in his hand, understanding what it must have meant to her. He used magic to create a chain, putting the ring on it like a pendant, and putting it around his neck.

An appropriate sentiment, the blue dragon thought.

He nodded, *Hopefully, the energy it contains will help us match Obsidian's power.*

Hopefully . . .

The next day, they flew into Chyia, landing before the sapphire and silver palace. This was the kingdom responsible for the art and supplies of the realm, including clothing, saddles, and furniture. The craftsmen were visible throughout the city, working steadily on their various projects. As soon as they landed, they were escorted inside, and to the throne room. Shelbara sat upon her throne, waiting. She had dirty-blonde hair and pale skin. Her aqua eyes and armor matched her dragon, Marina.

"Welcome," she said, "What can we do for you?"

Callisto stepped forward, once again explaining the situation.

Shelbara sighed, "I'm afraid we cannot help you. There aren't many warriors here in Chyia. We're a kingdom of artisans and pacifists."

"Perhaps, instead of telling you, I can simply show you," she said.

The queen stepped down from her throne. After a pause, she said, "If you must," and held out her arm.

Celestia took her hand, and they closed their eyes, standing there. Orion now knew what was happening, as she shared a vision with her of what's to come. Finally, Shelbara stepped back, looking at each of them steadily. After a long pause, she turned away, saying, "I'm sorry. We cannot help you."

"What do you mean, you can't help us?" Orion demanded, "Even after you saw what will happen? Why not?"

She turned back toward them, tears in her eyes. "Because we've already been taken over," she said.

"What?" he cried. No sooner had he said it than several smirking dragon riders came through the doors with their dragons.

"Dredon sends his regards," one of them said. With that, he charged straight for Orion and Saphron.

Kendreil and Citrine took on another pair, and Celestia teamed up with Tanzanite, taking on another. Even Shelbara and Marina joined in, trying to help.

Xharia and Mithrel had no dragons, but they wanted to fight. There were no other dragons or riders left to face, however. They watched helplessly for a moment, before Mithrel saw Shelbara struggling, and rushed to her aid.

The rider Orion was facing was a formidable foe, and he struggled against him. He pushed him into his dragon, who knocked him down. As he struggled to reach his feet, the rider smirked, shaking his head. He raised his sword to kill him, but was shoved forward, falling beside Orion.

When he looked up, he saw that Xharia had shoved him. She smiled, offering him her hand. He took it, getting up, and together they tag-teamed him. They fought back and forth as Saphron tore into his dragon. With two against one, they were able to dispatch him quickly, much to the horror of his dragon.

As he attempted to wreak his vengeance upon Saphron, they hurried to his aid. The blue dragon lifted each of them with one of his claws, and together, they plunged their swords into the dragon's heart. They turned to see Celestia and Tanzanite had been victorious as well. The two of them hurried to aid Mithrel, Shelbara, and Marina in their battle. So, Orion, Xharia, and Saphron rushed to the aid of Kendreil and Citrine.

It didn't take long for them to claim victory. Once the dragons and riders sent by Obsidian and Dredon were killed, the rest of them regrouped in the middle of the room.

"We need to get out of here," Kendreil said.

"Go," Shelbara said, "I'll try to gather what dragons and riders I have left, and join you on the battlefield tomorrow. I can't promise you it'll be much."

"That's okay," Orion said, "Anything's better than nothing at all."

"Come on," Callisto said, "Let's get out of here. We'll lie in wait in the mountains until tomorrow's fight."

The rest of them nodded, hurrying back to their dragons. On the way, Orion grabbed Xharia's arm. When she turned toward him questioningly, he said, "I've made up my mind. Yes."

She shot him a confused look, "Yes, what?"

"We can be friends," he said.

A smile spread across her face, "Really?"

He nodded.

"Oh, thank you, Orion!" she exclaimed, hugging him.

"Come on!" Kendreil yelled, "You can kiss and make up later!"

They separated, turning red. "Oh. We're not—" Orion began.

"Yeah, yeah, I don't care!" she cut him off, "Let's go!"

They leapt upon Saphron and Tanzanite's backs, exiting the palace and taking off. They heard cries behind them as several of his other followers realized what had happened. The whole city was under siege. Some of them spotted them flying away, and hurried to chase after them.

Follow me, Tanzanite thought. She led the way for Saphron and Citrine, heading into the mountains. They had to struggle a bit to keep up with her as she weaved and turned and tried to lose their pursuers. Finally, when they could no longer see them, she dove behind a mountain suddenly, and the other two followed. They ducked down, burrowing into its side.

The other dragons appeared, trying to find them. They flew straight past, not even noticing they were there. The rest of them breathed a sigh of relief, looking at Tanzanite in awe.

How did you do that? Citrine thought.

I know these mountains like the underside of my wing, she said.

He shook his head in amazement.

She was *the flying instructor,* Saphron thought.

You knew? she asked in surprise.

Of course, he replied, *I wanted to know as much as I could about the teachers of the training mountain, in hopes that Orion and I might one day make it there.*

Yes, well, I don't suppose any of that matters now.

Saphron looked down sadly, *No. I suppose not.*

They watched and waited until the dragons and riders flew back past them the other way before they finally moved from the side of the mountain. It was nearly dusk, and they moved to a secluded area of the mountains to make camp. They weren't far from Cabri, and they would easily make it before the battle commenced the next day.

Though I'm sick of training, Orion thought, *I can't help but be glad we were able to fight those other dragons and riders today. I think we need as much practice as we can get.*

Saphron sent him waves of agreement.

Goodnight, big guy, he thought as he faded out of consciousness.

Orion awoke to a deafening *crash!* When he sat up, he saw that the last two stars had collided. "No!" he shouted. *We're too late,* he thought, *We only had one more day, and we're too late!*

Everyone else was awake, too, sitting solemnly, staring up at the sky.

"We have to go!" Orion said, "Now!"

Everyone remained motionless as he started packing up his things.

He looked around at them in disbelief, "Come on!"

"Orion," Celestia said softly, shaking her head slightly.

He stared at her, "I don't care what any of you think. I'll go myself!" He leaped upon Saphron's back, thinking, *Let's go.*

"Orion, please, wait," Celestia said. When he looked at her indignantly, she sighed, "I'm going with you."

He nodded, and she leaped upon Saphron's back behind him. The others looked at each other. As Saphron took off into the night sky, Xharia and Mithrel climbed upon Tanzanite's back. She launched herself up, following them. Finally, Kendreil sighed, leaping onto Citrine's back and joining them in the air.

The three dragons set out for Cabri, soaring over the mountains. Orion's mind went dark as he thought of their queen being murdered by Dredon. *Not Lorena,* he thought, nearly choking on tears of rage, *We can't be too late. We can't.*

We'll find out soon, Saphron thought, shielding his internal thoughts from his rider. Orion could feel his mind was going just as dark.

We don't know anything, yet, Tanzanite thought, trying to soothe Saphron's mind.

The Oracle said we had until the last stars collided to prevent this from happening, Orion thought, *We're too late.*

The indigo dragon sighed, disheartened.

As the city lights of Cabri appeared in the distance, they flew faster, darting through the shadows so as not to be seen. Tanzanite guided them around the training mountain, where The Oracle's vision had taken place. No one was there.

Wasn't the vision in the daytime? Saphron thought.

Yes, Orion replied, *Was it today, and they cleaned the scene already? Or is it tomorrow?* He felt his hopes rise at the thought, but he tried to repress them, not wanting to get them too high until he knew.

We have to find them, he said.

Orion sent his dragon waves of agreement.

They circled the mountain, not seeing any signs of life.

Do you think they're in the city? Citrine thought.

Perhaps, Tanzanite replied.

Do you know where Obsidian and Dredon live? Saphron asked.

Yes, Tanzanite responded, *But, I doubt they would be there. He would hide them somewhere less conspicuous. They could very well be in the city.*

Or, they could be in the same place he hid the bodies from his slaughter of the leaders, Orion thought, *If so, we'll never find them. Even their best investigators: Morgalina and Austinian, and their dragons, Turq and Amaline, couldn't find them.*

Let's search the city, Kendreil thought, *It's worth a shot.*

The others sent her waves of agreement, and the three dragons swooped low to the ground, approaching the city and trying not to be seen. As they neared, they could see several of Dredon's followers posted around the city. Tanzanite knew a back way into the city, only known to its leaders. She led them toward it, and it opened at her approach, allowing them to pass through the narrow gap in the city wall. Once inside, the dragons landed.

It would be easier for the five of you not to be seen, Tanzanite thought, *The three of us will remain hidden here until you return.*

Orion nodded, and climbed down from Saphron's back, trying to gesture to the others to follow. Celestia, Mithrel, Xharia, and Kendreil climbed down, joining him, and they snuck through the city, avoiding the view of Dredon's sentinels. They made their way to the castle slowly and cautiously.

Once they got there, Orion whispered, "I think we should split up. We can search faster, and we have a slimmer chance of being seen in smaller groups. Callisto, come with me. Mithrel, Xharia, you two go with Kendreil. She can communicate with me with her mind through our dragons. We're not far enough away to be out of range from here. If something happens, meet back by the dragons."

"We'll take the east wing," Kendreil said, "You two take the west wing."

Orion nodded. They snuck through the courtyard and into the back door quietly, splitting up once they were inside. He and Callisto searched the main floor first, catching a glimpse of the throne room. Dredon was inside, asleep on the throne. Celestia patted his arm, seeing his reaction. When his hopelessness subsided, he began to wonder where Obsidian was. He was too big to enter any of the buildings, so he had to be outside somewhere.

They finished searching the main floor with no sign of them. They headed upstairs, searching the corridors of the palace, and still nothing. Finally, they crept back down the stairs, and to the lower floor of the castle, to the dungeons. They could see that the cells no longer had criminals in them, but warriors of Cabri. Orion's eyes widened.

When they reached the end of the row of cells, they saw amber and bronze scales. *Aeramen! Solstra!* he thought.

They didn't respond. He looked at Callisto, panicked. *Please, don't be dead,* he thought. He reached through the cell, touching Aeramen's bronze-scaled back. The massive dragon shook, waking and turning toward him, jaws open.

Aeramen! he thought, *It's Orion!*

She looked at him, *Who?*

Saphron and I were the ones who came to warn you about Dredon and Obsidian.

So, you came here to say "I told you so?" she thought angrily.

No, he thought, *We came here to save you.*

You can't save us! she snapped, *Get out of here!*

Where's Lorena? he asked, *And Kirstiana?*

Solstra turned to face them then, *They're not here.*

Where are they? he demanded.

He separated us, she said, pained, *They're out of mental range. He plans on killing us at dawn, and then making an example of them . . .* She paused, unable to continue.

I know what he plans, Orion said sorrowfully, *I've seen it.*

Solstra looked up at him in shock, *How?*

The Oracle shared a vision with me, he replied. After a pause, he said, *We have to get you out of here. We'll go to the mountain tomorrow and rescue your riders.*

Which mountain? Aeramen asked.

The training mountain, he said, *That's where he's going to kill them.*

The keys are by the stairs, Solstra said.

Orion nodded, turning and running back to the staircase to grab the keys. When he reached the bottom, he heard footsteps. Someone was coming down the stairs. His eyes widened, and he signaled to Callisto to hide. She rushed over beside him, and they moved into the shadows at the bottom of the stairwell.

Orion drew his sword, and Celestia drew her wand. When they got to the bottom, they charged forward, stopping when they saw that it was Xharia, Mithrel, and Kendreil.

"Xharia!" Orion whispered loudly.

"Orion! Celestia!" she replied.

"Come on!" he said, grabbing the keys and running back down the corridor. The rest of them followed as he unlocked the cells holding Solstra and Aeramen. Then, they went to each of the other cells, releasing the rest of Cabri's warriors.

The five of them hurried back up the stairs, sneaking out of the castle, and through the city to their waiting dragons. Once they reached them, they scrambled onto their backs, taking off through the opening, and back toward the mountains. Then, the liberated dragons took off out of the dungeons, attracting the attention of the sentinels.

A battle ensued as they tried to escape. They formed a group around Solstra and Aeramen, protecting them as they flew out of the city. Orion looked back, trying to ensure they escaped. The sentinels were focused on the two of them, going straight for them. The other dragons fought hard to protect their queens, but they were being slaughtered.

No! Orion thought, *What have we done? We just wanted to help, but we might have done more harm than good.*

As they watched from the relative safety of the mountains, the group surrounding Solstra and Aeramen flew out of the city, avoiding their pursuers, and bolting for the mountains on the opposite side. He breathed a sigh of relief when they made cover, happy that they got away.

Several of the others were still struggling to flee, fighting the sentinels for their lives. Just then, a looming, black shadow appeared behind the escapees. Obsidian let out a terrifying roar, tearing through the remaining dragons.

No! Orion thought, horrified. At the same time, Saphron, Tanzanite, Citrine, and Kendreil thought the same thing. He was sure the others did, too. *This is all my fault,* he thought.

No, Saphron said, *It's not.*

You saved our queen, Tanzanite thought.

He turned his eyes away from the slaughter, unable to look as Obsidian unleashed his wrath upon the warriors of Cabri. Celestia placed her hand on his arm in solidarity, a single tear streaming down her face.

Let us leave this place, Citrine thought.

Orion turned toward him angrily, thinking that he didn't understand, since he and his rider weren't from Cabri. But when he saw Kendreil's tear-stained face, he knew they did understand. Citrine grimaced, turning his head away. Finally, he nodded, and the three of them flew deeper into the mountains, finding a place to hide out until morning.

The Final Battle

19

A s soon as the blood-orange light of dawn appeared, Orion was awake and ready. He had one goal: save Lorena and Kirstiana. They had come up with a plan, and were ready to execute it. *Before they get executed* . . . he thought.

The blue, indigo, and golden yellow dragons set out for the training mountain, trying to stay out of view. When they arrived, they stuck to the side of the neighboring mountain, watching carefully. Solstra and Aeramen were nowhere to be seen, much to their relief. Orion had been worried they'd be found and still get killed before dawn.

As they watched, Dredon's followers slowly gathered on the mountaintop. Finally, the massive black dragon, Obsidian, landed atop the mountain, casting a shadow over everyone gathered there. Then, Dredon walked up, white teeth gleaming against his dark skin as he grinned. His black armor had a shine to it, and stretched across his massive muscles. Even from that distance, he looked intimidating. Orion gulped, looking from him to his dragon. Saphron was the size of Obsidian's leg. *How can we possibly beat them?* he thought.

It was then that he saw that Dredon was dragging something. As he struggled to see around the side of Obsidian's wing, he finally realized what it was. He threw Kirstiana and Lorena down, stepping on the chain between them to hold them in place. It was just like The Oracle's vision, except for the fact that Solstra and Aeramen were alive and safe.

Lorena, he thought, *Come on, we have to hurry.*

Wait, Kendreil thought, *Stick to the plan.*

He looked over at her, golden blonde hair and golden yellow armor illuminated by the rising sun, *Then, let's put the plan in motion.*

She nodded. With that, Citrine took off, straight toward the queens. Orion looked over at Xharia and Mithrel, nodding. They climbed off Tanzanite's back, clinging to the side of the mountain, and Callisto leaped from Saphron's back to Tanzanite's. He took a breath, and they bolted out from hiding, following. Taking Dredon by surprise, as he was saying, "Today, the dragon rider realm is ours!" Citrine knocked him over, and clutched the queens in his claws, flying off.

As Dredon rose angrily, preparing to mount Obsidian and follow them, Saphron and Tanzanite bowled him over, Orion drawing his sword to stab him. Before he could, Obsidian lunged forward, jaws open. Orion could see the curves of the inside of his mouth, the saliva dripping from its roof, each massive tooth the size of his entire body. His eyes widened as Saphron darted out of the way, avoiding getting snapped in half by the force of his jaws.

He maneuvered to his underbelly, trying to gain a vantage point. Orion raised his sword to stab the great dragon, but he swung his claw down, batting Saphron away. Tanzanite quickly darted in after him, Celestia pulling out her wand and blasting Obsidian with a magical attack.

The black dragon let out a deafening roar, maneuvering his body around to snap his jaws around Tanzanite. She moved quickly, avoiding him, but just barely. He shot out a jet of flame, and she had to grab Saphron by the scruff of his neck, pulling him out of the way.

The sapphire dragon looked at her in awe, *You just saved my life.*

Move it! she thought in return.

Orion looked over his shoulder to see that Kendreil and Citrine had gotten away with Lorena and Kirstiana. *You're right!* he thought, relieved, *We should wait for the army to get here! Right now, we're too vulnerable!*

The two dragons started to head back to the neighboring mountain to grab Xharia and Mithrel and make a flight for it, when they were frozen, unable to move. Slowly, the two dragons turned around, but not of their own will. When they were facing the training mountain once more, they saw that Dredon had a magical hold on them.

Tanzanite? he thought in surprise, *You're supposed to be dead.* After a pause, he said, *I should've known.*

Surprise, traitor! she thought angrily.

He looked at Celestia steadily, *Who's this? She's not your rider.*

She didn't answer.

She's not a rider at all, he said, *She can't hear my thoughts.*

She's the keeper of The Oracle, Tanzanite spat.

Suddenly, he grinned, *You mean this oracle?*

He waved to a few of his followers, who tossed a body to his feet. Orion could see it was The Oracle. She had golden and amber hair, white eyes, and a sheer turquoise ensemble on her cold, pale body. She was no longer glowing, and they could see she was dead.

I guess she wasn't a very good keeper, he said.

You bastard! Tanzanite thought.

Callisto stared wide-eyed at The Oracle's body, unable to react.

So, this must be the famous Orion, he thought mockingly, *The one she prophesied to defeat me.*

Orion glared at him, feeling his rage well up inside him.

Descendant of Derekkian? he scoffed, *This is the best this world has to offer? Pathetic. I mean, look at your dragon, and look at mine. Obsidian could swallow your beast in a single bite.*

The massive black dragon licked his lips, hovering behind his rider.

But listen, he said, *I'm not here to kill everyone. This whole rebellion is a waste. All I want is a little reform. If you all would just cooperate with me, no one would get hurt.*

A likely story, Saphron thought, disgusted.

You've got a brain, he said, *So, use it. You can't beat me. We fight, you die. All of your friends and followers die.* He paused, *You join me, you live. I give you your own territory, to run however you see fit. We avoid this whole conflict, and no one gets hurt.* After another pause, he said, *I leave it up to you.*

With that, he released his hold on them. Orion exchanged glances with Celestia, seeing the tears that had welled up in her sparkling blue eyes.

He felt the waves of pain and rage emanating from Tanzanite. *What do we do?* he asked Saphron, *We have to plan our next move carefully.*

Yes, the sapphire dragon replied, *We do.*

Should we pretend to join him?

No, he said, *He's too smart for that. He's prepared for betrayal from anyone at any moment.*

Well, we can't join him for real, he thought, *And, we can't face him, yet. I don't even think we can make a run for it. What can we do?*

We have to risk it, he said, *Fleeing is our only choice.*

"We've made our decision," Orion announced.

Dredon grinned cockily, looking up at them, "Yes?"

"Yes," Celestia said, surprising them all. They looked at her, panicked. She illuminated in blue magic, shouting, "You can go to hell!"

With that, she launched a burst of magic at him, taking him by surprise, and knocking the smug grin from his face. In the split second after casting the spell, Saphron and Tanzanite took off, flying away as fast as they could.

That worked out better than I thought, Saphron thought.

Orion sent him waves of agreement as he grabbed Mithrel's hand on their way past, pulling him into the saddle behind him. Celestia grabbed Xharia at the same time, and they sped through the mountain skies, trying to get away.

Dredon leapt upon Obsidian's back to follow, the giant black shadow darkening the peaceful skies. They went as fast as their wings could carry them, Tanzanite leading the way. She showed them more secret pathways, eventually ducking into a large cave system. They flew through it, finally arriving inside the stronghold of the mountain leaders, where she and her rider had lived.

This way! she thought, diving straight down.

Saphron followed, confused, as they dove into another secret underground tunnel beneath the mountain. Finally, she stopped, and the two dragons hovered breathlessly, waiting.

He can't fit inside, she explained, *But that won't stop him from bringing down the mountain. We'll be safe beneath it. There's another way out.*

It got dark as Obsidian flew overhead, and they all looked at each other. He roared in frustration, but he couldn't see them through the opening at the top of the stronghold. So, he flew off, presumably back to the training mountain.

That was brilliant! Saphron thought.

"Can someone please explain what's happening?" Xharia asked.

"He killed The Oracle," Celestia said numbly, "It's all my fault."

"It's not your fault," Orion said. After a pause, he said, "He tried to get us to join him. We were planning to flee, and then Callisto gave us an opening. I'm not sure how you knew what was happening, as you couldn't hear our conversation, but thank you."

"I didn't know what was happening," she replied, "But, what else would he be asking you to make a decision on?"

He shrugged, "Good point. Anyway, Tanzanite led us here, since Obsidian can't fit. I think he headed back to the training mountain. Citrine got Lorena and Kirstiana to safety. Now, we just have to wait for the armies to arrive, and . . . "

"And," Celestia continued, "somehow figure out how to beat Dredon and Obsidian."

"Is that all?" Mithrel asked sardonically.

Obsidian may be massive and intimidating, Tanzanite thought, *Powerful and deadly. But, his great size is a weakness as much as a strength.*

How so? Saphron asked curiously.

It makes him slow. You are much quicker than he is. You can use that to your advantage. Stay out of the way of his teeth, talons, and flames, and wear him out slowly. Go for his underbelly when you can, and Orion can use his sword once there. If nothing else, it causes him to have to maneuver a lot more to avoid his blade, which can only help in wearing him out.

Orion and Saphron shared the same thought, *That just might work.*

Tanzanite nodded.

"Mithrel," Xharia said, "We knew this would be almost impossible when we signed on."

"Yes," he agreed, "*Almost.*"

"We'll figure something out," Celestia said.

"Tanzanite already has," Orion said.

They all looked at him.

He smiled, "We have a plan to face Obsidian."

"What about Dredon?" Xharia asked.

Orion sighed, "We'll just have to wing it. I have to trust that my training was enough, and that The Oracle was right."

"I've never doubted her," Callisto said, "Not since I became her keeper. But . . . what if she *was* wrong? I mean, how did she not see her own death?"

Xharia patted her comfortingly.

"Maybe she did see it," Orion said, "Maybe she just . . . "

"Sacrificed herself," she finished breathlessly.

He nodded.

Everyone was silent.

In the distance, they could hear war drums and thunderous footsteps as the armies drew near. "It's time," Orion said.

They all nodded.

The two dragons flew out through the top of the mountain, circling the training mountain widely, and joining their troops. They could see humans, elves, dwarves, and wizards alike gathered below. On the other side of the mountain, Dredon's troops were arriving as well. More humans, elves, dwarves, and dark wizards assembled, forming the ranks of their army.

They landed, Xharia and Mithrel dismounting. They went to stand near Queen Gizella and King Tunxst. The dark-skinned queen of the elves and the strawberry-bearded king of the dwarves were standing proudly at the helm of their armies, ready for battle.

"We'll lead your army into battle, Orion," Mithrel said.

Xharia took his hand in solidarity, adding, "You can trust us. We'll fight alongside your troops with honor."

He smiled, giving her a nod, "I know you will."

With that, Saphron and Tanzanite took to the skies, trusting Xharia and Mithrel to lead their ground troops. Celestia planned to ride upon Tanzanite, so they could both join the fight with the riders. They had all agreed she would be the best candidate, due to her skill with both a bow and a blade. Not to mention, her ability to wield raw power.

As they soared above the mountain a safe distance away, they saw the entirety of Dredon and Obsidian's followers. Orion and Saphron's ground forces were two-thirds the size of theirs, the opposing army supplemented by kodrizans. Not to mention, he had hundreds of riders flying overhead, waiting for the battle to commence.

Whatever happens, Tanzanite thought, *We will fight.*

What if it's just the two of us against all of his riders? Orion asked.

It won't be, she replied, *Haaka will come, and any survivors from Cabri and Chyia will be here.*

But, will they be here in time? Saphron asked.

Orion sighed, *Tanzanite's right. Whatever happens, we fight. We have no choice. There's no turning back now.*

Saphron sent him waves of agreement, adding, *We came here to fight Obsidian and Dredon, and that's exactly what we're going to do.*

As soon as he'd said it, Michaël appeared on the horizon, Sardonyx letting out a mighty roar as they led the dragon rider troops of Haaka to the battle. The army below cheered at the sight, and Orion knew they were as relieved and elated as he that they wouldn't be alone in this fight.

The red dragon flew over to them, Michaël saying, "So, what's the plan?"

Orion looked over at the red-eyed king of the dragon riders of Haaka, and said, "It's simple. Our ground troops face theirs. Your riders face Dredon's followers, and we take on Dredon and Obsidian."

He smiled as he said, "At first, I was afraid for my troops, learning that we would be the only ones on your side to face his followers. But, facing the two of them directly will be far greater a challenge, so now, I feel lucky." He turned serious, "I fear for you, though, my friend. Good luck."

Orion nodded, a knot forming in his stomach. He clutched the ring Callisto had given him, looking over at the mountain. *Ready?* he thought.

Let's do it, Saphron replied, full of determination.

Michaël gave them another nod, Sardonyx flying over to their waiting army and getting them in battle formation. At the same time, Dredon's troops moved into position, and the ground troops on both sides formed their ranks.

As the armies on the ground let out battle cries, it began. They charged toward each other, swords and spears clashing. Then, the dark dragon riders launched their attack on the warriors of Haaka. Sardonyx led the charge as they met them in midair, a blur of colored wings and flame.

Celestia exchanged glances with him, and they nodded, making their way to the mountain. At the same time, the dark mass of Obsidian rose up into the air, causing the battle to pause as they all stopped and stared. Orion swallowed his fear, and Saphron flew faster, ready to finally face them. They could see Dredon's gleaming grin all the way across the battlefield.

They charged straight toward them, plowing right into Obsidian. The massive black dragon twirled, trying to snap his jaws around the blue dragon, but he moved out of the way at the last second. Saphron maneuvered quickly, trying to do what Tanzanite had said, and use his speed to his advantage. He had only to steer clear of his talons and jaws, and wear him out slowly.

He attempted to maneuver around to his underbelly so Orion could stab him, but he hit him with his tail. As they moved in for another attempt, he flipped suddenly, and Dredon held out his sword, grinning. Orion had to swing his sword up quickly to block him, and they engaged for a short duel on the way past, before Saphron maneuvered out of the way again.

Though he is slow, Orion thought, *he can flip quickly.*

Saphron maintained their strategy, trying to pace himself and keep a level head. Without being able to dive for the underbelly, however, he was wearing himself out more than Obsidian.

You're getting tired, Orion thought, *I can feel it. This isn't going to work.*

What else can we do? he replied, *Fighting them openly is suicide!*

Debating a strategy? Dredon thought suddenly, *Don't bother. There's no way you can win! Just give up now, call off this whole battle, and I'll let you live.*

Saphron breathed a jet of flame across him, making him cover his face. The momentary distraction allowed Orion to swing his sword down upon him. But it merely hit his armor, and he looked up, unharmed.

Very well, he thought, *No more trying to be nice, then.*

He raised his sword, black eyes gleaming, and engaged Orion. He fought and fought, somehow managing to put up a fight. He surprised himself as much as he surprised Dredon. His training had not been for nothing. Despite the obvious difference in strength, he had become quick enough to duel an elf. Speed was, indeed, their advantage.

Finally, he was able to get a good swing in, slicing into Dredon's side between the front and back of his black armor. He looked up at him furiously, blasting him back with a black ball of magic. Obsidian roared in anger at his rider's injury, snapping at Saphron.

The blue dragon maneuvered out of the way, but the black dragon wasn't done. He chased him, swirling his body every which way, trying to catch him. After a few attempts, he caught Saphron's tail, yanking him back. As he spiraled backward, trying to stop his momentum, Obsidian managed to plunge his giant teeth into him.

No! Orion yelled, *Saphron!* He could feel his dragon's pain as he was tossed to the side.

I warned you, boy, Dredon said as Obsidian landed, towering over the injured dragon.

Orion closed his eyes, holding onto his dying dragon, realizing this was the end. Obsidian opened his mouth wide, and Dredon laughed as he lunged forward to swallow them. Suddenly, he let out a roar as he was knocked off-balance.

When they looked up, they could see Tanzanite and Celestia fighting them off. The indigo dragon maneuvered expertly around Obsidian, working on wearing him out. Callisto was aglow with raw power, firing off spells at the black dragon and his rider.

Orion's eyes widened, and he turned toward his dragon quickly, wiggling out from under him and healing him. As his blue ball of magic left his hand, entering the tooth mark that spanned half of his dragon's stomach, he felt the drain of his energy. Healing such a large wound took a lot out of him. He collapsed against him when he was finished, unable to continue. There was still a minor injury on his tail, but he didn't have enough strength to heal it, too. At least they were both still alive.

Have . . . to fight . . . Saphron thought, *Tanzanite . . .*

They both tried to get up, but neither of them had the strength. They looked up at their mentors, fighting their battle. Dredon was no match for Celestia's use of raw power, and they were completely overwhelming them. Tanzanite bobbed, weaved, and dodged, tying Obsidian in knots.

How did people think we could stop them? Orion thought, *They're much better than us.*

They're stronger, faster, wiser, more powerful, and they've seen more battles, Saphron agreed, *And, I don't mean only our mentors, but our opponents as well.*

What were we thinking?

We trusted The Oracle, he replied.

Orion looked at his dragon earnestly, and they looked back at Celestia and Tanzanite. They were obviously wearing Obsidian and Dredon down, and Celestia's magic blasts were clearly doing damage. But, as they looked to the battlefield, they could see their army wasn't doing as well. The warriors of Haaka weren't enough to defeat the dark riders. The ground troops were being swarmed by kodrizans.

Then, he caught a glimpse of Mithrel and Xharia. He was stuck under a fallen horse, and she was fighting off the troops around them, trying to save his life. As he watched, she was knocked down, and she cast herself over the horse, covering Mithrel. *Xharia!* he thought, *No!* But, before the soldier could cut her down, King Tunxst intervened, stabbing him, and helping her push the horse off of Mithrel. Orion let out a sigh of relief. It was short-lived, as he turned back around in time to see Obsidian's tail bat Celestia from Tanzanite's back.

She was slammed into a boulder protruding from the mountain. Orion scrambled over to her. "Are you alright?" he asked frantically.

"I'm fine," she replied, sitting up.

As he looked at her worriedly, he knew it had to be he and Saphron who fought this battle. The moment he thought it, his dragon swooped under him, lifting him onto his back. Together, they locked into battle with Obsidian. Tanzanite joined them, double-teaming the dark rider and his dragon.

I'll distract him, Tanzanite thought, swooping into Obsidian's view.

As she did, Saphron moved to his underbelly, and Orion raised his sword. He plunged it into him as hard as he could, but it wasn't enough. He couldn't pierce his hide. *No!* he thought.

Problem? Dredon asked, sneering.

Obsidian slammed himself down upon them, squashing them.

Under the weight of the black dragon's body, they started to suffocate.

Saphron! Tanzanite thought, panicked. She began attacking Obsidian, trying to get him free. Finally, Celestia blasted him with her raw power, knocking him off. *Thank God!* Tanzanite thought, *I was so worried about you! Are you alright?*

Saphron blushed as he tried to catch his breath, *Yes. Tanzanite?*

Yes? she asked.

We may not make it through this battle, anyway. So, I suppose it wouldn't be putting you in a difficult position to admit how I feel. This secret dies with us. But, I just wanted you to know . . . I'm in love with you.

She paused, warm feelings radiating from her, *Me, too.*

Really? he asked excitedly.

She nodded, *But right now, we have more important things to worry about!*

Obsidian's tail came down between them, and they separated quickly, diving out of the way. As they did, a large claw came around, knocking Orion from his saddle.

Orion! Saphron thought, rushing toward him.

Obsidian blocked his path, and the three dragons locked into a fight. Dredon leaped from his dragon's back, landing a short way from Orion. As he struggled to reach his feet, legs wobbling from the force of the fall, Dredon drew his crossbow, notching an arrow.

Orion looked up, seeing the blurry, dark rider, and spat out a mouthful of blood. He stood, fighting the dizziness that threatened to take him down again. If he was going to get shot, he was going to be standing.

Dredon grinned, firing his arrow straight at Orion's chest. Suddenly, Celestia leaped in front of him, taking the arrow.

"No!" he yelled, dropping to his knees. His audible shout was echoed by the thoughts of Saphron and Tanzanite. The two dragons fought their way past Obsidian, Tanzanite keeping him distracted as Saphron closed his jaws around Dredon, throwing him.

Orion crawled to Celestia's side, taking the old witch in his arms. He stared at the blood flowing out of her around the arrow in her chest in horror. His hand trembled as he reached for the arrow, so he could pull it out and heal her.

"No," she said softly, grasping his hand, "Save your energy. You need it more than I do. The arrow has already pierced my organs. You can't save me, now."

"No!" he said, "Why did you do that?"

"Because," she replied, "You're my great-great-great-grandson."

Obsidian

20

"What?" Orion gasped.

Celestia smiled, "I was waiting until you were ready to hear it."

"How do you know?" he asked in disbelief.

"My daughter, Nastazya, became the queen of Chemsson when she got married. I kept track of the lines of my children—at least, the ones that remained in Duwazo. Your mother, Isadora, is my great-great-granddaughter." She clutched her ring, which was hanging around his neck, "Use it well, Orion. It's my final gift to you." Her eyes glazed over, and she gasped, whispering, "Bridgot . . ."

He felt her body go limp, and tears formed in his eyes. "No!" he yelled, shaking her. His tears streamed down as he rocked back and forth, holding her, not wanting to believe she was gone.

He hardly had time to mourn before Dredon stormed over to him, fury in his eyes that Saphron had tossed him. The force of Saphron's jaws had loosed his arm from its socket, and it was hanging useless at his side.

Somehow, it made him look even more intimidating. Yet, Orion wasn't scared. The emotions that were building inside him were agony and rage—the perfect recipe for vengeance.

Orion stood, calm and focused.

When Dredon looked at him, Orion could see a flicker of fear in his eyes. He suppressed it quickly, saying, "Look around you, Orion! There is nothing but death and defeat! You could have avoided all of this! *You* chose to fight! And now, you will all die!"

Just then, there was a loud *crack* from the neighboring mountain, and a fleet of dragon riders flew out. Kendreil and Citrine joined Haaka's troops. Shelbara and Marina joined them as well, along with the remaining warriors of Chyia. Then, they saw the rest of Cabri's troops fly out. Morgalina and Turq, Austinian and Amaline, Kirstiana and Solstra, and, at the helm, their queens, Lorena and Aeramen.

They all soared into battle, taking down Dredon's troops with ease. The other riders on their side cheered, rushing the dark riders with renewed vigor. Orion smiled as he watched the chocolate-haired Lorena swing her sword from her bronze dragon's back. She looked, to him, like an avenging goddess. The ground troops looked up, letting out cheers of their own. Their efforts redoubled as the battle raged on.

Dredon and Orion looked at each other as he said, "The only one who's going to die is you!" With that, he charged forward, swinging his sword, and the two riders locked into a fight. Dredon swung his sword with one arm, still managing to fight with force. Orion kept up with him, waiting for an opening. He was blinded by anger as he fought, unable to think clearly. His mind was a black mass of sorrow and despair at the loss of his mentor and relative.

Tanzanite and Saphron fought harder against Obsidian, holding him off, and wearing down his energy. Saphron felt a mixture of emotions. He was devastated by Celestia's death, same as his rider. He was also giddy about Tanzanite feeling the same way about him that he did about her. It made it tough for him to focus, but he knew they had to win this fight, for Celestia.

Orion felt the same way as his duel with Dredon continued. He was, by far, the most skilled opponent he'd ever faced. Even with one arm, he was formidable. They fought back and forth, neither one making any progress. Finally, the dark, muscled rider knocked Orion to the ground, raising his sword.

As he brought it down, he stopped, gasping. Orion stared at him, wide-eyed with confusion. As he dropped to his knees, he could see that Tanzanite had sunk her teeth into his armor. Orion hurried to finish the job, but Dredon blocked him just in time, rising and spitting blood. He let out a yell, swinging his sword and continuing to fight.

Obsidian hurried to aid his rider, but Tanzanite and Saphron blocked him, fighting him from two fronts. Dredon sliced into Orion's leg, causing him to yell out in pain, putting all his weight on his other leg. Saphron looked over at him worriedly, and Obsidian used the opening to charge him, jaws open. Tanzanite yanked him out of the way by his tail in the nick of time.

Orion stared down his opponent with fierce focus. They charged each other, metal clashing against metal, pushing each other back and forth across the mountaintop. They were evenly matched—Orion on one leg and Dredon down to one arm. Finally, Dredon knocked Orion down once more. As he tried to bring his sword down on him, he kicked him back with his good leg, hopping up.

Dredon looked up at him, choking on blood. His kick had worsened the damage done by Tanzanite's bite. Obsidian stared, unsure what to do. Before they could gain their bearings, Orion rushed forward, running his sword through him.

"Not even death can stop me," he sputtered, dropping to his knees, "As we fought, as our ancestors fought, so will our descendants."

"And, like us," Orion responded, "Like our ancestors, my line will always win."

He laughed, choking again, "You've proved a worthy adversary. But, you're wrong." He spat out a mouthful of blood as he stood up, grasping his sword, "My descendants will not underestimate yours. Yours will have no time to train. Mine will kill them before they have the chance. My line will not end with me. But yours . . . yours may very well end with you." He swung his sword, still trying to fight.

Orion leaped out of the way, avoiding his blade. He was defenseless, his sword still protruding from Dredon's gut. He hobbled over to Callisto as fast as he could, grabbing her sword. He turned just in time to see his enemy swinging his sword down on him. He blocked it, and they engaged again, fighting back and forth.

Dredon yelled, thrusting his sword toward Orion's chest. He side-stepped, yanking the sword from his chest as he did. The dark rider finally collapsed, blood pouring from his open wound. "You . . . you have not won. Your descendants will know the cold sting of death by the hands of mine." He grinned, laughing, as blood foamed up in his mouth. Finally, his black eyes faded to brown, and he fell back, releasing his final breath.

Obsidian's roars of agony echoed across the battlefield. Though the warriors knew it meant Dredon was dead, they also had the fear of God put into them by the sounds the massive dragon emitted. As Orion looked up at the terrible beast, he knew this battle was far from over. He leapt onto Saphron's back as Obsidian grabbed Tanzanite by her tail in anger, tossing her into a large boulder on the mountain. She was knocked unconscious by the force of it.

Tanzanite! Saphron thought worriedly. He looked back at the massive black dragon in anger, his focus narrowing.

Orion was on the same wavelength as his dragon. Now, he was able to focus his emotions enough to use them to their advantage. *Let's finish this,* he thought.

Saphron sent him waves of agreement, charging straight for him. At the last second, he swerved from the path of Obsidian's open jaws, diving for the underbelly. He was going too fast for Orion to use his magic and aim an arrow.

When they turned around, he had to maneuver out of the way quickly, as Obsidian had spun on them already. He was determined to kill them for what they did to his rider. It wasn't the first time they'd faced the fury of a wrathful dragon. The fight wore on, Obsidian too angry to get tired anymore. They needed a new strategy, and fast. Their energy was waning, and they wouldn't be able to keep maneuvering clear of his jaws much longer.

I've got a plan, Orion thought, *But, it's completely insane.*

What is it? Saphron asked.

Callisto gave me this ring for a reason, he said, *And, I intend to use it to win this fight. I just need you to fly beneath him fast enough that he can't dodge, but slow enough that I can kill him.*

He nodded, focusing.

Orion climbed down to Saphron's underbelly, as Kendreil had taught him, readying himself. He held himself up with one hand, clutching his sword in the other.

Where's your rider? Obsidian laughed, not seeing Orion dangling beneath the sapphire dragon, *Did he run away? Or just fall off?*

He wouldn't abandon me, Saphron replied weakly, trying to keep up the act.

The black dragon laughed even harder, *You're pathetic. And your rider's a coward! He will pay for what he did to Dredon!*

He lunged forward to devour Saphron, but he dove down quickly, avoiding his jaws once more. He flew as fast as he could, trying to keep up with the black dragon. He had to use some of the energy from the ring just to keep himself going. Obsidian began to look for him, unable to see him flying beneath him.

Orion swung himself back into the saddle, aiming his sword like a spear. He clutched the ring around his neck, thinking, *This is for you, grandma.* With that, he launched his sword, using the energy in the ring to propel it with magic.

It plunged into Obsidian's heart, piercing his hide easily. The shockwave from the magic blast hurled them all into the rocks on the mountain. Orion hit his head, and the world went black.

When he came to, he crawled over to his dragon. Using the stores from the ring, he healed his and Saphron's wounds, giving them a bit of energy as well. They went to Tanzanite's side worriedly, Orion healing her wounds, too.

S-Saphron? she said as she woke.

Tanzanite! he thought, *Are you alright?*

She gave a slight nod, *What happened?*

Orion stood, walking over to where the black dragon lay. Blood had streamed from his chest on all sides of the place where his sword protruded. His great, black eyes had glazed over. He was dead. *We killed Obsidian,* he thought, *We saved the world. We completed this quest.* He paused, *We did it.*

Then, *The Oracle was right,* she thought, sighing with relief.

Saphron nodded, *Yes. She was. It's over now.*

As his dragon curled up beside her, offering his comfort, Orion went over to Celestia's body. He gently closed her eyes and folded her arms over her chest. "Thank you," he whispered.

"Orion," a voice said softly from behind him. He turned around to see that it was Lorena. Her bronze eyes brimmed with tears as she said, "You were right. You were right about everything, and we didn't believe you. I'm sorry."

He stood, crossing over to her, "It's alright. It's not your fault. You had to get the facts before you could blindly take action."

She looked up at him, "You had no reason to lie about such a thing. I should've followed my own instincts and listened to you, instead of doing everything my mother tells me."

Aeramen stirred beside her, and Orion could feel her agreement.

"I've got to stop living in her shadow and become my own queen."

He looked at her, her bronze armor blinding in the light of the dawn. He realized the battle had raged all night. "I think you should," he said, "You would make an amazing queen."

She smiled, "I know it was you that saved us. You snuck into the city and freed Aeramen and Solstra. And, you organized the plan that saved my mother and me." After a pause, she added, "Thank you."

"You're welcome," he said, unsure how to respond.

Lorena looked at him steadily, "You saved us all. I would be honored if you and Saphron would become warriors of Cabri."

He bowed deeply, saying, "The honor would be ours."

She smiled, looking as though there was more she wanted to say. After a pause, she looked away sheepishly, which was most unusual for a queen. "Well, alright then," she said, turning to walk away.

It occurred to Orion that perhaps she was seeing him the way he saw her. He wasn't sure what gave him such unfounded courage—probably the leftover adrenaline—but he found himself saying, "Wait."

"Yes?" she asked as she turned around, biting her lip.

He crossed the distance between them in three strides, taking her face in his hands and kissing her.

Orion! Saphron thought in shock, *What are you doing?*

That's our queen! Tanzanite added.

But, Orion didn't care. In that moment, he felt more confident, brave, and carefree than he had in his life. Not to mention, she kissed him back. When he finally stepped back, he felt a bit dizzy, but he couldn't stop smiling. Nor could she.

After a long pause, all she could say was, "Wow."

"Yeah," he said, checking her out, "Wow."

Lorena raised an eyebrow at him, smirking, "Too bad your dragon isn't available, too. Aeramen's still single." She looked over to where Saphron and Tanzanite were still cuddling.

Thanks for that, Aeramen thought sarcastically.

"A gorgeous dragon like her?" Orion said, "She won't stay single for long."

The bronze dragon sent waves of approval, *I like him.*

Me, too, Lorena thought, meeting his eyes.

He smiled, biting his lip and reaching his arm up to scratch his back as he started to feel awkward again.

"Young man," Kirstiana said, breaking up the tension as she rode up on Solstra's back, "You have saved us all." She waved her arm over the crowd assembled before the mountain. He stepped to the edge of the precipice, looking out over their army. None of Dredon's followers remained—either having run off or been killed. The remaining dragon rider warriors were hovering ahead in solidarity, and the ground troops were celebrating below.

He wasn't sure how to feel as he looked at all of them. It was all finally over. They'd completed their quest. All of these warriors had fought with him. It was bittersweet, thinking about all they'd accomplished, and all they'd lost along the way. He knew in that moment that he would never be the same again.

Suddenly, he felt Saphron nudge him as he came up to stand beside him.

Orion knew he was the only one who truly understood. He leaned against his dragon's snout, patting him. Whatever happened in life, he knew he could always count on him. *We'll always have each other, Saphron,* he thought.

Yes, the blue dragon agreed, *We will.*

Epilogue

"**O**rion, come on!" Lorena shouted. She had brown hair, pale skin, and bronze eyes.

"Coming!" Orion replied. He had black hair, and his skin was a mixture of light and dark. His mother was from the land of Duwazo, which was a land famous for its light-skinned residents. His father was from the land of Cardeas, which was mostly darkly complected individuals. It wasn't often the two came together, so he was the product of an unusual love affair.

Orion put on his sapphire blue armor—the uniform of the dragon rider warriors. He now lived in the city of Cabri, in their hall of warriors, where only the elite could call home. Ever since he and his dragon, Saphron's quest, they commanded the respect of their fellow riders. It was quite the change from their life in the mountain stronghold.

However, he wasn't in Cabri today. Today, he was in Korga, the land of the dwarves. King Tunxst, of the kingdom of Dirthix, had taken them and their dragons in for this most festive occasion.

"What's taking so long?" Lorena asked, swooping in upon her bronze dragon, Aeramen's back, "Let's go. We're going to be late!"

He leapt upon Saphron's back, shooting her a wry smile. She was the queen of Cabri, and also, newly, his girlfriend. "What?" he said, "I'm ready."

She shook her head, "Must you always make an entrance?"

He chuckled, "Of course."

The two of them met up with Saphron's mate, Tanzanite, and they made their way to the main hallway of the dwarven tunnels. There wasn't much room for their dragons to spread their wings, so they had to go slowly.

When they arrived, the two riders dismounted, Lorena's bronze gown flowing around her. "You look beautiful," he whispered.

Saphron, Tanzanite, and Aeramen sat together at the back of the room, so they wouldn't take up too much space. Orion and Lorena took their seats in the spacious hallway beside the other guests. They were just in time, as the music started, and the bridal party made their way down the aisle.

Elves and dwarves alike were gathered there for Mithrel and Xharia's wedding. Xharia's sisters, Queen Gizella of Garellis and Kamine, were bridesmaids. Her parents, Boreas and Annalisa, were there as well. Mithrel's siblings, Ljuis, Zimera, Crastanza, Crarstos, and Diethro, were also in the bridal party. His parents, Ghabriel and Ljourdes, were front and center. King Tunxst himself was performing the ceremony.

The halls of Dirthix were decorated with a stunning array of dwarven *and* elven masterpieces. There were elven lanterns strung up above them, and dwarven-made carpets beneath their feet. It was a true display of unity between the races, and Orion knew that was exactly what his friends wanted.

Mithrel stood at the end of the aisle beside his brothers and King Tunxst, wearing black armor with white accents. His black beard and hair were slicked and braided, in an attempt to look clean-cut. His brown eyes gleamed, and his terracotta cheeks flushed with anticipation.

Finally, the elven wedding march began to play, and Xharia came down the aisle. She wore a flowing white gown and cape, which accentuated her bust and narrow waist, billowing around her gracefully. She held a bouquet of white orchids from the forests of the elves, and her black, silky hair flowed over her ebony cheeks, accented with a silver band around her head. She smiled all the way to her hazel eyes as she glided down the aisle.

Orion shot them both a smile as the ceremony began, truly happy for the two of them. Saphron had been right: his feelings for Xharia had faded away. They were no more than a distant memory now. They had been replaced with feelings of friendship, which he knew could never fade. After everything the three of them had been through together, regardless of how it happened, they would always be friends.

As he thought that, he also thought of Celestia. They had attended her funeral in the realm of the wizards shortly after the final battle. The three of them, along with the blue and indigo dragons, had mourned her loss more than anyone. She was honored in The Wizarding Museum as one of the greatest witches of all time. But, to them, she would always be more than that. Especially Orion, since he'd learned of their relation.

When the ceremony ended, they wandered into the neighboring corridors as the dwarves transformed the main hall for the reception. He took Lorena's hand, guiding her around Dirthix, and showing her the intricate dwarven carvings embedded with jewels.

"It's beautiful," she said, marveling at the craftsmanship, "But, you know what's more beautiful?"

He looked at her, "What?"

"The open sky," she said, "The world from above. Soaring through the very clouds, feeling the wind on your face, and knowing . . . nothing can touch you."

Orion smiled, "You're right. That is the most beautiful thing in all the world."

Lorena smiled back at him, retaking his hand, "Come on. We've been wandering long enough. Aeramen says the reception is beginning."

The feast consisted of the meats and cheeses of the dwarves, as well as the fruits and vegetables of the elves. Everyone was able to enjoy the meal, as the drinks started flowing, and the dancing commenced.

Orion and Lorena joined in, celebrating with the happy couple. Mithrel and Xharia danced the night away, long after most of the guests had gone.

"Congratlations," Orion slurred, giving them each a hug, "An thanks for in-nviting me. I'm glad we can . . . put the pass behine us and . . . and be friens."

"Yes," Lorena said, just as drunkenly, coming up beside him, "We had a . . . great time!"

Mithrel laughed, and Xharia chuckled. "Thanks for coming," she said, "It was wonderful to have you both."

"Goodnigh, then," he said, and the two of them stumbled to their respective rooms, swaying every which way.

The next morning, Orion awoke with his head pounding. He got up and dressed, grabbing some coffee from Curtis and some water from Isaac. When Lorena joined him, they said their goodbyes to Xharia and Mithrel, who were due to set out for their honeymoon in the far reaches of Gliken, and headed over to their dragons.

The five of them set out from the dwarven tunnels, the two riders mounting their dragons once they were outside. They took to the skies, making their way back to Abyumo. As they flew, and Orion regained his senses, he smiled, breathing in the fresh air.

Lorena was right, he thought, *This is the most beautiful thing in the world.*

Actually, Saphron replied, *I can think of something more beautiful.*

Oh, yeah? he chided, *And what's that?*

Tanzanite's pregnant, he said.

What? Orion thought excitedly, *Really?*

The indigo dragon nodded.

I'm gonna be a father, Saphron thought.

I can't believe it! he said, *A little baby dragon!*

Not exactly, Tanzanite thought.

What do you mean? Orion asked.

Dragons lay eggs, she replied, *And, those eggs go to the vault. They won't hatch until they're touched by their rider.*

His disappointment was matched only by Saphron's sadness.

Did you ever know your parents? he asked Tanzanite.

Yes, she replied, *If they're still alive when you hatch, you're allowed to see each other. They found me shortly after I hatched. So, I had the opportunity to know them.*

What were they like?

They were wonderful, she said softly, *And, they were so pleased to see me. We actually got to have a relationship with each other, until they passed away . . .*

I'm sorry, he said sympathetically. After a pause, he turned to his dragon, saying, *Saphron, we should find your parents.*

He sent them waves of uncertainty, but he finally said, *I have wanted to meet them my whole life. But, what if they're dead?*

We'll find out together, he thought, *If you're going to have an egg of your own, you should know the dragons who conceived you.*

He's right, Tanzanite agreed, *I'll help.*

I hope it doesn't take too long for ours to hatch, he thought, *I really want to meet our child.*

Me, too, Orion thought.

Tanzanite sent waves of agreement.

They continued the next few days across Gachichken, and back into Abyumo. When they reached the realm of the dragon riders, the three of them began their search for Saphron's parents, while Aeramen and Lorena went back to their duties at the palace of Cabri.

It didn't take long for Tanzanite to track them down, as she was well-connected amongst the high-ranking leaders. She arranged a meeting with them, giving her and Orion time to prepare Saphron.

It's going to be okay, she thought, trying to ease her mate's anxiety, *We'll be right there with you.*

I'm always here for you, Orion said, *When have I ever let you down?*

Saphron sent waves of gratitude, tinged with uneasiness.

They journeyed to the mountains, landing right beside the training mountain. Orion slid off his dragon's back, standing beside him. It wasn't long before two dragons were flying toward them. They were large and old, one blue and one green.

Saphron! the blue one thought, *Is it really you?*

M-Mother? he replied timidly.

Yes, my darling. Oh, how I've longed to see you, ever since the day I laid your egg.

Saphreya! the green dragon said, *Let the boy breathe.*

Sorry, Emer, she replied, *I'm just so excited!*

Father? Saphron said, looking at the green dragon.

Yes, son, he answered, *I'm your father.*

There was a pause, before Saphron lunged forward eagerly, embracing his parents. The overwhelming surge of emotion coming from him caused Orion and Tanzanite to turn away, giving them some privacy.

We thought we'd never find you! Saphreya said.

We searched the whole of Cabri when we received word you had hatched, Emer added, *But, you were nowhere to be found.*

Orion and I lived in a mountain stronghold, Saphron explained, *We were working toward making it to the training mountain. That is, until we discovered our destiny, and embarked on a quest to save the world, defeating the famed Obsidian and his rider, Dredon.*

That was you? the green dragon asked in amazement.

He nodded.

Oh my! his mother gasped, *Our son is famous!*

He's a hero, his father said, beaming with pride.

Saphron blushed, unsure how to respond. He had so many emotions running through him, he wasn't sure what to say. After a long pause, he said, *I'm going to be a father soon myself.*

What? Saphreya asked in surprise.

My mate, Tanzanite, is pregnant, he said, nodding to the indigo dragon.

They looked at her. After a pause, his mother said, *So, that's why you came to find us.*

She nodded.

Congratulations, she said warmly.

Thank you, Tanzanite replied.

A most beautiful mate you've found, his father said, *Well done, son.*

Emer! Saphreya said.

What? he replied, *It was a compliment.*

And this, Saphron said, changing the subject, *is my rider, Orion.*

They looked at him, then. *It's so wonderful to hear what success you've found in your life,* Saphreya said, *We're so proud of you. And we're going to be grandparents! This is all so wonderful!*

As she embraced her son again, nuzzling him affectionately, he said, *I actually wondered if I could ask you about that.*

About what? Emer asked.

About becoming parents, he said, *What's it like? How do you know when your child hatches? How can you find them? What if you never get to meet them? Is it all worth it?*

We don't really have a choice in when our children hatch, his father replied, *Dragon eggs only hatch when they are touched by their rider. You never know when that will be. But, we each get to name our child, and the riders keep track of every single egg, registering them to their parents. When they hatch, the rider council informs you. You then have the ability to find them, hopefully in the same city. You never know where their rider will choose to go. Unfortunately, Cabri didn't have record of the mountains. They were treated as a separate city. That's why we were unable to find you. But, we're lucky to have met you at all. Some parents don't live as long as it takes for their child's egg to hatch.*

To answer your other question, his mother continued, *Yes. It is all worth it. If you do get to meet them, it's the most wonderful thing in the world. If not, it's still worth it, just knowing you did your part, and continued the species.*

Knowing that your bloodline won't end with you. Knowing that one day, your child will hatch—that they will live. She sent waves of warmth and love to her son.

It's hard, being a dragon, Emer said.

Harder than I ever realized, Saphron agreed.

Tanzanite nodded, *Yes, it is.*

But, now we can get to know you, my child, Saphreya said, almost tearing up, *And, for that, I'm truly grateful.*

They embraced once more, welcoming Tanzanite in as well.

Orion stood by, watching his dragon embrace his family, and he couldn't help but smile. Though it was bittersweet, expecting an egg that may or may not hatch in their lifetime, he knew that one day his dragon would have a child. And, for now, he had a mate, and he had parents.

He looked over at the training mountain, seeing the new mountain leaders training the recruits, and he knew what he had to do. He had to petition the dragon rider council to include the mountains in Cabri's registry, thereby allowing more dragons to find their hatched children.

Thank you, Saphron said, reading his thoughts, *I'm proud to call you my rider, Orion.*

And I'm honored to call you my dragon, he said, *If your child hatches, I'll help you find them.*

As he felt the wave of raw emotion his dragon emitted, he could tell what it meant to him. He looked up at him, as the other three dragons were still nuzzling him to death, and they locked eyes. A single tear escaped down Orion's cheek as he smiled.

THE END

Pronunciation Guide

Characters:

Orion	(oh-rī-on)
Saphron	(saff-ron)
Callisto	(kuh-list-oh)
Celestia	(seh-less-tee-uh)
Epsilon	(epp-sill-on)
Moonstone	(moon-stone)
Xharia	(zah-ree-uh)
Mithrel	(mee-threll)
Tanzanite	(tan-zuh-nite)
Dredon	(dray-don)
Obsidian	(ob-sid-ee-an)
Helado	(ay-lah-doh)
Tunxst	(tungst)
Kendreil	(ken-drayl)

Cities/Kingdoms/Villages:

Cabri	(kah-bree)
Chyia	(chee-uh)
Haaka	(hah-kuh)
Garellis	(guh-rell-iss)
Dirthix	(der-thix)
Khanjgi	(con-jee)
Batosque	(bat-osk)
Chemsson	(shem-son)
Gachich	(gah-cheech)

Chichka	(chich-kuh)
Kiken	(kee-ken)
Cartouche	(car-toosh)

Countries/Lands:

Duwazo	(dew-way-zo)
Katangalo	(kat-ann-gall-oh)
Gliken	(glī-ken)
Korga	(core-guh)
Gachichken	(guh-cheech-ken)
Abyumo	(ab-bee-you-moh)
Cardeas	(car-dee-yes)
Fluorasti	(floor-ah-stee)
Mashang	(muh-shang)
Kogatsa	(koh-got-suh)
Kuttub	(kut-tub)
Millhaymae	(mill-hay-may)

Learn Dwarvish

Bie	I/me
Sie	us/we
Gyo	you
Yaug	he/she/they/them/it
Es	is/are
Ie	and
O	or
U	on
I	from
In	negative (no/not/nor/won't/wouldn't)
Frug	friend
Feinedo	foe
Haill	come/originate/hail
Yatren	trust/truth/true
Vraden	hurt/harm
Zatrage	orders
Draigyhr	dragon

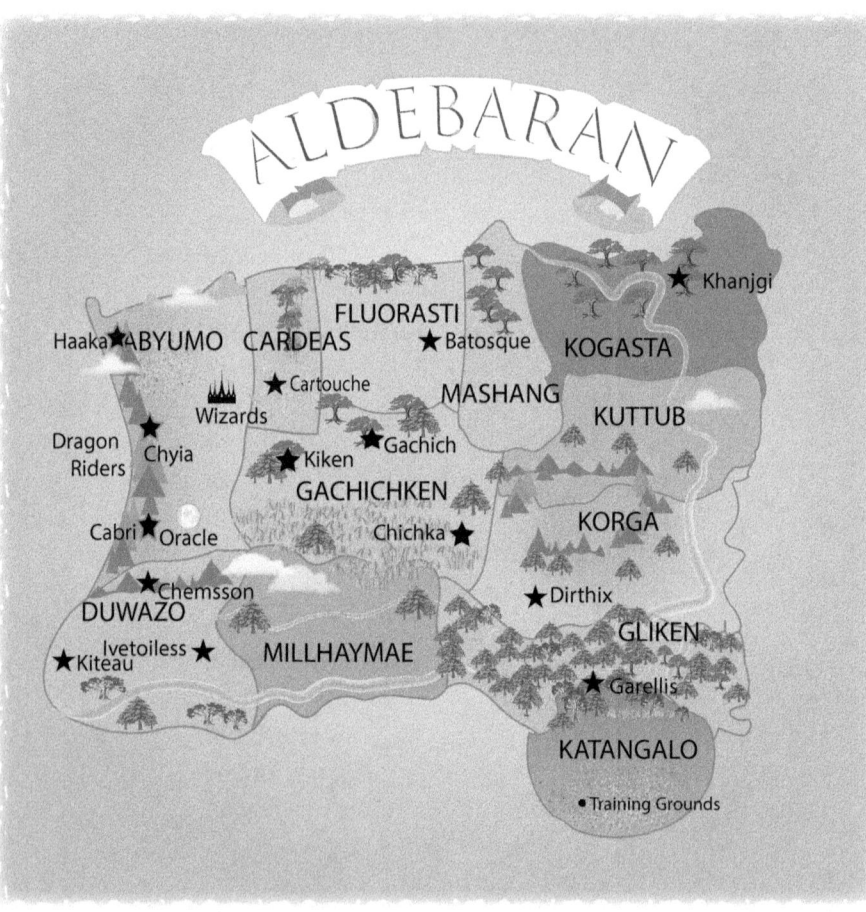

ALDEBARAN

Khanjgi

Haaka ABYUMO CARDEAS FLUORASTI Batosque KOGASTA

Cartouche MASHANG KUTTUB

Wizards

Dragon
Riders Chyia Gachich

Kiken KORGA

GACHICHKEN

Cabri Oracle Chichka

Chemsson Dirthix

DUWAZO GLIKEN

Ivetoiless MILLHAYMAE Garellis
Kiteau

KATANGALO

• Training Grounds

The Star Chronicles

Book 1: *When the Stars Align*

Book 2: *When the Stars Fall*

Book 3: *When the Stars Collide*

Book 4: *When the Stars Form*

Coming Soon!

www.ingramcontent.com/pod-product-compliance
Lightning Source LLC
Chambersburg PA
CBHW051830020726
47502CB00005B/1713